ALSO BY KARYN MASTERS

When Deep Sleep Falls
Silent Storm
God, Fix it!
Spiritual Warfare, My Battle
Arion and Azura (The Adventure Series)

The Girl Inside

Karyn Masters

Book Cover Design: Chase Jentz
Editing/Proofreading: Polgarus Studio
Formatting: Polgarus Studio

Aris Publishing
Copyright © 2017 by Karyn Masters
ISBN-13: 978-0-9990599-0-6
Printed in the United States of America
First Edition 2017

Illusions commend themselves to us because they save us pain and allow us to enjoy pleasure instead. We must therefore accept it without complaint when they sometimes collide with a bit of reality against which they are dashed to pieces.

~Sigmund Freud

Chapter One
Evangeline

MARCH 8
WEDNESDAY MORNING

Thick black eyeliner caked around my upper and lower lids. I'm going gothic today. It's my mood. Dark. Black. I've swung in and out of melancholy, basically my entire life. My makeup will reflect where I stand most days. If I'm going princess, my cheeks will be rosy and my lips the color of pink petunias. Maybe a touch of light shimmery shadow dusted across my eyelids, like fairy dust. If I awake feeling angry and unsatisfied, I break out the Kat Von D. It screams black studded attitude. She's really more my style.

But Greta, poor, poor Greta. She's the princess. She's the sweetheart, so everyone believes. Weak girl with a conscience. Pfft. She likes everything in her life to be orderly and calm. She works hard at creating a peaceful environment. The sun always shines and the birds always sing in Greta's world. We are complete opposites.

Where was I? Ah, that's right ... my mood. My clothing reflects my lifestyle, which is chaotic and unsettled. Sometimes people stare at me when I go out, not sure what to make of me. They know I have problems. I can see it in their eyes as they look me over, trying to figure out where life has done me wrong. I can hear their thoughts: *Was it a man? He beat her down until she had nothing left. Now she's a mess.* If something's wrong with a woman there's always a man to blame. Men drive women crazy and then it's the women who get labeled as psychotic.

Nothing has beaten me down; not life, not a man. I am who I am. I was born into this dark world as a dark soul, and now I lead a dark life. It's not complicated. My princess days exist because many times life calls for me to be a princess in a fairy tale so that I can get everything I possibly can out of it. Nothing gets handed to people like me. You have to steal, lie, and fake your way through the finish line.

Greta wouldn't know anything about that, though. She came from wealthy, loving parents who coddled her ... still do. She's a thirty-two-year-old spoiled brat who married the man of her dreams ... the man of every woman's dreams, for that matter. He's a doctor. A shrink. Big education, big salary, big house. I'm not jealous. I'd hate to be her. She's got nothing I want. Even her man is a little too prissy for me—with his perfectly manicured nails and Armani suits. Silk ties with matching pocket squares. Puke!

I laugh at the thought of him prancing around like a big shot—all five feet, nine inches of him—and I spit coffee all over myself. Never a hair out of place, that guy. That doctor.

Greta's husband. He's a little slim for my taste, although I do admit he's got nice muscle tone.

I reach for some napkins sitting on the table in front of me and clumsily sop up the puddles of coffee. The couple sitting close by are stealing glances at me, but I don't care. I'm used to being gawked at. The chick leans in and whispers something to the guy seated to her left. He nonchalantly glances over his shoulder at me and then they both stifle their laughter. For a fleeting moment, I wish I had a companion with me today so we could stare and laugh back at them. As petty and childish as it sounds, sometimes what's good for the goose is good for the gander.

I roll my eyes and toss the soggy napkins on the table.

Where was I? Ah, right, Mr. and Mrs. Perfect. Greta and Jax Kavanagh. What a name. Jax Kavanagh. I believe it's Irish. It makes a statement, though, doesn't it? Doctor Kavanagh. Speak of the devil, here he is now. Every Wednesday morning at precisely 7:43 he zips up in his dark blue BMW 5-Series and prances into the coffee shop. He orders a grande, quad, nonfat, one-pump, no-whip mocha, with almond milk. I know this because I've stood in line behind him a time or two. Maybe five, or more. He always orders the same thing. He pays using his phone and then stands off to the side and scrolls through—who knows—emails, maybe? Sometimes he'll make a quick call. I think people who use their phones in public are obnoxious and self-absorbed, but who am I to say? I'm no shrink. I chuckle at my own joke, this time covering my mouth with my coffee cup, denying the mindless couple next to me another reason to snicker at my expense.

I watch him impatiently pacing the floor. He's not in a hurry, he's just too good to stand in line. He has more important things to do. He's wearing a black slim-fit suit today. Ralph Lauren, maybe? I'm not sure. Crisp white dress shirt with a blue and red silk tie. He looks sharp, I admit, but that's not unusual. I couldn't deny his sense of style if I tried. His black hair is forced into place by hair paste, giving it a nice sheen. Okay, so he might have good hair, but his flaws totally outweigh any physical benefits.

Occasionally, he'll glance my way, but always pretends he doesn't see me. But, oh, he sees me. He knows I'm here every Wednesday morning at precisely 7:43. He knows if I'm not standing in line behind him, I'm right out here on the patio, sipping my chai latte, watching him closely. I think it creeps him out a bit, and maybe it should. I guess it *is* a little unsettling … to be watched.

Here he comes, rushing through the door—snobby, overpriced coffee in hand. He glances in my direction. Bam! He sees me, but he acts as if he doesn't and keeps a fast pace to his car. He swings in behind the wheel and is gone in under ten seconds. It's over. This is my Wednesday morning routine. I'll see him again later today, in the afternoon at my 3:00 appointment. I'll tell him I saw him this morning and he'll act surprised. Then he'll tell me he was in a rush and didn't see me, although we'll both know he's lying.

He'll only meet with me at his home office. He never allows me to visit him at his practice in New Orleans. He says it's not proper. I think he's embarrassed he has a crush on me, and doesn't want anyone to figure it out. What if they revealed his crush to Greta? She has the tendency to pop in unannounced some days and surprise him with lunch. I'll never understand what she sees in him. He's nothing but an overeducated buffoon.

I can't wait until 3:00 rolls around.

Chapter Two
Greta

MARCH 10
FRIDAY EVENING

"Honey. Have you seen the box with all my shoes?" I wait for an answer, but get nothing except a moment of silence, so I yell louder this time. "Honey. My shoes. Where are they?" Still nothing. I sigh loudly and hop to my feet. It's a good little trek from the master bedroom to the kitchen where Jax, undoubtedly, will be polishing individual pieces of silverware and placing them meticulously in their new home.

"Jax," I say breathlessly as I round the corner into the kitchen. He jumps and drops a knife, which goes clanking to the floor.

"Good lord, woman! You startled me," Jax says as he bends over and picks the (fortunately) small knife up.

I stifle my laughter. "Do you know where my shoe boxes are? They didn't make it into the bedroom. The movers must have placed them in another room."

"Check the guest room. I think I saw some wardrobe boxes in there earlier. How's it coming in the bedroom? Will we be settled enough to have a comfortable night tonight?" Jax asks, cocking his brow.

"Only if I can find my shoes in a timely manner." I smile mischievously.

"Are you asking for my help?" Jax rolls his eyes and sighs.

"You are too kind, my dearest husband," I say, tilting my head to one side while batting my eyes wildly.

Jax is no pushover, but this method seems to work well for me. He comes running for a damsel in distress. Not that misplaced shoes constitutes a woman in dire straits, but he knows I won't stop whining about my missing wardrobe until it's found.

"Here's the deal: I'll find your shoes and carry them to the bedroom if you promise me you'll have everything put into place by bedtime," Jax says sternly.

"Deal," I say and extend my hand toward him. We shake on it and off we go.

We're upgrading. Moving up. We sold our eighteen-hundred-square-feet home to buy something larger. Jax was looking at new construction. He said he wanted something easy to keep up, so new was the way to go. But not me. I wanted something with character. A history. A story. I found a recently renovated mansion tucked away in a small city called Mandeville. It's across Lake Pontchartrain from the city of New Orleans, which is where we last resided. Three years ago, Jax and two of his colleagues joined forces and started their own psychiatry practice. They've done better than projected, hence the reason we're able to upgrade.

I can't stand the noise and ruckus in New Orleans now that I'm older. Not that thirty-two is old, but my priorities have changed. I'm no longer concerned with partying on the weekends. Quite the contrary. The weekends are used to catch up on time with my husband and sleep. New Orleans is fast-paced, and way too touristy for my comfort these days. Jax suggested we buy something on the outskirts, even though it's a bit of a commute for him—thirty-five miles. In rush hour, it can sometimes take forty-five minutes, or more, one way. He'll adjust. I need my peace and he agrees. He, of all people, can understand how anxious I become in the wrong environment. It makes me dysfunctional and then he has to babysit me. He grows irritable when that happens. He agrees, moving out here was a necessity.

Now here I am, standing in my beautiful forty-eight-hundred-square-feet home. We don't nearly have enough to fill it up, but that's my department. Interior design is my expertise. I've been decorating homes since straight out of college. I worked for one of the biggest design firms in Louisiana, but not anymore. I went solo several years ago. I'm Greta Kavanagh Designs now. Although I do decorate homes on occasion, my clientele is mostly made up of the filthy rich. I get calls from some of the biggest plantations in the area. I worked on Oak Alley last year. I redid some of the guest cottages. It's a beautiful place—that old mansion, so much character. Just like my new home. Old with history. The only problem is, I'm not quite sure what the history of my home is … yet. I only know it's around a hundred years old, but I'll be finding out soon enough. I'm sure Google will be spilling this old house's secrets to me without a fight.

"Where do you want this?" Jax asks through gritted teeth, his face turning redder by the second as he balances the large box on his forearms.

I hurry to the back of our closet where the shoe rack is located. "Drop it here, to the right."

Jax lets it drop and it hits the hardwood with a loud thump.

"Good thing I purged my wardrobe before we moved, huh?" I smile proudly.

"Woman, if you call this purging, I'm in trouble," Jax says as he gives the collection of packed boxes a once-over. "Good luck to you. Remember, tonight. I want this room functional if we're going to spend the night here. I don't want to be digging around for everything."

"It's a deal. I said I would, now get out of here." I shoo him away with a wave of my hand, but he leans in and gives me a quick peck on the forehead.

"You never let me down," he says over his shoulder on his way out.

Of course not—I'm Wonder Woman.

I drop to my knees and start pulling shoes out of boxes. Great! They're all mixed up. I'm going to be here a while. I grab my stepstool from the corner and then search for my least favorite and least worn shoes. They'll go at the very top of the rack. That way I won't be climbing up and down this stool every day. I start placing shoes along the top shelf when I notice one of them won't slide back, as if something is in the way. I stand on my tiptoes, straining to see if there's anything blocking the shelf. There is. Looks like a book. I reach for it, barely able to grab it with the tips of my fingers. I slide it toward me.

It's a journal covered in green material with gold embossed letters across the front that read:

PROPERTY OF EVANGELINE

This is interesting. I flip through the pages and notice it's almost full. Someone has forgotten their diary. They've left it behind. When they—Evangeline—discovers this ... well, I'm sure she'll be beside herself. I flip to the first page to see if there's an address or phone number. I can call and tell her I have her journal. I bet she'll be grateful to get it back. No one in the world would want their innermost secrets floating around, making their way into someone else's hands. Secrets she's probably never told a soul could be resting between these pages.

There's no address. No number. No name. Just **EVANGELINE** on the front cover. I flip to the next page, but it starts Evangeline's thoughts.

HE'S AT IT AGAIN. TRYING TO MANIPULATE ME. HE LIKES CONTROL. HE THINKS HE'S SMARTER THAN ME.

I quickly slam the book closed. I didn't mean to read any. I was just checking to see if I could find out something about the owner so I can return it to her. I press the words I read out of my mind and head toward the kitchen, journal tucked under my left arm.

Jax is lying under the sink, faceup with a wrench in hand.

"What happened?" I ask, disappointed. Our first day and we have a leak? Already?

"Not a big deal. It just needed a slight turn. I think it's good now," Jax says as he jumps up from the floor and turns the water on full force. We both stand frozen, staring at the pipe under the sink. "See? It's all good. Fixed ... this time."

"What do you mean by that?" I ask.

"I mean, this is an old house. We can expect things like this to occur regularly. That's why I wanted a new house," he says as he shoots me a stern look.

"But you love it," I say happily.

"I do love it. I won't lie." He grins broadly, and I can see joy on his face, into the depths of his eyes.

I get down to business. "I found something that belongs to the previous homeowner. I need to return it."

Jax glances at the book tucked beneath my arm. "What? That? A book?"

"It's more than a book. It's a journal."

"So what? Toss it."

My jaw drops. "Are you kidding me? I'll do no such thing. This is someone's life! Their energy and emotion live among these pages. I'm not going to throw it away like a piece of trash. I need to find the owner so I can return it to her."

"Her?" Jax raises a brow. "How do we know it's a her?"

"Because it has her name on it." I keep it tucked tightly under my arm as if I'm protecting it; like removing it would put it in danger of being destroyed.

"Well, I've got bad news for you. Because this house was bank owned, there's no way we can find out who the last *real* owner was. And if I remember correctly, this house sat empty for many years at one point. It wasn't until last year that it was bought by an investor and renovated, so good luck." Jax turns the faucet off and bends down, feeling for any more leaks around the pipe.

"There's got to be some tax records I could check, or something of the sort," I argue.

"Yeah, you can probably do that." He closes the cabinet doors and turns to me.

"Why are you looking at me like that?" I ask.

"Have you finished upstairs?"

I wince as though I'm in pain, and physically I am. I'm completely exhausted, but calling it a day isn't an option. Not until I have the bedroom and bathroom put together in a functioning manner. I start out of the kitchen and then pause. "Pizza and red wine?"

"As soon as you're done," Jax promises and flashes me his pearly whites. His smile gets me every time, and he's fully aware, so he uses it to his advantage at every opportunity.

I finish emptying the last of our wardrobe boxes into the closet, putting everything in its new place. It all fits nicely, but that's because this closet is three times the size of the closet in our previous house. I loved that home. That's where Jax and I started out our marriage. We experienced some good times there. Many memories were made in that house; family, friends, celebrations and shed tears will always be a part of that home, but it was time to move on and that's just what we did.

Now I have a big enough space to work out of. I've got my own office. Jax will have the study while I take over the mother-in-law suite located on the first floor. This works best for me. Not only is the room larger, but it has its own bathroom. It's like being at the office except I get to enjoy working from home. There's nothing better. There are also French doors that open onto a beautiful travertine patio surrounded by every blooming flower imaginable. On cool days—and there aren't many—I can enjoy sipping coffee on the patio while catching up on phone calls.

I've already ordered the biggest desk I could find. Solid oak with a mahogany finish, intricate marquetry top with a decorative hand-carved border. It cost a small fortune, but we have more than enough money for important items such as this. Jax won't mind the splurge—he knows how important my work is to me. Besides, I bring home a significant chunk of change every year. I'm very successful at what I do and it shows. All one has to do is look around my own home to see how talented I am at what I do. This is another plus about working from home. My clients get to see my work firsthand when they meet with me at my office.

I turn the lights out in the closet and then check the bathroom to make sure everything is in its place. Jax hates disorder. He won't have it. I always tease him about being OCD when he's a psychiatrist and all. For Jax, everything has got to be clean, tidy, and in its place. I stand in the doorway and take a long look around the bedroom. No one would ever guess this is our first night in our new home. By the looks of this bedroom, we've been here for some time. The furniture is perfectly positioned, linens are creaseless and folded back for bedtime, and each throw pillow, painting, and piece of decor is carefully placed. The furniture is a distressed ivory, and then I've added a light touch of gray. I'm in love with vintage

French design; can't get enough of it, actually. Our sanctuary looks like a picture out of a magazine. We'll be sleeping good tonight.

I nod in satisfaction and head downstairs. Jax is just finishing the kitchen, so he orders pizza while I grab a bottle of 2005 Château Léoville-Las Cases. It *is* a special occasion. No paper plates and plasticware for us. He has managed to unload, clean, and put away every dish and piece of silverware we own. I pop the cork and set the wine on the counter. This is one that needs time to breathe, unlike cheap wine, which hasn't been a part of our lives for a long time. I collect two wineglasses and set them beside the bottle.

Jax and I eat mostly in silence, not for any other reason except pure exhaustion. Once finished, we sit for a while and go over our "to do" list for tomorrow while we polish off the wine. Then it's off to the bedroom. After a shower, Jax collapses on the bed and in less than five minutes I can hear him lightly snoring. I take my time, allowing the heat from the shower to penetrate my sore muscles. The steam feels good to my sinuses as I inhale deeply. My mind returns to the journal I found. Evangeline's journal, and I make plans to do some research tomorrow so that I can track her down and return what's hers.

I quietly and gently climb into bed, Evangeline's journal in hand, thinking I'll take another look at it to see if there's something I missed—a name, number, or email address. I carefully flip through the first few pages, but I don't see anything except a few scribblings in different colored pens, as if they were written at different times, on different days. One page, written in red ink, says: LOVE, HAPPINESS, HOME, BEAUTY. She's drawn several hearts and messily filled them in. I turn the page and find where she's written just the opposite in black ink: HATE, JEALOUS, UGLY, EVIL, MEAN. She's drawn a picture of a girl's face, black streaks running from her eyes down her cheeks, mouth curved into a frown, long black hair framing her face, brow furrowed in anger. She looks evil. Self-portrait, maybe? I wonder how old she is.

I feel a bit uncomfortable, yet intrigued, so I continue to snoop. I flip to the next page and, again, I read the first few lines:

> HE'S AT IT AGAIN. TRYING TO MANIPULATE ME. HE LIKES CONTROL. HE THINKS HE'S SMARTER THAN ME. HE'S ALWAYS THE ONE WHO CALLS THE SHOTS. I NEVER GET A SAY-SO. AND MY IDEAS ARE ALWAYS DUMB, WHILE HIS ARE BRILLIANT. AT LEAST, THAT'S WHAT HE BELIEVES. I CAN'T STAND HIM SOMETIMES.

I quickly shut the book. I'd never be able to live with myself if I stooped so low as to read someone's diary. *Well, it's not like anyone would know, Greta.* I quiet my inner voice immediately. I'm not that kind of person. *Oh, aren't you? Maybe you could offer this poor woman some help. You'll never know if you don't at least try.* I give in, sickening easily, I might add. I'm weak. I've never claimed not to be.

I turn back to the page and continue to read.

> SOMETIMES I THINK HE JUST USES ME TO DO HIS DIRTY WORK FOR HIM. I'M ALWAYS THE ONE PUTTING MYSELF OUT THERE

WHILE HE STAYS UNDERCOVER. INCOGNITO. *I HAVE A REPUTATION TO PROTECT*, HE SAYS. A REAL STELLAR KIND OF GUY. WHAT COULD ANY WOMAN SEE IN THIS WIMP? YEAH, MAYBE HE'S DOING THE PUBLIC A SERVICE BY HELPING PEOPLE, BY RIDDING THE COMMUNITY OF ITS LOSERS, THE MENACES TO SOCIETY, BUT OUTSIDE OF THAT, HE'S REPULSIVE.

I hear something, so I stop reading and listen. After a minute, I notice I'm holding my breath; I slowly exhale and get up from the bed. It sounds like banging. Three short thumps. There it is again. I cross the room and look out the window. The neighbors to our right are awake. I can see lights. Now I see shadows—silhouettes dancing along the curtains. There's that thumping again. The front door swings open and a man emerges. He rushes over to the trash cans sitting alongside the house and starts rummaging through them. He looks fit, dark hair, slim build, disheveled. Although I can't see his face, I can tell he's angry. His body language says it all: rigid and forceful movements.

He must have found what he's looking for because he's stomping back toward the front door, something in his hand. I can't make it out. I hear him yelling as he closes the door behind him. At an upstairs window, I notice curtains being pulled back, and I get a glimpse of a woman with long straight hair. I can't tell the color, it's too dark. She looks down toward the trash cans and then pulls the curtains shut tight. I hear words being exchanged, angrily, followed by silence. I put my ear to the glass and listen to see if they're still fighting, but I hear nothing.

I tiptoe back to my bed and climb in. I hope we don't have a dysfunctional couple living next door. The last thing I need in my life is neighbors who like to fight at all hours of the night. Jax won't like this. No, Jax won't like this one bit. Maybe it's best not to tell him. He'll probably find out on his own anyway. I drift off into an exhausted sleep, completely forgetting about the mysterious journal sitting on my nightstand.

Chapter Three
Evangeline

MARCH 15
WEDNESDAY AFTERNOON

"I saw you this morning—at the coffee shop. You pretended not to see me, again," I say, tilting my head inquisitively to one side.

Jax is sitting at his desk, writing, ignoring the fact that I'm sitting across from him in a chair, waiting on him to start playing doctor. He's going to tell me how sick and twisted I am, but that's what he likes about me. We have one meeting a week where we catch up, exchange notes, make "to do" lists, and then it's over. He forbids me from coming around any more than that, and unless I feel like making trouble for myself, I happily oblige. I don't have a choice. He said he'll get rid of me if I don't respect and obey his rules, and I believe him. He's very good at what he does—genius, in fact—so there's no reason not to believe he has the power to vanquish me if he so desires.

He stops writing, sets his pen on the desk, and leans back in his chair. His eyes meet mine and don't move, not even to blink.

"Must we do this every Wednesday?" He sighs.

"Let me guess … you didn't notice me, right?" I roll my eyes. "Stop playing games, Jax."

"You're the only one playing games, Evangeline, and it's getting old. Let's get down to business. I don't have time to waste."

I glance over his new home office. It's big and fancy. I wouldn't have expected less from him. His desk is neat and orderly, sitting away from the wall, toward the middle of the room. Behind him there's a built-in bookcase extending from one side of the room to the next, pecan-colored stain. It's filled with medical books, awards, and degrees. One thing Jax is not, is an underachiever.

"I bet Greta is just loving this big fancy house, though it's not quite my style …"

He interrupts me. "We're not here to talk about Greta. We're here to talk about *you*."

I smile and look down at my shoes, my favorite black combat boots. "You're too sensitive when it comes to her. You never allow …"

"I said to stop. Now if you want to continue with me, things will have to go my way. If this no longer interests you, then we can part ways. I have no problem with that. You're not bringing much to the table lately anyway." He smiles as he picks up his pen and resumes writing. He's got me again, and he knows it. He's in full control and no matter what I do, the power will always lie in his hands.

"I could tell Greta everything," I threaten.

He rolls his eyes. "This again? I've already explained why that won't work. Do you really want me to go through the steps once more?" He cocks his head to one side, a wry smile forming across his face. "Whatever you *do*, I can *undo*. I'm the psychiatrist here; a noted one at that. You could leave her numerous signs and messages, but I'll be able to explain them all away. There's no part of her that distrusts me. Besides, what a whacko of a story you'd be forced to confess to. Who in their right mind would even believe you?" He sighs heavily. "Do we want to go down this tired old road again?"

My hands clench into fists, and I can feel burning in my chest. The acids in my stomach are churning as my anger reaches new heights. I've tried for so long to beat him at his own game, but I fall short every time. I can't even come close. I feel beads of sweat forming on my forehead as my anger and frustration rise. "I don't have anything to offer today. Just charming conversation. How about you?" I say through gritted teeth, and I force a smile.

Jax laughs wildly. He has won again and he relishes in his victory. He doesn't treat Greta like this. He cherishes her. He even babies her, seeing to her every need, as if she's so fragile she could break if something semi-toxic were to come her way. It makes me sick, the way he treats her. She's his whole world, yet I'm completely expendable. I think he'd love to get rid of me once and for all, and I don't doubt he could do it. That's why I have to bite my tongue and instead be on my best behavior. I have to sit here and smile as if I actually like him. One wrong move, and I'll be history. No one would ever miss me. They wouldn't know I was gone, because they have no idea I even exist. He keeps me hidden. Stifled. It's smothering.

"Then we're done for today. There's nothing more to discuss. Agreed?" Jax says, pausing to watch my expression so he can analyze me, no doubt.

I nod. Deep inside I want to pick up the letter opener sitting on his desk and stab him through the heart, but instead I smile and blow him a kiss. It makes me want to gag. I lean down to pick up my bag, and I notice he eyeballs it suspiciously, but doesn't say anything. Normally he has the gall to ask me what's in it. I always lie. He hates my makeup and my sense of style. He says I have no style at all, and that I only dress like I do to gain attention from others. He's constantly putting me down, making me feel like I'm worthless. Then he compares me to Greta in detail, pointing out her strengths and my weaknesses—her class and my unruliness. He says I'm uncouth, and that I'll always be overshadowed by her.

I start slowly toward the door.

"Evangeline," Jax says, jotting something in his notebook, "stay away from the coffee shop on Wednesday mornings."

I pause long enough to nod, but I know I won't stay away. He knows it, too. I'll be there next week, just like I always am.

And he'll pretend not to see me, just like he always does.

Chapter Four
Greta

MARCH 17
FRIDAY EVENING

I've just finished setting the table when I hear Jax come out of the study. I quickly light the two ivory-colored tapers and place them accordingly on the table.

"Perfect timing, my love. Dinner is served," I say as I peck Jax on the cheek. "Sit and I'll serve the food. Roasted chicken, potatoes, and carrots. I made a raspberry torte for dessert."

"What's the occasion?" he asks with a chuckle.

"Ouch. Does that mean you aren't impressed with my everyday meals?" I furrow my brow.

He raises his hands defensively. "Not at all. I just feel like you went out of your way for this meal today, so I'm wondering if you're going to spring something on me." He chuckles once more, but this time it's more of a nervous giggle.

I get a good laugh. "Not this time, but you know me well," I say as I pile food onto Jax's plate. "I just thought it would be nice to have a really great meal in our new home. We've been here a week and it's been frozen food or takeout every night, so I thought I'd take the afternoon off and cook something we can really enjoy."

"I'll toast to that," he says, looking around for a drink.

"Oops. Hold that thought." I quickly grab the bottle of red wine I left sitting on the island and pour us some.

Jax raises his glass. "To love, marriage, and our new home."

I quickly add, "And our first home-cooked meal." Our glasses chime as they touch and we sip our wine for a minute before digging in.

We share small talk throughout dinner, both anxious to call it an early night. Jax heads upstairs while I stay behind and clear the table, put the food up, and wash the dishes. I drink another glass of wine before following suit.

I find him in bed with an open medical book across his chest. He's snoring. I gently lift the book and place it on the nightstand, but not without glancing at the title first: *Crazy Minds Think Alike*. Interesting title. Jax loves his medical books, that's for sure. Always reading, always learning, always a student. That's why he's so wise. He never stops the learning process. A narcissistic person would feel he's educated and learned enough—he's earned a doctorate, what's left? Not my Jax. It's never enough for him. He always wants to know more. That's why he's so successful in his field and so highly respected.

I have a shower and climb into bed. The house is quiet. The sheets are cozy and I can imagine myself dropping off in only a minute or two. I think about the book Jax was reading and suddenly remember I was reading something not too long ago as well. Evangeline's journal. I remember tossing it aside the first night in our new home, when I heard the ruckus next door. I haven't thought about it since because I've been too preoccupied to bother with it. I must have stuck it into my nightstand. I open the drawer and reach for it without hesitation. I don't need to have the conversation where I battle back and forth with myself arguing whether it's right for me to read someone else's journal—I already know I'm going to do it.

I open the book and turn to where I last left off. The guilt is gone. Was there ever any?

RANDOM THOUGHT: IS IT POSSIBLE TO LOVE SOMEONE YOU HATE?

I RAN INTO AVA TODAY AT THE CANDY BOX. SHE WAS PICKING UP MARDI GRAS CHOCOLATES, AND I WAS STOCKING UP ON PRALINES, OF COURSE. SHE'S STILL MOURNING THE LOSS OF HER HUSBAND. HE WAS SUCH A LOSER. A VILE MAN, REALLY. I WONDER HOW SHE CAN GRIEVE OVER SOMEONE WHO WAS SO HATEFUL TO HER. HE'D SLAP HER IF SHE DISAGREED WITH HIM. A BACKHAND RIGHT ACROSS HER FACE.

I WITNESSED IT, MORE THAN ONCE. I ALMOST CAME UNGLUED THE FIRST TIME. I WANTED TO GET UP FROM MY CHAIR AND PLANT MY FIST IN HIS MOUTH, BUT INSTEAD I SHRIEKED, AT LEAST I THINK I DID. I FOUND MYSELF

STANDING AND REALIZED AVA HAD HOLD OF MY ARM AND
WAS PULLING ME TOWARD THE FRONT DOOR, ASKING ME TO
LEAVE. MY EYES NEVER LEFT STAN, HER ADORING HUSBAND.
I WANTED TO KILL HIM. HE STARED RIGHT BACK AT ME,
DARING ME TO SAY SOMETHING TO HIM. HIS EYES WARNED
IF I TOLD ANYONE, OR CALLED THE COPS, HE'D COME FOR
ME.

I WASN'T SCARED, I WAS FURIOUS. MEN LIKE HIM AREN'T
TOUGH GUYS, THEY'RE COWARDS. HE WOULDN'T TREAT
ANOTHER MAN IN THAT MANNER, I CAN PROMISE THAT. HE'D
BE TOO SCARED OF GETTING THE CRAP BEAT OUT OF HIM
... BUT HE CAN DO IT TO A WOMAN. BULLY!

I COULD BARELY GET MY FEET MOVING. WHEN AVA AND I
GOT TO THE DOOR, I ASKED HER TO COME WITH ME, BUT
SHE REFUSED. I TOLD HER SHE'S SO MUCH BETTER THAN
THIS, BUT SHE DIDN'T WANT TO HEAR IT. MADE ME THINK
SHE'S HEARD IT ALL BEFORE. PROBABLY FROM OTHER
FRIENDS AND FAMILY. STAN YELLED AT HER FROM THE OTHER
ROOM, DEMANDING SHE GET RID OF HER "TRASHY FRIEND"
AND GET HIS DINNER READY. I HAD TUGGED ON HER ARM,
COAXING HER TO LEAVE WITH ME, BUT SHE REFUSED.

THIS HAPPENED TWO MORE TIMES IN FRONT OF ME. EACH
TIME I BEGGED HER TO COME TO MY PLACE. I COULD HELP
HER. SHE ALWAYS REFUSED. A FEW MONTHS LATER, I RAN
INTO HER AT THE MALL AND SHE INFORMED ME STAN HAD
BEEN IN AN ACCIDENT WHILE FISHING. HE'D GONE

OVERBOARD, OR SOMETHING. HIS BODY WAS FOUND HOURS LATER BY SOME OTHER FISHERMEN. HE'D HAD A LARGE AMOUNT OF ALCOHOL IN HIS SYSTEM. POLICE THOUGHT HE LOST HIS BALANCE AND FELL OVER THE SIDE, MAYBE HITTING HIS HEAD ON THE BOAT. THEY FOUND A LARGE BUMP ACROSS HIS FOREHEAD.

AVA CRIED AS IF IT WAS A TRAGEDY. I CALLED IT DUMB LUCK. SHE WAS RID OF HIM, BY NO MEANS OF HER OWN, AND HAD A NICE LITTLE SUM OF CASH FROM THE INSURANCE COMPANY. WHAT MORE COULD A BATTERED WOMAN ASK FOR?

BUT SHE WHINED AND CRIED OVER THE SLOB LIKE THERE WAS NO TOMORROW. THE CHICK MUST BE COMPLETELY BONKERS. IF MY ABUSIVE HUSBAND SUCCUMBED TO HIS INJURIES, I'D BE CELEBRATING ON EVERY DIME HE LEFT ME! LATER, I CALLED HER TO SEE IF SHE'D LIKE TO TAKE A TRIP TO HAWAII AND SHE THOUGHT I WAS OFF MY ROCKER. I TOLD HER SHE NEEDED TO ENJOY HER NEWFOUND FREEDOM, BUT SHE DIDN'T FIND ME AMUSING. IN FACT, SHE EVENTUALLY HUNG UP ON ME.

I DON'T HAVE THE FREEDOM TO TRAVEL ANYWAY. I'M KEPT ON TIGHT REINS THESE DAYS, BUT THAT'S ANOTHER STORY THAT I WON'T BE GETTING INTO, AT LEAST NOT HERE.

KISSES FOR NOW!
EVANGELINE XOXO

I close the journal and quietly place it back into my nightstand. I'm going over every word this woman wrote. Wow! What a psychopath! I understand her anger toward the abuse, but celebrating the death of anyone is a bit sociopathic, isn't it? I'm no psychiatrist, but I *am* married to one, and I may know a thing or two. Besides, do I really need to be an expert in order to recognize that this woman has major mental issues?

I breathe in deeply and then slowly exhale. I regret reading this journal, even though it was just a small portion. It serves me right. I shouldn't have been invading this woman's privacy. Now I must pay the price for allowing my curiosity to get the better of me. I should try to return it to her. I'll search online for the previous homeowner tomorrow. There's got to be something I can find out. Jax said our house had been abandoned for some years, yet this journal seems to be rather new. It's not worn looking, the pages are fresh enough, and it wasn't dusty when I found it. This makes me wonder if the investor who renovated the house left it behind. I'll start with him. If he doesn't recognize it, he may be able to point me in the right direction.

With that thought, I close my eyes, and it takes only seconds before I drift off to sleep.

Chapter Five
Greta

MARCH 20
MONDAY MORNING

I lean back on my wicker chaise lounge, allowing the morning sunrays to barely brush my face. I can feel the warmth, and I think about how I won't be able to sit out here and enjoy coffee on my patio for too much longer. The Louisiana heat will destroy my morning routine. Spring doesn't last long in these parts. A month or two, if I'm lucky. I hold my coffee mug against my forehead; the heat feels good. I awoke with a slight headache this morning, which happens quite often once life makes its way back into the yard. The flowers start to bloom and my allergies kick in like clockwork. That's my life.

"Hi, there!"

I'm startled at the sound of a voice and I jump, spilling hot coffee in my lap. I wince in pain and quickly set my mug on the table beside me. I look up to find a woman making her way over to me. She's got dark red hair, clearly dyed. I notice a purplish hue to it. Some may call it burgundy, but I see violet. It's long and straight, with just the tips slightly curled, which frame her face beautifully. She's tall and thin, but built. This woman works out—I can tell by her broad shoulders and tapered waist. She's wearing formfitting black jeans paired with a snug maroon top that almost matches her hair color. A cropped black leather jacket accentuates her matching five-inch peep toe booties. She looks totally chic, and I immediately feel mousy.

I may be a bit jealous.

"Hi," I say and quickly swipe at the coffee stains on my pants, trying to hide them.

"I'm so sorry if I scared you. I noticed you sitting out here and I thought I'd come by and introduce myself. I'm Isabella, your neighbor next door." She waves her hand in the direction of her house. "I meant to get by here sooner, but I didn't want to bother you guys while you're trying to get settled." She smiles warmly, revealing perfectly straight, perfectly white teeth.

"I'm Greta. So glad to meet you," I say as I stand and extend my hand to her. Shaking hands is such an odd thing for women to do. I'm old school, I guess. Men shake, women smile. I attempt to cover the coffee stains on my khaki slacks by resting my free hand over them, but it seems to accomplish the opposite effect, drawing her attention downward.

"I'm so sorry. I didn't mean to make you spill your coffee...."

I cut her off. "No problem. I'm a klutz, anyhow. Speaking of coffee, would you like a cup?" I offer.

She looks over her shoulder toward her house and pauses briefly. "Uh—sure. I'd love a cup." She smiles and follows me into the kitchen. At five-four, I'm definitely shorter than she is. She's got a good five inches on me, even more wearing those neck-breaking high heels. I check out her long luscious locks when she turns away to look around. I tug on the band around my ponytail and pull it out, shaking my head to loosen the waves. I wear it curled, on most days, but felt a little lazy today.

"Wow! This is some place. And I can't believe you guys just moved in and you have everything unpacked. You even have paintings on the wall. I'm impressed. I can't believe what Tom has done to the place." She looks around with wide-eyed amazement.

"Tom?" I ask curiously.

"Oh, yes. Thomas Young. He's the investor who bought this old house. You know, it was in really bad shape. It sat empty for over a decade. It was the only house out here."

"What do you mean?" I ask as I grab a coffee mug from the cupboard. She has definitely piqued my curiosity.

"All this land …," she moves her hand in a circular motion, "it belonged to this house. This whole area—not sure how many acres it is—sat untouched for many years. Tom purchased it and divided it up into lots and had a few houses built on it. He put in this street and small cul-de-sac, Sleepy Elm Drive."

I'm blown away, and I try to concentrate on making Isabella's coffee. "Cream and sugar?"

"Both would be great," she says as she moves around the kitchen, glancing over even the fine details, such as the crown molding and chandeliers.

"How long have you lived here?" I ask.

"Owen and I have been here since the beginning of Tom's project. We were his first buyers, so our house was the first one to be built. He hadn't started renovations on your home yet. He had originally planned to finish it before even attempting to sell the other lots, thinking it would hurt sales to have an old, shabby, dilapidated house next door—and it should have. But once word got out that he was building several mansions back here, people started fighting over the lots. This house was slow to start and even slower to finish. Tom had his hands full, that's for sure." She smiles and takes her coffee from me.

"I wonder why no one snatched this house up immediately?"

"But didn't you?"

"How do you mean?" I ask curiously.

"From what I understand—and correct me if I'm wrong— you guys had a deal with Tom on this house from the beginning. No?"

I laugh. "Oh, no. Quite the opposite. We happened upon this home purely by accident. In fact, we'd been looking in a completely different area when, one day, I received an email from our realtor suggesting this home. I initially turned it down because I thought it was too large and too expensive. I thought Jax, my husband, would never go for it, so I didn't even show it to him. My realtor started hounding me to take a closer look, so I eventually showed Jax the listing and he agreed to view it. We both loved it. It didn't take much coercing on my part before dear Jax was sold on the idea."

"He may have played a bigger part than you know." She chuckles and sips her coffee.

What in the world does that mean? Did she just insinuate my husband is a liar? A trickster? She starts going on about Tom again, and I try to wrap my mind around what she just implied about my husband. I only hear half of what she's saying.

"… so I got to see most of what he was doing, but I haven't seen it finished. You guys moved in so fast, I didn't get the chance."

I'm not listening to her anymore. "By any chance, do you know who used to live here? The very last owners…" My voice trails off. I'm trying not to rouse suspicion with my questions. I don't want anyone to know about the journal I found. My invasion of Evangeline's privacy is bad enough. I wouldn't want other people trying to read her journal, too.

"It was owned by the bank when Tom purchased it, and had been sitting for a long time before that, as I mentioned. That's all I know. Why do you ask?"

"I'm just wondering who'd ever let a place like this go downhill. Let it fall to pieces like that," I quickly respond.

"I assume that happened once it went into foreclosure. I don't think the previous owners could afford it. Of course, I'm just guessing, since it was owned by the bank, and all." She nods and sips from her mug.

"Of course," I agree. "And Tom? Is he married? Kids?" I try to sound nonchalant, but I feel like I'm being obvious.

"He and his wife have three grown kids. Two in college and the other one married. Do you mind if I look around a bit more? I'd love to see the rest of the house now that it's finished."

"Be my guest." I smile and decide that's enough questioning for the day. I have plenty of time to be nosy. I like Isabella, so I invite her and her husband, Owen, I believe it is, to dinner next Friday evening.

MONDAY EVENING

"I met the neighbors today. Well, I met *a* neighbor, anyway," I tell Jax as he's trading out his suit for his black lounging pants and a red cotton T-shirt.

"Did you?" He acts surprised. "Which one?"

"The lady next door. Her name is Isabella. She's drop-dead gorgeous," I say, catching a glimpse of myself in the Queen Anna style floor mirror sitting outside the closet. I moan inside as I run my fingers though my blonde highlighted hair. I need a trim. I like to keep it shoulder length so it's easier to manage. Have I gained weight? I feel around on my abdominal muscles. This used to be a six-pack. I make a mental note to start up my core routine I've slacked on lately.

Jax laughs softly. "And what are you? Chopped liver?" He smiles crookedly and shakes his head. "Where's your self-confidence, woman? Have you ever bothered looking in the mirror?"

I steal another quick glimpse of myself, and I don't understand what he means. There's nothing strikingly beautiful about me, but maybe that's his attraction to me. Some men prefer plain. It's less problematic that way. Having a wife other men fall all over every time he takes her out could be a pain. A lot of unnecessary drama. I'm average height, average weight, and average build. I'm plain and average.

"I invited them to dinner next Friday. She and her husband," I say, trying to keep my focus on point.

"Nice. That's a good way to get to know them. I'd like for us to be friends since you'll be working from home a lot. It'll be good to have someone to talk to when you're not working." He nods in approval.

"Isabella said something curious to me when she was over here this morning. She insinuated you already had dibs on this house before it was even finished being renovated." I watch his face closely.

He pauses dressing for a second and then continues. "What a crazy thing to imply. What would make her say a thing like that?"

"That's what I'd like to know." I don't take my eyes off him.

"How would she even know who has bought what house and when? It's ridiculous." He rolls his eyes.

"She knows Tom Young." I notice Jax's eyes dart in my direction and then he quickly turns away.

He leans down and tucks his shoes back on the bottom shelf. "Who's Tom Young?"

"Apparently, he's the investor who bought this house. In fact, he bought all of it. The whole subdivision. He's the developer. Do you know of him?"

"I've never heard that name. Why would I? We dealt strictly with the realtor, remember?" His face turns solemn. Why is he so serious suddenly? Have I caught him in a lie? If Jax is lying … what's the purpose? What would he have to gain? He could have easily come to me and suggested this house. Why keep it a secret and do it behind my back? It doesn't add up.

"You wouldn't, or shouldn't. I just felt it was peculiar for her to say such a thing."

"She doesn't know what she's talking about. Blow it off," he says and waves his hand in the air as if he's swatting at an annoying gnat that has lingered too long in his face.

I change the subject. "Do you have reading tonight?"

He pulls on his T-shirt and smiles at me. He must see the hope and desperation on my face, wishing there may be a chance I get to spend some time with my husband this evening.

"I don't have anything on my mind but spending quality time with my wife."

"I'm a lucky woman."

I don't bring up Isabella, Tom, or our house again.

I *blow it off*.

At least for this evening.

Chapter Six
Evangeline

MARCH 22
WEDNESDAY MORNING

I enjoy the cool breeze as I sip on my spiced chai latte. I'm
sitting on the patio, close to the windows so I can see inside.
Jax is standing at the far end of the counter, waiting on his
tongue twister of a coffee. A young attractive blonde has
started a conversation with him. She shoots him a roguish
smile; her body language flirtatious. Jax looks irritated and
bored. I think it's more about me than her. He knows I'm out
here, watching him, and he can't stand it. He shifts his weight
uncomfortably from one leg to the next. The more I watch
him, the more I can see his fury growing inside. He'd love to
explode in anger right now, I can tell, but he never does. He
always keeps his composure, no matter the situation. He wants
to look at me, but he won't. If he allows himself, he may lose
all control.

Blonde chick finally gives up on him and moves on. I want

to go inside and ask her, *Did you not notice the wedding band he purposely flashed in your face several times? How dense can you be?* I give her points for trying. A young, good-looking doctor (of course, she doesn't know his profession), dressed to the nines … and if she saw his car when he pulled up…. Gross. I can't stand him. It's hard for me to see his good qualities, although I will admit he has some. He's leaning over the counter now, looking for his coffee. *They'll call your name when it's ready, dude. Calm down!* He's antsy.

I think about approaching him, but the consequences could be deadly for me. I like playing with fire, though. I love a good challenge. Actually, I like getting under Jax's skin. He gets so irritated with me, but pretends my actions don't faze him. His body language speaks differently. He'd love to kill me off. I sense it quite often, but he needs me. I'm a vital part of his operation. Plus, I can tell him things about Greta he wouldn't otherwise know, although he hates for me to talk about her. He wants to choke the life out of me if I bring up her name. I see it in his eyes; they're his tell-all. The window to his soul.

It may seem as if Jax holds all the power, but that's not accurate. Not at all. I hold a tremendous amount of power because he has no way to get ahold of me. He can't contact me. It's always up to me to contact him. If I stopped, he'd never see me again. Then this deal between us, this operation, would cease to exist. I'm the one who holds this power in my hands, not him. That's why we have a standing appointment every Wednesday afternoon. I'm never to miss it, because outside of our weekly meeting time, he can't reach me. Either I show up, or I don't. Maybe I need to remind him, once more, today in session how important I am to him. I smile impishly as I take another sip from my latte.

Here he comes, coffee in hand. Oops, he gets stuck holding the door. I can see his impatience. He's angry. He's frustrated, yet he won't mention my being here when I see him later. I'll tell him I saw him, and he'll act surprised, just like he always does. He's moving through the door now, stepping out onto the patio. No glance in my direction today. He'll usually cock his head to the side and catch a quick glimpse of me, but not today. I think it has a lot to do with my attire. He hates it when I dress gothic. He says I look like a LA vampire. I suppose he's referring to the Hollywood vampire look. I'm not attempting to look like anyone but myself. I dress according to my mood, and my mood is black today. Black moods call for black clothing. I'm sorry I can't be more like his precious little wife. She's so innocent. If he only knew half of what goes on in that chick's head. She's a basket case. As a psychiatrist, he's got to know this; he's just in denial.

I watch as he pulls out of the parking lot fast and recklessly, revealing how angry he is with me. He'll get over it. He always does.

Chapter Seven
Greta

I sit down at my new desk and pop open my laptop. I type in **Tom Young New Orleans, LA.** Multiple sites come up. *Real estate developer, Thomas Young. Soon to be shopping center in downtown NOLA, owned by Thomas Young. Thomas Young and Associates.* I click on this last listing in hopes of a phone number or business address. I scan the page and viola, I've got his info. I pick up my desk phone and dial his number; it goes to voice mail. "Good morning, Mr. Young. My name is Greta Kavanagh. My husband and I bought the home you recently renovated on Sleepy Elm Drive, and I have a couple of questions for you. I'd appreciate a call back. I promise, I won't take up much of your time." I leave my number and then hang up.

I've got to be careful how I word my questions so that he doesn't think I'm trying to pump him for information about my husband. I can't let him know I'm suspicious over the purchase of this home. I'll bring up the journal first and ask him if it belongs to someone he knows. Then I'll ask him about the previous owner, although I already know it doesn't belong to anyone who used to reside here because it's too new. This book has not been sitting for many years in an old, dilapidated vacant house. Someone has left this journal here recently. I wonder if this person wants it to be found. I open the top drawer of my desk and pull it out. I keep it here now so that Jax won't find it. He seems to have forgotten about it, and I haven't mentioned it to him again.

After I ask Tom about the journal, I'll nonchalantly bring up the renovation and find out if he knows Jax. I lean back in my chair and gaze out the French doors to the patio. My perfect patio, outside my perfect home office, that even has a bathroom for my clients to use so that they don't have to wander into our home. I get up and walk into the kitchen. My perfect kitchen with the huge island I've always wanted. It's even the right colors, a mixture of teal and seafoam blue. The eating area is separate and off to the side. I walk through to the great room. My eyes stop at the vintage French fireplace surround. It's stone with an antique parchment finish and black fossil stone top. How perfect! What are the chances the designer has the exact same taste as me? What are the odds they'd decide to finish out this house in a French vintage theme? My favorite.

I continue into the dining room, where I pay special attention to the wainscoting. I added wall to wall wainscoting in the foyer and dining area of our previous home. I turn toward the foyer, which is also done in wainscoting. The first time I walked through this house, I thought it was just pure luck that it had everything I loved, that the builder shared my taste in design. Now I'm not so sure it was *luck* at all. I'm starting to think my husband may have had a hand in the design process. But why? Why would he do this and keep it a secret from me? He risked a great financial loss if I would have hated the house when we did the first walk-through. Ah, but he made sure I'd love it, didn't he?

I go back to the kitchen and fill a glass with water. My head is spinning. I feel faint as I attempt to take it all in. Did Jax plan this whole thing? Was the realtor in on it? Tom, too? Was this whole thing one big charade? I feel like a fool.

He's a shyster, Greta. You've always known that.

No, he's not. Don't jump to conclusions.

Oh, please, you've never trusted him, have you?

Jax is a good man.

Think about it. From the very beginning of your relationship you were catching him in lies.

Jax is an honest man.

Then explain this house. Is it really just luck?

I'm not the only one who likes French design.

He's a liar. Think about when you first met. How about all the times he was late to a date with some lame excuse about working overtime? What about the times he never even showed up, and then you'd receive a phone call the next day explaining why he stood you up? You always forgave him.

He always had a reasonable excuse and would be terribly sorry.

Stop! Get out of my head!

I drink down the water and place the empty glass on the counter. I've got to clear my mind. It feels like a mass of jumbled thoughts. I've always had trust issues, and I can't allow them to interfere in my marriage. Jax taught me years ago these thoughts are unhealthy and toxic to our relationship. He showed me how to talk myself out of them, but I feel like I do just the opposite. I seem to talk my way into believing things, or situations, that don't even exist.

I hear the phone ringing in my office and I rush to get to it.

"Hello," I say breathlessly.

"Hi. Mrs. Kavanagh? I received a message from you. This is Thomas Young."

"Mr. Young." Oh, no. I need to get my thoughts straight. I feel like a mess. I've got to concentrate. I've got a game plan. I'm supposed to ask him certain questions in a certain order. Think! "Uh, hi. My husband, Jax, and I bought the house on Sleepy Elm," I stumble over my words.

"Uh-huh," he says slowly.

"I-I found something in the master suite closet. A journal. The cover has the name Evangeline embossed on it. I was wondering if it, maybe, belonged to you? Er, not *you*, but maybe your wife … or daughter." I quickly add, "I mean, if you even have a daughter." I sound like a rambling moron. I nervously twist a strand of hair around my finger out of habit.

"Uh, no. Actually, I'm not even sure how that would've gotten there. In the closet, you say? Maybe the interior designer left it behind, but her name isn't Evangeline. It could belong to an assistant, I suppose. Um, I could give her a call, I guess, and then if I find out something I could ring you back."

Is he nervous? I swear I can hear a nervous tone to his voice.

I mean, I've never talked to the guy, but I get the impression he'd like to get rid of me as soon as he can.

"That would be great. I'd hate for someone to be panicking over losing something so private," I say, trying to keep the conversation going. "You mentioned an interior designer. I'm an interior designer as well." I chuckle and pause for a reaction. I get none, so I continue. "Let me ask you, who did you use for the design in this home, because I'd love to get some paint color names and I have a few questions I'd like to ask?"

He pauses. "Let me have my assistant get back with you on that. I've got to take a call …"

I quickly interrupt him. "One more thing …" I feel like just blurting it out: *Did you secretly meet with my husband and plan this renovation, keeping it undercover the whole time?* "I was talking with a neighbor the other day, and she informed me that the houses you built sold so quickly people were getting into bidding wars. I was wondering why this house didn't sell quickly like that?"

"Actually, we—the realtor and I, Missy—didn't advertise or show your home until it was fully finished. I didn't really have a price point until the interior was completed. You could say I dragged my feet a bit with that one."

"You mean, we were the first people to even view it?" I find that hard to believe.

"Um, no. But you were the first ones to offer what I was asking," he says slowly.

"So, you received other offers?"

"Correct." He clears his throat. "I've got to return a missed call. It's been a pleasure chatting with you. My assistant will get back with you about that journal if she finds something out. Goodbye, Mrs. Kavanagh."

We hang up and I sink down into my desk chair. I feel like he was being hesitant in his answers, like he was caught off guard. Why would he possibly be nervous about answering my questions regarding this home if he had nothing to hide? One thing I can't stand is a liar.

I head to Jax's study. There's a part of me that already feels guilty for what I'm about to do, but I won't be able to function until I know whether Jax planned on buying this house without my consent. I head straight for his desk and start rummaging through drawers, and discover the bottom right-hand one is locked. That's odd. Why lock a drawer in our home? I can understand locking things up in a public office, but at home where only he and I have access to it?

I feel my heart beating faster and I notice I'm breathing heavy. I quickly search the other drawers for the key. That would a bit obvious, no? I run to the kitchen and grab a small paring knife from the wooden block sitting next to the stove and rush back to the study. I go to work on the lock, twisting the knife to the left and then the right. It's not budging and I've left a few scratches around the exterior. I better stop. It's not right to invade Jax's privacy like this ... but if I feel he's lying...

He is lying, you nitwit! Check the file cabinet in the corner.

I glance across the room to a large mahogany file cabinet situated in the corner. It's got a lock on it as well, and I make up my mind that if it's also secured my husband is definitely hiding something from me. I head toward the cabinet.

"Well, hello there."

I jump so hard the paring knife flies out of my hand and onto the hardwood with a thud.

"Oh, my gosh. Are you okay?" Jax laughs. "I didn't mean to scare you." He walks over to the knife and picks it up.

"I—I was just—" I take a deep breath. "Wow, you really startled me." I put my hand to my chest and force a laugh.

"You dropped something," Jax says as he spins the knife handle around and holds it out to me.

I hesitate and then take it from him.

"This is peculiar. You in my study with a knife. Are you looking for something? Did you lose something, perhaps?"

"No," I say breathily, and force another laugh, as if he's being humorous. "I was actually getting ready to cut myself some fruit when I thought I heard a noise, so I came to investigate. I didn't think bringing the knife was such a bad idea. What—what are you doing home?" I try to change the subject.

"It's Wednesday, Greta. You know I only work a half day on Wednesday. A noise? From my study?" He looks around the room curiously. "What did it sound like?" he says and raises an eyebrow.

He's messing with you now, girl. Don't play his game.

"Wednesday. Ah, that's right. Wow, I've been so caught up in trying to get my new office organized and making appointments that I totally forgot what day of the week it is. Would you like some fruit and yogurt?"

"That would be nice. Thank you. I'm going to get to work now." Jax strolls over to his desk, and I see him look it over thoroughly before taking a seat.

I can feel my heart pounding away in my chest. I've been caught red-handed. My husband is no idiot. He knows I was snooping, and I'm sure he's put it together that I tried to open his locked drawer with the knife. How did I lose track of the day? I know he always works a half day on Wednesdays. He likes to come home and catch up on paperwork, phone calls, and anything he may be working on. Many times, he's solicited by editors to write articles for different medical publications. He likes to follow up on Wednesdays.

"I'll be back shortly with your yogurt." I hurry into the kitchen and breathe a sigh of relief. Thank goodness I didn't have the knife stuck into the lock when he came into the room. This is humiliating enough. I dish some Greek yogurt into a small glass bowl and then top it off with sliced strawberries, blueberries, honey and granola. I pour a glass of raspberry tea and head back to the study. Jax is on the phone. I place the bowl and glass off to the side on his desk and he smiles at me and silently mouths, "Thank you."

It seems like he's already over my snooping incident. He's such a busy man, he doesn't have time to worry over petty stuff like this. He makes the big bucks because he's a hard worker. He's very serious about what he does and never allows himself to be distracted. That will work in my favor today. He'll have forgotten all about this by dinnertime.

Chapter Eight
Evangeline

WEDNESDAY AFTERNOON

"I saw you this morning at the coffee shop. I was sitting on the patio, by the window ... but you know that already, don't you?"

I get no response, as usual.

"You looked good in your Armani suit." I pause. "Did you like my outfit? I wore one of your faves." I raise my leg up to show off my black fishnet stockings and clunky combat boots. Still nothing. Jax hates the little games I play with him, and ignores me when I do so. He's so nonreactive. "Looks like you had an admirer while you were waiting on your coffee." I watch as he scribbles in his notepad at his desk. I've been sitting in this chair across from him for twenty minutes. No conversation, just waiting for him to finish what he's doing so we can get started. I finally can't take it anymore so I stand up, lean across his desk and slam the palm of my hand down in the middle of his notepad. He stops writing, but remains imperturbable. He doesn't even look at me.

"Pay attention to me," I demand.

"Stop! And sit down," he says, irritation in his voice. I don't budge. He grabs my wrist and forces it from his notepad and shoves me backward. "Sit down!" He yells it this time, so I do as I'm told.

"Pay attention to me. I'm bored." I lean back in my chair and sigh heavily.

"I'm not here to entertain you." He continues writing.

"And I'm not here to watch you work. You treat me as if I'm not a real person. Like I don't have feelings, or like my life has no meaning."

Jax sets his pen down on the notepad, leans back in his chair, and stares me in the eye. I've got his attention now.

"You always put Greta above me."

"Greta's my wife!" he barks. "You'll never be on the same level as her."

"I know. I know. I get it. You don't have to keep reminding me." I roll my eyes.

"Do you have something you want to discuss with me today?" he asks in a sincere tone, but I know he's faking it.

"Can we move to the sitting area so I can get comfortable?" I raise up from my chair.

"Sure. Let's move." He gestures with his hand and then follows along behind me, waiting until I choose my spot before sitting across from me. "What's on your mind?"

"I'm feeling neglected."

"And what do you want me to do about that?" He doesn't hesitate with his answer.

"We need to talk," I inform him.

"Just come out with it. I'm listening," he says and throws his hands in the air. He's such an impatient creature.

"I think you're keeping things from me." I smile roguishly.

"Not this again. What is it you *think* you know?" He sighs as he runs his fingers through his heavily pasted black hair.

"I think you did a clever little thing … getting Greta out of the city, and playing like it was her idea." Jax is frozen in place, eyes glued to mine. The air in the room just became unusually thick. Do I see concern forming on his baby face? Are his blue eyes now turning fiery red?

"Wh-What do you know about that?" he stutters.

"It wasn't hard to put the pieces together, Jax. You'll need to cover your tracks with her, but don't lie to me. I hate it when you lie to me." I feel like I've got him in a tight spot right now. The ball is in my court, so I push my luck. "Can I have a drink?" I tilt my head toward the coffee table, eyeballing the bottle of scotch sitting on a silver tray with two glasses.

"No, you cannot. You're not allowed to drink, you know that. Quit trying to push my buttons." I can see his wheels turning. He's worried, trying to figure a way out of this. "What does she know?"

"She doesn't *know* anything … yet. She's still putting the pieces together. You should probably give Tom a call and tell him not to take her calls anymore. He seemed uncomfortable. I don't like finding things out in this manner, Jax. You know I don't like surprises. You said you'd always keep me informed." I raise my voice to let him know I'm serious.

"I tell you everything I can. Some things I have to keep from you. I'm not having this conversation again." His eyes narrow, but it's not me he's upset with, it's himself. He thought he was clever enough to get away with this deception, but now he's been caught.

"Do you really believe moving out here is going to change anything? A home office she can work from? It's very nice, by the way." I smile wryly. "Isolation is not the key."

His focus is on nothing but me now. He's thinking about something. He's plotting right now as we speak. I think he wants to get rid of me. "What's going through that head of yours?" I can hear the anxiety in my voice. He takes the bottle of scotch sitting on the table and pours some into one of the glasses. He shoots it back and then pours another. I'm dying for a taste. I feel my mouth watering as I watch him sip from his glass. He gets up and starts pacing, drink in hand.

"Thinking of more lies to tell her in order to cover up your previous lies?" I laugh sarcastically. "You need me, Jax. I'm the one who always fixes everything for you, remember?" I need to remind him of this.

He paces and sips, and then paces some more.

"She thinks you're Mr. Perfect. Her whole image of you will be shattered if she finds out the truth ... that you lied and tricked her into this house."

"Shut up, Evangeline," Jax snaps. "Stop talking so I can think."

He may feel a bit flustered right now, but in a matter of minutes he'll have come up with a plan to cover his tracks. He's a genius at manipulation. In fact, he's king. He'll be back to his superior, arrogant self in no time flat, so I need to enjoy what little time I have watching him squirm.

He smiles smugly and takes his seat back on the sofa across from me. He throws his head back and empties his glass.

"That quick, huh?" I smile, but I'm disappointed his distress didn't last longer. "You've already figured out how to fix it, haven't you?"

He smiles wickedly. "What else do you need to talk about today?"

"Aren't you even going to thank me for revealing what I know? I could have kept it a secret, you know—let it backfire in your face. I may have even enjoyed watching that."

"Oh, please. Spare me the crap lecture. You only mentioned it because you were upset that I kept it from *you*. You could care less about anything else."

"You may be right about that," I say as I grab the scotch and pour a small amount into the other glass. Jax grabs the bottle from me, but he's not quick enough to get the glass out of my hand. I toss it back and then close my eyes in pleasure as the scotch smoothly rolls down my throat.

"You just keep testing me," he says and goes for the glass in my hand. I pull back and he misses. "At least wipe the lipstick off the glass. I don't need any more trouble."

I laugh wildly, pour another shot and toss it back. Jax stares at me in disgust and then shakes his head.

"You do this in an attempt to get a rise out of me. You're like a child," he balks.

"Compared to you, I *am* a child. I'm only twenty-one, Jax. Like it or not, you have to treat me like I'm twenty-one, not thirty-five." I smile and lick the scotch from my lips. My head feels like it's floating. I can already feel the effects from the liquor and I feel great. I don't want to stop. "Maybe I'll go out tonight."

"The hell you will. Stop messing around, Evangeline." There's fury in his eyes now, and I know it's time to stop. Deep down inside, Jax has a soft spot. I smirk at the idea of him having an emotional side, since he's so stoic all the time.

He checks his watch and stares at me for a minute, undoubtedly thinking about how he's going to fix this huge deception. "Help me."

I roll my eyes. "On one condition … you start acknowledging me at the coffee shop."

"Never! Now, help me. I'm not playing around."

"One more shot." I smile, tilt my head to the side, and bat my eyelashes at him.

"No."

I pick the bottle up and take a swig straight from it. "Wow, that was good!"

"Wipe your lipstick off and wash both of those glasses."

"Yes sir, boss man." I giggle and then lose my balance as I lean over to pick the glasses up. I laugh even harder at my clumsiness.

"This is why I don't allow you to drink. You get sloppy drunk and act like a fool." Jax rips the glasses from my hands and heads out of the room. "Follow me," he commands over his shoulder.

Chapter Nine
Greta

WEDNESDAY EVENING

"Look at this! And it smells wonderful. What do we have here?" I say as I walk over to a huge spread of food covering the island in the kitchen.

"Well, you did it for me the other night … cooked a great meal, so I decided you deserve to be cooked for as well. So here you go." Jax smiles at me and hugs me tightly.

"This is wonderful! I'm in shock. Now tell me, who cooked all this food for you?"

Jax's eyes widen, and then he laughs. "Very funny! I know how to cook, a little."

"No, you don't." I don't let him take the credit, mainly because I'm too curious how this meal came about. Baked salmon, mashed potatoes with chives, green beans in a creamy white sauce sprinkled with bacon, and what looks like homemade rolls. Not to mention it's laid out as if it were catered.

"Ever heard of Food Network?" he says with a sly grin.

"Really!" It's more of a statement than a question.

"Don't worry about how I managed to fix it, just come sit down and enjoy it." Jax grabs me by the shoulders, leads me over to the table and pulls out my chair. "I'll make your plate," he says as he hurries back to the spread of food and starts dishing it onto a plate. "Did you have a nice nap?"

"Yes, I guess I did. I don't even remember lying down. I've been sleeping good, it's so peaceful out here. It's quiet. I shouldn't need to nap." I chuckle at the thought that maybe I'm just getting older and napping is one of those things that will become a habit. "Where's the wine? How about white tonight?" I ask as I start toward the built-in wine storage located in the island.

"Wine? Are you sure you feel like drinking right now?"

"What does that mean?" I ask, confused.

"I don't know. I just thought maybe we'd skip it tonight." Jax shrugs.

"That's an odd thing to say."

"No, it's not. We don't have to drink wine every night with dinner."

"We don't … do we?" I'm perplexed by Jax's behavior.

He pauses. "I don't know. Open a bottle." He smiles warmly.

I hesitate, standing motionless by our wine collection. Jax comes over and pulls a bottle from its cubby.

"How about a rosé?" He sets it down on the island, grabs the corkscrew from a drawer, and proceeds to open the bottle. I stand watching, trying to figure him out, but I remain quiet.

He glances up at me every few seconds and smiles. What's going on here? What have I missed? We don't drink much, and when we do decide to have a glass of wine, it's never an issue.

"Sit, my love. Let me serve you tonight." Jax grabs two wineglasses from the rack and pours them half-full as I take my seat at the table. He hands me a glass and then slightly raises the other up and says, "To a peaceful evening with my wife." He smiles and then clanks his glass against mine, causing the crystal to whistle. Although I feel Jax's behavior is bizarre, I decide to stop trying to analyze him and instead enjoy this magnificent meal he's cooked for us. That sounds crazy. Jax cooked a meal?

We eat for a few minutes before starting our dinnertime small talk.

"This is delicious. Maybe I should nap more often," I joke as I bite into the flakiest biscuit I've ever had.

"I'm glad you like it." He smiles warmly. "Hey, have you spoken to your mom recently?"

I shake my head and finish chewing so I can answer properly. "I need to call her. The last thing she said was she and my stepdad were going to come visit once they get back from Italy."

"When will that be?"

"I'm not sure. They decided to extend their vacation, so there's no telling." I shrug.

"I bet you're excited for them to see our new house," Jax says with a smile.

I nod. I am excited. I want them to see what we've become.

It's been a while since they've come down for a visit. We usually go to them in Seattle. They've got the big gorgeous house with plenty of room and they adore houseguests. They love to host and entertain. That's why we usually end up there, so they say, but I think they didn't like staying in our little home. Of course, eighteen hundred square feet isn't all that small, but when one considers what they're used to, it probably feels like the walls are closing in on them.

The last time they were here, which has been a few years, they tried to stay at a hotel downtown. They said they wanted to be closer to the action, meaning the French Quarter, Jackson Square, and Bourbon Street. I immediately got upset, so they cancelled their reservations and stayed with us instead.

My parents are snobs. There's no denying it. They enjoy the finer things in life, have worked hard for them, and won't settle for less. Now I want them to see how we're living. We've worked hard to get where we are and this is just the beginning. We've still got years of working and accumulating yet to come. But here we sit in this gorgeous home in one of the most sought after areas of town. What a great accomplishment! I'm proud of Jax, and I'm proud of me.

Mom and Paul have always been career oriented, though they're retired now and spend the majority of their time traveling the world. Mom was a high-powered attorney, and my stepdad owns numerous real estate firms which his oldest son, Trey, now runs. They don't have any children together. My sister, Hannah, and I are from Mom's previous marriage. My biological dad wasn't the best man. I don't know much, actually, because it's not Mom's favorite conversation to have. But I did find out a few family secrets years ago at a family reunion. Put a couple of drinks into my aunt Steph and one will soon learn she loves to divulge family gossip.

My father was an abusive man. He liked to smoke crack and then beat women. He was a real piece of work. I've always wondered what Mom could have possibly seen in him. He rarely had a job, and when he did it never paid more than minimum wage, and he never kept it long. Mom was working as a paralegal and going to night school while my dad was out hitting the bars and, apparently, the crack pipe. What a winner! How did someone intelligent like Mom end up with such an ignoramus?

Their marriage lasted for almost a decade, but apparently my dad wasn't always a heathen. He'd been a pretty decent guy when Mom met him and they tied the knot. He was in med school, but I guess once the drugs started to rule his life, that career was nothing more than a faded memory. Before my dad lost himself to drugs, I was born and then seventeen months later Hannah came along.

"What about your sister and Aiden? Are they going to come as well? We have plenty of room now, that's for sure," Jax says as he takes a bite of potato.

"They want to come. Hannah said for me to let her know as soon as I get a date and they will arrange it. Not a bad drive for them. Just a few hours from Monroe."

My dad eventually succumbed to his drug use. Not by overdose, though, by murder. He was murdered in a back alley. Beaten and robbed. What a waste of life. He had two choices, and he chose wrong. He picked the coward's way. He had a loving wife and two beautiful daughters and he threw us all away so he could live like an animal. A cowardly animal.

At the time of his death, Mom had already started the divorce proceedings. I was almost ten, yet I barely recall anything about the man. I've got a few flashes of him, his face, in my mind, but other than that I can't remember much. Hannah recalls a lot, though. She says he would yell all the time and call us all names. He was an angry man with a hot temper. That's not unusual behavior for a crazed druggie. They all have a complete loss of their emotions. A disconnect with life and relationships.

Jax can't stand it when a drug addict comes to him for therapy. He won't treat them. He refers them to a drug specialist. He can't even stand the sight of an addict. He says they're criminals and liars. He's been stood up, lied to, threatened, and stolen from. He won't touch a druggie client with a ten-foot pole. Who could blame him?

"Well, I hope it's soon. We haven't seen your parents, or Hannah and Aiden, in a while. It'll be good for us to get together. There's nothing better than family, right?"

I nod and take a sip of my wine. I feel a slight headache coming on, almost like I have a hangover, but it's probably my allergies just acting up again. Spring is the season for allergies.

By the time I climb into bed, Jax is already sleeping. That's not unusual, and I don't mind. In fact, I prefer it. I like my quiet time at night. I like to read, or get on my iPad and check my messages, or look at design pictures. I'd already planned how I'd be spending this evening. I'm going to invade Evangeline's privacy some more.

Atta girl!

Oh, shut up. I don't need anyone's approval. I can do whatever I want. I can make up my own mind. But I'd never want Jax finding out I'm the kind of person who would read someone's diary. He'd think ill of me. In his eyes, I'm perfect and flawless, and I plan to keep it that way.

I open the book and turn to the page where I left off last time.

WHAT A BLOODY MESS! LITERALLY. I'M TIRED OF CLEANING UP AFTER THE PRINCESS. WHY DOES SHE GET TO HAVE ALL THE FUN, YET I'M LEFT HOLDING THE BAG? WHY DO I HAVE TO BE THE MATURE ONE? SHE'S OLDER THAN I AM. IT'S NOT FAIR. I SHOULD BE THE ONE OUT SOWING MY WILD OATS, INSTEAD I HAVE TO BABYSIT ALL THE TIME. I HAVE TO KEEP TRACK OF WHAT SHE'S DOING, WHERE SHE'S GOING, AND WHO SHE'S TALKING TO.

I'M SO TIRED OF ALL THE QUESTIONS AND NOTE TAKING. I'M SO TIRED OF BEING HELD RESPONSIBLE FOR HER ACTIONS. I'M MY OWN PERSON AND I HAVE MY OWN LIFE. I SHOULDN'T LET HIM CONTROL ME LIKE THIS. I'M TIRED OF HIM, AND I'M TIRED OF HER. AND I'M TIRED OF CLEANING UP THESE BLOODY MESSES. I'VE GOT TO GET OUT OF THIS SITUATION. I'M WONDERING IF I'D BE BUYING MY FREEDOM IF I REVEALED THE TRUTH TO HER, OR WOULD I BE KILLING MYSELF? COMMITTING SUICIDE? AS LONG AS I DO AS HE ASKS, I'LL ALWAYS BE SAFE. IT'S WHEN I DISOBEY HIM THAT HE TRIES TO GET RID OF ME.

MAYBE I SHOULD JUST LEAVE. DISAPPEAR. I WANT TO, BUT
I KNOW HE'LL FIND ME. I CAN COVER MY TRACKS, NO
PROBLEM; IT'S HER I CAN'T TRUST. SHE'LL GET ME CAUGHT
FOR SURE. SHE'S SO SELFISH, THINKING ONLY OF HERSELF.

I NEVER THOUGHT I'D SAY THIS, CONSIDERING I'M THE
MASTER OF MANIPULATION AND MY IQ IS HIGHER THAN
MOST PEOPLE'S, BUT ... I'M TRAPPED.
I'M TRAPPED IN A LIFE I DON'T WANT BECAUSE I'M
SURROUNDED BY SELFISH AND CONTROLLING PEOPLE.
THERE'S GOT TO BE A WAY OUT.
I NEED HELP TO BREAK FREE.

I'm rattled out of my peaceful state by a loud-sounding crash coming from outside. I jump out of bed, careful not to wake Jax, and rush over to the window. I scan the area for a minute, but see nothing. As I'm closing the curtains I catch a glimpse of movement and pull them back open. I see Isabella running down the sidewalk to her car. She flings open the door and slides in behind the wheel as fast as lightning. Then I see Owen. Well, I assume it's Owen. It's not like I've ever gotten a good look at him. Not in daylight, anyway.

He tries the door handle, but it's locked. I can hear his voice as he yells something through the car window at Isabella. She starts the car and the headlights light up the driveway. "Get out." I hear him loud and clear now, yelling for her to get out of the car. He punches the car window and yells at her again. She's not obeying. I hear the engine rev as she puts the car in gear and it jolts backward. He punches at the window again, but it's out of his reach now. She backs out of the driveway and speeds off down the street.

I look back at Owen and watch as he paces back and forth. He rubs the knuckles of his punching hand, and then I hear him yell out once more. I can't make it out, but I can hear the anger in his tone. I'm watching a man out of control, and then he looks straight at me. His body is stiff and rigid as he stares up at me standing in the window. I quickly close the curtains and back away. He saw me. He knows I witnessed what just happened. He's aware I know his secret now ... he's got a temper and he likes to take it out on his wife.

I'm not sorry he saw me. He needs to know others are aware of his weakness. That's what it is—uncontrollable anger is weakness. Owen is angry at the world, his parents, his childhood, his boss, his bullies, and Isabella gets the brunt of it. Later, he'll apologize and try to convince her that his outbursts are not a big deal, just small peccadilloes that all married couples experience. That's a load of crap. I'm not a psychiatrist like Jax, but I've learned a thing or two about abusive behavior from the years of volunteer work I've done at the women's shelter. I think Isabella may be a battered woman. Obviously, she felt threatened enough to get out of there. She ran to her car and took off.

I crack the curtains open just enough to see out. I watch as Owen slowly walks toward the front door and back inside. He doesn't know how long I was watching, or if I heard anything. I could have had the window open, for all he knows. The weather has been cool outside. It's a perfect time for open windows. They're supposed to come for dinner this Friday.

Won't that be awkward? I bet his mind is going crazy right now, already thinking about what he'll say about this scene I just witnessed.

I won't let him get away with it.

I won't allow him to minimize his abusive treatment of her.

Chapter Ten
Evangeline

MARCH 24
FRIDAY MORNING

I wake up with a raging headache. Every muscle in my body aches. I slowly raise myself to a sitting position and wince in pain. It's dark. I can't see, but I can tell I'm on the floor. Where am I? I carefully stand, every movement causing pain, and I feel my way around the room until I find a light switch. I flip it on and the bright light stings my eyes. I blink until they adjust to the light.

I'm in someone's living room. Nothing looks familiar. I glance around for my purse, but don't see it anywhere. In fact, I don't see any of my belongings. Where's my phone? I'm dressed up. I'm wearing high heels, Louboutin, a nude-colored short skirt and matching silk blouse. Crap! What has happened? I try to piece the night together, but I'm coming up blank. I don't remember anything. Am I drunk? I don't seem to be. I glance over my legs and arms, holding them out in front of me. I'm not hurt, just a bit stiff from being on the floor.

Suddenly, I freeze in fear.

Am I alone?

The rest of the house seems dark, like no one's home, or they're sleeping—maybe not aware of my presence? I see a glass sliding door and quietly move toward it. On the way, I notice a picture hanging on the wall. There's a brass nameplate attached to the bottom of the frame: *The Spencers*. Husband, wife, and two young teens—one boy, one girl. Typical good-looking American family, but they mean nothing to me, so I move on.

I'm in the kitchen now. It looks tidy and clean, but unfamiliar. As I head to the door, I spot a purse, a set of keys, and a phone neatly sitting on the table. I recognize all three, quickly snatch them up and slide open the door as softly as I possibly can. I'm in the Spencers' backyard. I look up at the house and see it's a two story. I rush around to the front, but the car in the driveway isn't familiar.

I feel panic race through my bones and my legs begin to shake. I have no idea where I am, who I was with, or how I got here. Why does this have to happen? And why now? I thought things would be different now. I thought Jax had … fixed it! He promised these blackouts would fade, but here I am, once more, waking up with no memory of the previous evening.

I stand on the curb at the edge of the driveway and look both ways, studying the parked cars lining the dark street. I see a flash of silver as the wind blows, allowing the streetlight to peek through the tree branches. The car looks familiar. I start in that direction so I can get a better look. I click the remote and the parking lights flash. Oh, thank goodness. I jog lightly, and carefully, in my four-inch heels. I throw open the driver's door and slide in, quickly locking it.

I look at the phone for the first time. It's three a.m. I search for calls and texts and find nothing that shouldn't be there. There's nothing to give me any kind of hint as to where I am, or who I was with. I start the car and put it in gear. Everything I do sounds incredibly loud against the still of the night. I coast slowly past the mystery house and take note of the black metal numbers attached to the pillar by the front door: **10038**. I get to the end of the street and strain to see the street name: **Shelby Dr**. None of this rings a bell.

I feel sick to my stomach and have to pull over until the sensation fades. Why do I have to live like this? It's not fair. I feel like I'm trapped inside my own mind. It doesn't matter how careful I am, or how good I live; whatever happens when I black out could be the death of me. No matter how stable of a life I live, I'll always live in fear that something horrible is about to happen to me. This has got to end. I blame Jax. He's supposed to be counseling me every week, but instead he just orders me around, or worse, ignores me.

What if I went to someone else? A different psychiatrist. One who's on *my* side. Jax is *not* on my side in the slightest. The only thing he's ever concerned with is Greta. He doesn't care whether I live or die; in fact, when he doesn't need me anymore, he's going to kill me. I know he will. I can see it in his eyes. He's threatened to *get rid of me* numerous times over the years. Any time I disobey him, he reminds me how easy it would be to *let me go* and not have to deal with me anymore. He said it would make his life calmer—less chaotic. Then I remind him how much he needs me, that if he got rid of me his marriage would be a mess.

He threatens me and then smiles at me, unscrupulously. He loves to taunt me. It's all a power trip to him. He says he can do it with the snap of his fingers and, *poof*, I'll be gone. I believe him. He's very good at what he does.

I put the car back in gear and start to drive again. My hands shake as I grip the steering wheel, causing me to white-knuckle it. I'm scared. Not at what may have taken place tonight during my blackout, but at what Jax is going to do to me once he finds out that I fled the scene without checking things out first. Whenever I black out, I'm supposed to find out where I am, who I'm with and why, and what may have happened. I couldn't do that tonight. I was too scared. Besides, everything looked peaceful. Maybe I was out with a friend and we went back to her … er … his house, and then I fell asleep. I'm supposed to stay away from men. I moan as I think ahead about reiterating all this to Jax. He's going to kill me.

He will absolutely have my head!

Chapter Eleven
Greta

FRIDAY EVENING

"I'm thinking about starting with a 2005 Vieux Château Certan, what do you think?" Jax asks as he rolls the bottle back and forth in his hands, examining the label.

"Who are you trying to impress?" I smile as I pull four Waterford crystal glasses from the cabinet. Why is it if someone enjoys the finer things in life it automatically makes them a snob? Jax and I happen to have very good taste in everything from food and drink to décor. It has nothing to do with money, although we can more than afford our devilish splurges. If we had no money, our fine taste wouldn't automatically be nonexistent. It would still be there, it would just be a bit more painful because we wouldn't be able to afford anything we desired, like we can now.

"The neighbors, of course. Who else?" We both laugh and he pops the cork on the wine.

"Is everything ready? Any last-minute touches I've

forgotten?" I ask nervously as I glance around the kitchen at the food and drinks.

Jax yells into the dining room. "Rocio, please tell my wife everything is set and ready to go so she can stop worrying."

Rocio comes around the corner nodding her head. "Everything ready, miss. You have nothing to worry about. It's all good and perfect." She smiles proudly and gathers the four wineglasses I just set on the island. "You start in the living room with drinks?"

"Yes, Rocio. That will be splendid. Thank you," Jax says as he winks at me. "See? Nothing to worry about." He reaches out and gives me a tight hug, kissing me on the forehead. He always knows how to ease my anxieties—and so does Rocio. I don't know what I'd do without her.

Jax has known her since he was a young teenager. She worked as a nanny/housekeeper for his family for many years before his parents passed away. Both of his parents died way too young. When Jax was twenty-four and away at Harvard Medical School, his father, Michael, suffered a fatal heart attack. He was only fifty-two, and in great shape, according to Jax. His diet consisted of lean protein, organic fruits and veggies, and sprouted grains. He also jogged five or more miles every morning, never skipping a day, so I was told. His death was very unexpected and came as a shock to everyone. He was a highly respected psychiatrist in New Orleans, but that's not where he made all his money. He also invested in real estate, buying and selling. He owned several restaurants in the French Quarter, along with a few bed and breakfasts, but he was most dedicated to his psychiatry practice.

I didn't know Jax's father. He died a year before we met, but I did have the pleasure of knowing his mother, Evelyn. She was the sweetest woman I've ever met. She catered to Jax, but not in a smother-mother way. It was more along the lines of letting him know if he ever needed anything, she'd be there for him. She loved him dearly—you could see it in her eyes every time we'd visit together. Her face would light up and her eyes would sparkle any time he'd walk in the room. She adored him, and he returned those feelings. There was nothing Jax wouldn't do for his mother.

He hated that she lived alone in that big house. Rocio was a live-in, but Jax always said his mother needed to be with family, that is until his younger brother moved back. Preston was nothing but trouble. A drunken slob who despised his own family because they were successful, and he wasn't. He couldn't live up to his father's expectations of him, at least that's what he claimed, according to Jax. Preston had moved to California years earlier to attend UCLA, but instead his college partying became a full-time job. He eventually dropped out and then separated himself from the family because he knew they wouldn't approve.

Sometimes Jax's father would pay for Preston to come home for the holidays. Jax said it would always end in catastrophe. His brother would get drunk at dinner and start in about how he never had a fair shot. He'd blame his father for putting too much pressure on him, expecting him to follow along in his footsteps, like the goody-two-shoes Jax. By the end of the holidays, Jax's parents would be kicking him out, forbidding him to come back.

Evelyn died six years after Michael, due to complications from triple bypass surgery. I've never seen anyone so heartbroken. Jax mourned his mother's death for a long time. At several points I thought he'd never recover. His practice started to suffer. He was losing patients due to his long absences. Then, almost instantaneously, he bounced back and got back into his old routine. He said it was time to get back to life and move forward. I was relieved he was starting to get back to his old self again.

Jax couldn't stand to lose Rocio, so he offered her a job with us. She's not a live-in, but she's here several days a week, and sees to our parties when we entertain. She also keeps his office building downtown clean and tidy for him. He keeps her busy and the pay is good, so she sticks around. She loves him, though. She treats him like a son. I think that's why he can't let go. He misses that motherly attention. Rocio helps to fill that void.

"Mr. Jax, your guests have arrived. I seat them in the living room. You go and I grab the hors d'oeuvres." Rocio starts gathering the plates and platters of food, placing them on a large tray.

Jax says something as we make our way to the living room, but I don't hear him. I have only one thing on my mind ... meeting Owen. I'm wondering how he's going to react toward me. He wouldn't dare say anything about the other night. That would almost be a confession. He'd be making it obvious he has something to hide.

After introductions, the four of us take a seat in the living room. Rocio brings us wine, and Jax starts off the conversation asking Owen about what he does for a living. Typical male aim—defining each other by their profession. He's in pharmaceutical sales. That's a prosperous industry. He and Jax will have something in common to chat about since Jax, as a psychiatrist, knows plenty about meds.

I can sense Owen is relieved to direct his attention to Jax so he doesn't have to look at me. During introductions, he could barely make eye contact. He would glance at me and then his eyes would immediately shift downward and to the side. He knows I saw him acting like a madman, running after his wife like an animal; he was completely out of control. I think back to that night. He'd been breathing so furiously, I could see his chest heaving. There was nothing but pure rage radiating from this man. He would have brutalized her if he'd been able to catch her.

I tune back into the conversation at the mention of my name.

"Greta can tell you more about that. She's a fantastic decorator—well, just look around you. Looks like we're living in a French château, no?" Jax laughs and turns his attention to me.

I smile and tilt my head downward, embarrassed at his gracious compliments, although I know he believes every word. "What can I say? I love what I do, and I think that's the key. When a person lives out their passion every day, great things happen. But enough about that." I have a different topic I want spotlighted. "My true love and passion in life rests in helping battered women." Owen almost chokes on his wine and Isabella coughs.

"Greta volunteers at the local women's shelter downtown, House of Ruth. She may spend more time there than with clients, isn't that right?" Jax looks at me proudly and squeezes my hand.

Isabella leans forward and reaches for a crab cake from the coffee table between us. "Oh, how wonderful. How long have you done that?" Her voice is shaky, but she plays it off nicely.

"Over ten years now. If I could do it full time, I wouldn't hesitate. Some of these women are in real danger. They've been beaten, threatened, and even killed. It's heartbreaking."

"What does the House of Ruth do, exactly? How do they guarantee these women's safety?"

"Well, I guess safety is never a guarantee, but we do everything we can to keep the abusive men away and in jail. We also provide clothing, toiletries, food, and shelter to those whose lives are in danger. We help them to pick up and start over by assisting them in getting new jobs in new locations where they can't be found."

"And what keeps a deranged man from busting through the door and shooting up the place?" Owen asks, this time staring into my eyes intently. I guess his embarrassment has profoundly subsided.

"Nothing keeps a *deranged man* from doing anything, but because every volunteer in there is packing heat, he won't get very far before being filled with a lot of lead." I smile crookedly and sip my wine. "You see," my attention is directed toward Owen now, "the women needing shelter don't stay at the downtown location. They're taken to a private shelter no one knows about." I nod assuredly to Isabella, and we lock eyes briefly. I can see she's absorbing everything I'm saying. She doesn't know I suspect anything, but I can see in her eyes that she wants to tell me, and now she knows I'll understand. She knows I'm more than just the next-door neighbor. I'm a safeguard, I'm protection, I'm … a way out!

Owen clears his throat and shifts awkwardly in his seat.

Jax speaks up then, directing his attention to Isabella. "And you? What do you do?"

Isabella stares at the floor and smiles sheepishly. "I'm actually a housewife. Do we still use that term these days? Housewife?" She laughs awkwardly. "I used to practice law. Graduated from the University of Pennsylvania …"

Jax chimes in. "That's a great school. Quite an accomplishment."

"Yes, it is. I was good at what I did, too." She smiles and takes a large swig of her wine. Something has changed about her. She looks … hard. Suddenly, her facial features look sharp, and her voice crass.

Jax must notice it, too, because he calls out to Rocio. "Would you bring the bottle of wine, please, and then we'll be heading into the dining room for dinner." He turns again toward Isabella. "What made you decide to quit?"

She doesn't hesitate with her answer. "Owen couldn't stand me …"

"… working so much," Owen quickly interjects. "She worked all hours of the day, every day. It was wearing her down and was taxing on her health. I couldn't allow her to go on like that. We both agreed I made plenty of money and that it would be better for her to move on to something else."

Jax nods and slightly shrugs his shoulders. He's a hard

worker, so doing anything to create a quieter and more peaceful life wouldn't be something he can relate to. I glance at Isabella and her face is solemn. The bitterness in her eyes and small quiver of her bottom lip tell me she's about as peaceful inside as a Tasmanian devil.

"So what did you move on to then?" Jax directs his question to Isabella, but it's Owen who answers.

"She hasn't quite figured it out yet." He leans over and squeezes her hand in his. "Have you, dear?"

"I have a great idea. We could always use donations at the shelter. If you have any gently used clothing and shoes, and wouldn't mind buying a few toiletries or makeup, that would be a tremendous help," I say and raise my eyebrows in anticipation.

"I'm sure I can rummage through my closet and muster up something. I'd love to help in any way I can." Her face lights up, and she manages a smile.

"Well, then, I'll take it a step farther. How would you like to join me every week and do some volunteer work for House of Ruth?"

"I'd love nothing more," Isabella says with a broad smile.

I glance at Owen—who looks as if the veins in his neck are about to burst—and say, "Well, looky there, now we found something for her to do." I wink at him and stand up, ready to head to the dining room for dinner.

Dinner consists mainly of small talk. Lots of questions to help us get acquainted. No one is aware I know Owen's and Isabella's secret except for Owen and me. I never mentioned anything to Jax. I want to wait until I know for sure, but after this evening I'm more than positive Owen is an abuser. I can tell in his conversations, gestures, and mannerisms that he's most definitely a wife beater. That may sound like a peculiar thing for me to say, or to claim, but it's true. Call it a woman's intuition—a sixth sense. We can tell when one of our sisters is in trouble, and Isabella is most definitely in need of help. I can confidently say she is trapped in a situation, a loveless marriage, that has consumed her, and she needs help breaking free.

The problem is, an abusive man never lets his woman get away. Once the split is made, he will search, threaten, and even kill her if she doesn't come back to him. Abusive men are the most controlling of creatures.

Sometimes, the only way to break free is for him to die.

Chapter Twelve
Evangeline

MARCH 29
WEDNESDAY AFTERNOON

I'm sitting in my usual spot in Jax's office, waiting. He's not present. The door was unlocked, so I let myself in. I'm nervous to tell him about my blackout last week, yet it's something he needs to know. I can't keep anything from him—he'll just find out later anyway, he always does. He has a way of reading people. It's almost as if he can mind read; in fact, sometimes I think he can. I feel like he has mental telepathy when I'm with him.

What's taking him so long? He's never late to one of our sessions. I glance down at my watch. He's *not* late. I'm early. Anxious to get this over with, I guess. I hear a noise coming from the other room. Restless, I get up and follow the sound. It's ice clinking into a glass.

"Hello, Jax. I'm waiting for you," I say impatiently as I join him in the kitchen.

"You're supposed to wait in my office, Evangeline. You have no business coming in here." He doesn't even glance in my direction. He sets his glass of ice on the countertop and then pops the tab on a can of soda and slowly pours it in, pausing occasionally to allow time for the fizz to recede.

"I got tired of waiting. Could you please hurry up?" This time he stops what he's doing, turns and looks at me through narrowed eyes.

"I do believe you have something for me today. Am I correct in assuming this?" He tilts his head back slightly and chuckles. "Ah, that's why you're early. I should have guessed as much." He waves his hand toward me. "Go, and I'll follow you. This, I've got to hear. What could possibly be bothering you today?"

Back in his office I head straight for the beige suede sofa. I won't be sitting across from his desk like a paying customer. Today, I'll be sitting wherever I please, because I have something he wants. Information.

He chuckles once more as I make my choice for seating. "I can hardly wait," Jax says as he takes a seat in the chair across from me and sets his soda on the coffee table between us.

I immediately reach for the bottle of scotch because today I hold the power. He quickly knocks my hand away.

"I'll do what I want," I snap.

"Not until you tell me what you've got." His eyes widen in awareness. "You weren't at the coffee shop this morning. I thought I'd finally gotten through to you, and you'd given up on irritating me, but now I'm thinking it's because your mind is on something else." He runs his fingers through his hair in thought. "Tell me. What is it?"

"You won't be happy," I say, eyeballing the bottle of scotch. I need a drink to get through this. Jax isn't the easiest person to please, and if I don't do things his way, there's always hell to pay. He belittles me, talks down to me, and then ultimately threatens to kill me. Even though I fear him right now, I have to act as if I hold all the cards.

Jax furrows his brow and leans forward, resting his elbows on his knees. "Go ahead."

"I woke up Friday night, er, Saturday morning, I mean, and I didn't know where I was. It was the house of a stranger. Nothing looked familiar, and I'm not sure how I got there."

Jax raises his eyebrows in surprise and worry. "Wh-What was your state? What was the state of the house? Was anyone around? Did anyone see you?" Questions are flying out of his mouth, but none are registering with me. I just keep talking.

"It was dark … and quiet. I slipped out the back. My car was parked along the curb a few houses down."

"Your car?" Jax asks, surprised.

"Greta's. It was Greta's car. I was driving Greta's car." I quickly correct myself.

"Wow, woman! Did you find out anything? Like, why you were there, or who you'd been visiting?" I hear the concern in his voice.

"I-I don't know." I take a deep breath, because I know his anger is coming. "I'm starting to forget things lately. My memory is bad for some reason. Maybe I'm not sleeping well."

"What do you mean you don't know?" Jax says, ignoring my concern over my memory. "Why didn't you find out?" He runs his fingers through his hair again, this time in frustration.

"I was scared. I just wanted to get out of there. I mean, I looked around as I exited and everything looked in order, like there had been no trouble." My voice is trembling now.

"Were you clean? No signs of a struggle?"

"No signs of a struggle. My clothing was good, my body was fine. I found the keys and purse sitting neatly on the kitchen table ... everything seemed fine ..."

Jax interrupts me. "But you don't know for sure because you don't even know where you were or who you'd been with." He raises his voice. He's becoming angry now.

"At least I didn't wake up in a pool of blood, as usual. Can't you be happy about that? Can't you, just this once, be satisfied that everything was okay, and then let it go? Be grateful you didn't receive a phone call from me in the middle of the night with a mess to clean up."

He cocks his head to the side and gasps. "How do you know everything was fine, or that you weren't seen by anyone? Did you at least look in all the rooms?"

I shake my head. "No. It was three in the morning. It was the dead of night and you could hear a pin drop. I had to get out without making a sound. Once I saw I was okay and my clothes weren't covered in blood, I left."

"Are you sure no one saw you drive away?" Jax says as he jumps up from his chair and starts to pace.

"I'm as sure as I can be."

"Do you remember an address of where you were?"

"One, three, zero, zero, eight Shelby Drive."

His eyebrows raise in astonishment. "Crap, let me write that down." He rushes to his desk and jots it down on a sticky note. "Here's what worries me…" He looks me straight in the eye. "Why were you parked down the street?"

"I've already thought about that. Maybe something was planned, but for whatever reason, it fell through."

Jax stares at me, and I can see distress in his eyes as he tries to figure out what happened. There's a part of me that wishes his concern and worry was for *my* sake, but I know it's not. His concern, first and foremost, is for himself. He wouldn't want anything to interfere with his sanctimonious facade. Secondly, he's thinking about Greta. He certainly doesn't want the reputation of his little princess wife flawed. What would he ever do if his picture-perfect reputation as doctor, husband, neighbor, and friend was less than, well, picture-perfect?

"Oh, there's one other thing. On the way out, I noticed a photo hanging on the wall. The frame had a metal plate that read *The Spencers*. Mean anything to you?"

"Spencers?" Jax rubs his chin. "No. Wait … maybe. Jacqueline Spencer?"

I shrug.

"I have a patient, Jacqueline." Jax looks at me as if I can fill in the blanks, but I'm completely clueless.

"Does she have an abusive husband?" I chuckle, and prop my feet up onto the sofa.

"Yes, as a matter of fact, she does. He's a mean mouth." I can see his wheels turning as he pieces it together. "Get your feet off the sofa."

I do as I'm told, letting my boots fall to the floor with a thud. "Well, there you have it. Abusive husband. Now you gotta figure out how I knew about him and what I was doing there. Good luck with that," I say sarcastically.

I smile wickedly as I envision Jax's world crashing down on him, and quickly cover my mouth with my hand so he doesn't see. It takes a lot of trust on his part … when I wake up after a blackout. He must trust me to do the right thing, and to call him so that he can come to my aid, if need be.

"Don't go to that house again," he says demandingly.

I laugh incredulously. "As if I have any control. Remember, I'm the one who wakes up having no idea how I got there or what's transpired. I'm clueless after these blackouts and you know it. I don't have a choice, Jax. My decisions are made for me." I'm angry and resentful now.

"Oh, please. We're not going down that road again. *Poor Little Evangeline doesn't have a choice in life. She was dealt a bad hand.* Give me a freaking break. You shouldn't even be here and you know it. What else do you want? I already allow you to stay, to invade my life, not to mention my marriage!"

"How dare you. If it weren't for me, sweet little Greta wouldn't even have this life. YOOUU wouldn't have this life. I'm the reason your fairy tale even exists for the both of you."

Jax's face becomes flushed and I see fire in his eyes. "Get out!" He's furious now. He rounds the coffee table at such speed I think he's going to strike me. I move quickly, tripping over my own feet and stumbling in the process. I grab the corner of the table long enough to regain my balance and then I run out of his office. I head through the kitchen to the French doors, where I burst through them onto the back patio.

"You're going to be sorry one day, Jax. Sorry for the way you treat me. Wait and see what happens. Just wait and see,"

I yell at the top of my lungs. I trip again and realize the laces on my boots are undone. This infuriates me and I scream out, fists clenched. I could tear his head off right now. I hate him. I hate everything about his self-righteous... I stop myself. He's not worth my anger or my time. I take in a few deep breaths and then lean down and start to tie my boots. Someone is watching me. I swing around to find a redheaded neighbor staring at me, her mouth agape in shock.

"Mind your own business, lady." I start laughing hysterically. The look on her face is priceless. I guess she's not used to any commotion coming from *this* house. The Kavanagh mansion where everything is picture-perfect.

If she only knew the truth of what goes on behind these closed doors.

Chapter Thirteen
Greta

APRIL 10
MONDAY AFTERNOON

I arrive home earlier than planned. I've been hired to redecorate the Southern Oaks Plantation for a special charity event. They'll be holding an auction in the ballroom in a few weeks and are looking for a late-nineteenth-century theme. They want to change out the drapes, some furniture, and paintings. Easy-breezy. Quick money. The work I did out at Oak Alley seems to be gaining attention and other plantation owners are starting to ask about me, and *for* me. This is my third call. Bocage Plantation called me last week wanting a quote for some restoration upgrades. They are transitioning the plantation into an event venue and are planning a new ballroom to be added behind the plantation. Cha-ching.

Business is booming, but it has left me exhausted the last couple of weeks. I'm glad to be home a little early today and plan to soak in the bathtub before dinner. I kick my heels off and place them neatly on the shoe rack. Then I peel off my tan slacks and silk top and toss them into the clothes hamper. In the bathroom I already have a glass of chardonnay waiting for me. I place it next to the tub, not without taking a sip first, and then turn on the water. I like it hot to where it takes a minute for my body to adjust to the heat before I can fully lower myself into the tub. My phone and Evangeline's journal sit on the edge, next to the wineglass.

After relaxing for a few minutes in the warm water, I reach for the journal. Let's see what this strange bird is up to. Her last couple of entries have been a bit disturbing, to say the least, but I'm curious just the same. Maybe even more so now.

I WOKE UP COVERED IN BLOOD LAST NIGHT. HERE WE GO AGAIN. I WANTED TO JUST RUN AWAY ... FOR GOOD THIS TIME. I THOUGHT ABOUT LEAVING AND NEVER COMING BACK, BUT THE LAST TIME I DID THAT, HE CAME AFTER ME AND IT TOOK NO TIME AT ALL FOR HIM TO FIND ME. HE THREATENED TO GET RID OF ME. HE SAID HE'D ALWAYS FIND ME, AND THAT I'D NEVER BE ABLE TO HIDE FROM HIM.

I BELIEVE IT. EVEN THOUGH I CAN'T STAND HIM, HE HAS SOME GOOD ATTRIBUTES, HIS IQ BEING ONE OF THEM. HE'S GENIUS LEVEL, AND I DON'T HAVE A PROBLEM ADMITTING HE CAN OUTWIT ME EVERY NOW AND THEN. I FEEL SO DESPERATE RIGHT NOW. I WANT TO ESCAPE THIS LIFE; IT DOESN'T BELONG TO ME. IF I WAS IN CONTROL, I WOULDN'T BE LIVING LIKE THIS. I'D BE DOING THE SAME THINGS OTHER TWENTY-ONE-YEAR-OLDS DO. I COULD BE GOING TO

COLLEGE RIGHT NOW. OR HOW ABOUT A BOYFRIEND? I'VE
NEVER EVEN HAD A BOYFRIEND BECAUSE HE WON'T LET ME.
HE KEEPS SUCH TIGHT REINS ON ME I CAN'T EVEN HAVE
FRIENDS, MUCH LESS A GUY IN MY LIFE.

ONCE, I GOT SO ANGRY AT HIM, I THREATENED TO END IT
ALL. HE GRABBED ME AROUND THE NECK, BUT ONCE HE
REALIZED WHAT HE WAS DOING, HE LET GO. HE MAY BE
ABLE TO GET RID OF ME, I DON'T DOUBT THAT PART, BUT
HE CAN'T HURT ME; NOT PHYSICALLY. HIS LITTLE PRINCESS
WOULD HAVE TO PAY THE PRICE FOR HIS ANGER, AND I'D
LOVE TO SEE HOW HE'D TALK HIS WAY OUT OF THAT ONE.
I LAUGH JUST THINKING ABOUT IT.

BACK TO MY EVENTFUL EVENING LAST NIGHT... I CALLED
HIM AND HE CAME IMMEDIATELY. WALKED THROUGH THE
DOOR LIKE IT WAS NOTHING. HE HAD THE USUAL IN HAND:
BLEACH, TOWELS, SCRUB BRUSHES, GLOVES. HE HANDED
ME A SPONGE, BUCKET, AND A BOTTLE OF BLEACH AND
TOLD ME TO GET TO WORK, WHILE HE DID THE SAME.

THEN IT WAS TIME TO MOVE THE BODY. IT WAS A MAN,
BUT THIS ONE WASN'T TOO BIG OF A GUY. IT'S ALWAYS
A MAN, SOMETIMES LARGE AND VERY HEAVY. I HATE THE
BIG ONES. IT TAKES US FOREVER TO MOVE A LARGE BULKY
BODY LIKE THAT. THE SMALL ONES ARE SO MUCH EASIER.
WE LAID DOWN A PLASTIC TARP ON THE AREA WE'D
ALREADY CLEANED AND THEN MOVED THE BODY. HE
GRABBED THE GUY'S TORSO WHILE I GRABBED A LEG IN

EACH HAND.

ONE, TWO, THREE, GO.

WE SET HIM DOWN.

ONE, TWO, THREE, GO.

IT ONLY TOOK US TWO TIMES AND WE HAD HIM ON THE TARP. WE ROLLED HIM UP TIGHTLY, ALMOST LIKE SWADDLING A BABY. NOT THAT I KNOW MUCH ABOUT SWADDLING, BUT I'VE SEEN IT DONE BEFORE.

I WAS TIRED AT THIS POINT AND WANTED TO STOP. I WANTED TO GO HOME, BUT HE DEMANDED WE FINISH. EVEN THOUGH IT WAS FOUR IN THE MORNING, IT WAS A SHADY MOTEL AND THERE WERE A FEW PEOPLE MOVING IN THE SHADOWS, PROBABLY DRUG DEALERS, CRIMINALS, AND THE SORT. ANYONE MOVING STEALTHILY IN THE NIGHT IS UP TO NO GOOD. AND WE FIT INTO THAT CATEGORY. NOTHING GOOD EVER COMES AFTER MIDNIGHT.

HE WATCHED OUT THE WINDOW FOR A MINUTE AND THEN WAVED FOR ME TO PICK UP MY END OF THE TARP. WE HURRIED OUT THE DOOR AND TO HIS CAR. HE CLICKED THE TRUNK RELEASE AS WE APPROACHED, CARRYING OUR SWADDLED BABY. WE QUIETLY SET HIM DOWN ON THE GROUND AND RESTED FOR A MINUTE. HE NODDED FOR ME TO GRAB MY END, SO I DID.

ONE, TWO, THREE, GO.

WE DUCKED BACK INSIDE THE MOTEL ROOM WHERE WE FINISHED THE CLEANUP PROCESS. AFTERWARDS, HE HELPED

ME INTO THE SHOWER WHERE I SCRUBBED SOMEONE ELSE'S BLOOD FROM MY CLOTHES AND MY FLESH. I PUT MY WET AND BLOODY CLOTHES IN THE LARGE PLASTIC BAG HE HELD OUT TO ME AND THEN HE TIED IT UP NICE AND TIGHT. IT WAS ALL ROUTINE AT THIS POINT IN OUR LIVES. WE DIDN'T TALK, WE JUST MOVED THROUGH THE STEPS, SILENTLY. HE HANDED ME A FRESH CHANGE OF CLOTHES AND THEN WASHED HIS HANDS GOOD AND LONG, SCRUBBING EVERY CREVICE AND GETTING UNDER THE NAILS THOROUGHLY.

WE WAITED UNTIL THE COAST WAS CLEAR AND THEN WE HURRIED DOWN THE SIDEWALK TOWARD HIS CAR. HALFWAY THERE, HE POINTED ME IN THE DIRECTION OF MY CAR. I HEADED OVER, AND SURE ENOUGH, THERE IT WAS, HIDDEN IN THE SHADOWS. I HADN'T BEEN SURE IF I'D DRIVEN THAT NIGHT, BUT HE ALWAYS KNOWS. I CAN COUNT ON HIM TO BE AWARE OF THE DETAILS BEFORE HE EVEN GETS TO ME.

WE WON'T SPEAK OF THIS EVENT AGAIN ... EVER. WHAT'S DONE IS DONE AND WE WON'T TALK ABOUT IT. HE WON'T LET ME, BUT I DON'T WANT TO ANYWAY. IT SICKENS ME. IT'S NOT FAIR I HAVE TO LIVE LIKE THIS. CLEANING UP OTHER PEOPLE'S MESSES. AND HE SHOULD FEEL THE SAME WAY, BUT HE DOESN'T. HE'S MORE THAN HAPPY TO BE AWAKENED IN THE DEAD OF NIGHT, DRIVE OUT TO SHADY LOCATIONS, AND CLEAN UP THE REMAINS OF SOME POOR SAP WHO WAS SLAUGHTERED IN HIS SLEEP. I ACTUALLY DON'T KNOW IF THEY'RE KILLED AS THEY SLEEP, BUT I'D

THINK IT WOULD HAVE TO BE WHILE THEY'RE AT A GREAT
DISADVANTAGE, AND THAT'S THE ONLY THING I CAN COME
UP WITH.

I TRY NOT TO THINK ABOUT IT, THOUGH. I DON'T WANT TO
KNOW THE DETAILS, AND I'M GRATEFUL I DON'T EVER
REMEMBER ANYTHING.

I slam the book closed and fling it onto the floor next to the tub, as if that will erase everything my eyes have just seen. What am I reading? What kind of a person keeps a-a … killing journal? What kind of a person kills? I've got to go to the police. I should tell Jax about what I've just read and then I'll take it to the police. I need to get rid of this book. I glance at it lying on the floor. There's a part of me that wants to pick it up and finish it, but that would be twisted and I can't allow myself to do it. But in my defense, there's also a part of me that is terrified to know what else lies within those pages.

The question is: Which is stronger, and which will win?

Jax smiles at me and takes a sip of his wine.

"Dinner is fantastic, by the way," he says and takes a bite of pasta carbonara. One of the easiest dishes to make, but he doesn't need to know that. I force myself to return the smile as I swirl noodles around my fork like I'm going to take a bite, but then I don't. I've been playing with my food for ten minutes, but I can't seem to eat; not after reading Evangeline's journal of murder.

"How was your day?" It was all I could think to say, but I believe I already asked him this question when he got home.

"You already asked me that." Jax wipes his mouth on the cloth napkin and sets it back in his lap. I can feel him studying me, although I'm not looking at him. Here it comes. "Okay, what's going on, Greta? Out with it. I've been home almost an hour and you still haven't told me what's on your mind."

When did psychiatrists become mind readers? I did everything in my power to hide the fact I'm troubled, but Jax saw through it immediately. This small talk at dinner has been nothing more than a game, while he waits for me to reveal what's bothering me. I guess I've been playing right along with him, waiting for the right time. I was hoping he'd be closer to having his meal finished before I ruin his appetite.

Just spit it out, girl. He'll be fine. Jax is a big boy. He can even help you!

I inhale deeply. "Do you remember the night we moved in and I found someone's journal?"

He pauses to think. "Yes, yes, I remember that. Did you find the author?"

"Not exactly." I twirl more noodles onto my fork. I fear Jax will judge me for reading it. "I—I flipped through the first few pages to see if there was a full name, address, phone number, social media account, or something written down so I could contact this person."

"Was there?" he asks, brow raised.

"No, but ... but I saw something else." I take in another breath. Jax is watching me intently now. His eyes are fixed on me. There's no turning back. "I ended up reading a couple of lines, which led me to read more." I wait for a response.

He hesitates. "Well, that's not right, but no harm done, I guess. If you can't find the owner, you need to get rid of it. Throw it away before you read any more." He takes his focus off me and resumes eating. Here comes the bombshell.

"After work today, I read a little more. The author of this journal gives a detailed account of cleaning up a murder she, apparently, committed."

Jax drops his fork and it clanks loudly against his plate, causing me to jump. "Are you kidding me? You can't be serious! This has got to be some kind of prank. Really."

"What if it's not? I mean, I've read quite a bit of it so far and it seems to be a legitimate journal."

Jax shakes his head, refusing to believe it. "Some prankster left it behind on purpose. They wanted it to shake someone up, stir up drama. That's probably all it is, but we've got to turn it in to the police, regardless."

I sigh with relief. He seems more concerned with getting rid of it than the fact I shouldn't have been reading it. "My thoughts exactly. I knew you'd help me figure out what to do."

"Go get it and let me take a look, then tomorrow you can stop by the police station and turn it in. Just say you were flipping through the pages looking for a way to return it when you noticed something that seemed suspicious, so you decided to give it to the police. If they ask you any questions, be vague."

"Let me run upstairs and grab it so you can read the part about the dead body." I hop up from my chair, almost giddy with relief. Problem solved. I'll turn it over to the police and then I won't have to think about it anymore. Jax is in full support and doesn't think small of me for reading it.

I race into the bedroom closet and reach up to the top shelf. It's hidden under my sweaters. Back in the kitchen, and slightly out of breath, I open it to the pages about the murder and hand it over to Jax.

"Read this part," I say anxiously. I watch him closely as he starts to read, waiting to see his reaction. I'm curious if he'll be as disturbed over it as I am. After a moment, I see his eyes widen and I notice his breathing quickens. He reaches up to his tie and loosens it. Beads of sweat are forming on his brow. He pushes his chair back and stands up, but his eyes never leave the page. I take two steps backward. He looks like he's about to have a heart attack. I'm shocked by his reaction, which is much more dramatic than my own.

"Where did you get this?" he pants.

I feel a lump in my throat and I cough. "What do you mean? You know where." He slams the book closed and examines the cover. "Evangeline. That's the only name on the book, but it's not enough to help me find her, if that's even her name. It could be referencing the Evangeline Home…" I stop speaking as Jax drops the book on the table and doubles over. He looks as if he's about to go into convulsions. His face has turned beet red and the vein in his forehead is bulging. "Jax!"

"Get me a glass of water," he chokes. He's barely able to get the words out. I rush to the sink, fill a glass with water and then race back to him. I try to push him down into the chair, but he pushes back. He wants to stand.

"Sit, Jax, you don't look so good. How can I help you?" Is he having a heart attack? I can feel fear rising through my body and into my chest. I'm about to call 911. "You need to breathe." I pick up my phone from the counter and he snatches it from my hand. I'm scared. I've never seen him like this before.

"It's okay. I think … I'm just having a panic attack. It will … pass," he says between gasps for air. "Give me a minute." I watch as he rips the tie from his neck, flinging it onto the floor. He gulps down the water and slams the glass on the table, making me jump. "Get me something stronger."

I don't argue. I head straight for the liquor cabinet in the living room and grab his favorite bottle of scotch and a glass. I rush back to him and pour a drink as quickly as I can. I hand it to him with shaky hands. He throws it back and hands me the glass.

"Another," he says, and takes in a deep breath. His color is looking better and he sits down, sliding the book off the table and into his lap where he covers it with his hand.

"Oh my gosh, Jax. What just happened to you? You scared me." I hand him the refill of scotch and squeeze his shoulder. "You started reading the journal and I thought you were having a heart attack."

"It has nothing to do with the journal, I can assure you of that. I've been having some mild anxiety lately…"

I interrupt him. "Mild? You call that mild anxiety? The vein in your forehead looked like it was about to burst," I say, placing my hand on his chest. His heart is beating fast.

"It's okay. I'm fine. I probably just need to get on a mild sedative for a while," he says, still a bit winded.

I pull my chair over to his and sit down, taking his hand in mine. I know he doesn't want the attention and is just being polite, but I feel like I need to attend to my husband's needs. As a wife, it's my duty.

"Give me the journal. I'll put it away until I take it to the police tomorrow," I say and reach for it in his lap.

He quickly yanks it away. "No. No, I'm going to handle this myself. You don't need to be involved. Let me take care of it."

"I thought you said it's probably a prank. I'll handle it. You don't need to worry yourself and cause another panic attack like this again. That was really scary."

"I'm fine. Don't worry about me, and don't worry about that journal. I'll take care of it." He drinks down his scotch and then stands, keeping the journal low at his side. "I'm going to take a shower."

I watch as he saunters out of the kitchen and up the staircase. What just happened? One minute Jax is perfectly fine, having a normal dinner, clearheaded as ever, and then within seconds he's doubled over clutching his chest like he's about to keel over. Could what's written in the journal have that profound of an effect on him? Certainly not. I even warned him what was in it beforehand. Of course, I didn't go into details of the murder cleanup, but I'm sure he's used to hearing some pretty whacked out things in his sessions from patients. Something seems amiss here. Why the strong reaction? Is my husband keeping something from me? Does he know more about the journal than he's revealing? How could that be?

He couldn't have known the previous owners because there

weren't any for many years, only the investor, Tom. Could he be having an affair? Is Evangeline a patient of his? She's clearly mental. Maybe they were meeting here for their secret rendezvous before we moved in. That doesn't sound like Jax. He's not a liar, or a cheater. He's a good hardworking man who would never do anything to hurt me. He loves me too much. What then? Why the heart-pumping reaction? Maybe anxiety can be set off by very small events. Maybe our conversation was enough to spark it, and then when he started reading the pages it quickly escalated, causing an attack. That sounds reasonable.

Puh-leeze! You make excuse after excuse for that man. Jax is sneaky. Open your eyes, Greta!

Oh, shut up. I don't need to listen to anything you have to say right now.

You never catch him sneaking around because you don't bother to look.

I don't need to look.

You'd be surprised at what goes on behind your back.

I said to shut up. All you do is try to poison me against him. Go away!

Fine! Find out the hard way. See if I care. I was only trying to help you.

I've picked up our dinner mess, washed the dishes, and turned off the lights. It's time to check on Jax now. I quietly climb the stairs and walk softly down the hall. Am I trying to sneak up on him? Maybe I want to see what he's doing when he thinks I'm not around. I silently enter the room to find him showered and lying on the bed in his lounging pants and T-shirt. He's reading one of his medical books. I laugh inside at my paranoia.

"How do you feel?"

"Come here," he says and places his book on the nightstand. I sit beside him and he pulls me down and hugs me tightly.

"Don't worry about me," he says and chuckles. "I can take care of myself, along with numerous patients. You're expending energy where it's not needed."

"But that journal just set you off. I had no idea it would affect you like that…"

"No. It wasn't the journal. I couldn't care less about that. It was just bad timing, I guess. Anxiety is a strange creature, it strikes when it pleases. There's no rhyme or reason. Did you know most people experience panic attacks while they're sleeping?"

"Sleeping? That's crazy. Isn't that when a person is in their most peaceful state?" I say incredulously.

"It's true. I prescribe a lot of sedatives, such as Xanax or Vistaril, to help people get through the night because they experience a lot of anxiety in the evenings. Sometimes the body winds down, but the mind doesn't and it causes severe anxiety." He reaches up and twirls a section of my hair around his fingers.

"Are you going to take something like that, a sedative so this doesn't happen again?"

"Maybe, but I don't think I need one. It's just been a long day, that's all," he says with a smile. I know he's trying to sound reassuring, but I still feel a sea of worry lurking in the pit of my gut. He pulls me down and pecks me on the lips.

I say goodnight and then head for the closet to change clothes.

You fool. He just handed you a load of crap and you're absorbing it like summer sun on a child's behind.

I'm not listening to you anymore.

I climb into bed thinking about Evangeline. The journal. Jax. Panic attacks. Murder. Mental disorders. Affairs.

I wish I had a sedative to ease *my* thoughts and put me into a restful sleep, free from the nagging voice in my head.

Chapter Fourteen
Greta

APRIL 11
TUESDAY MORNING

I rap my knuckles lightly on Isabella's front door. I made sure Owen had already left for work before walking over here for a visit. I can hear footsteps approaching and then the door swings open. Isabella's face lights up with genuine delight when she sees me.

"Greta! Good to see you. And you brought goodies. My, my, come in," she says as she eyeballs the basket of muffins in one hand and the French press full of coffee in the other. She's completely decked out. Full face of makeup, sharply dressed, and hair bouncing with curls. I glance down at her shoes and notice she's wearing slippers.

"I didn't catch you at a bad time, did I? Looks like you might be on your way out," I say and hesitate before entering.

"Not at all. This is just me. I get gussied up every day whether I'm staying in or not. I know it sounds crazy, but it gives me something to do." She gently tugs on my arm and pulls me into the foyer, closing the door behind me. She locks it. "What a wonderful surprise. You're not working this morning?" She gestures for me to follow her, so I do.

"I only have a few calls to make confirming appointments, that's all." That's not exactly true since I just landed the Southern Oaks gig, but I want to get to know her better and today feels like a good day.

"Sit. Let's have pastries and coffee. This is too kind of you," she says and smiles warmly at me. Her eyes are sincere, and maybe I detect a bit of loneliness in them.

"It was nothing. I love to bake, so any excuse is a good one." I head toward the large island, centered in the kitchen, where I unload the muffins and coffee. Then I take a seat on one of the brown leather barstools tucked underneath. The kitchen is large and modern. What one would expect in a new house this size. It's grey and white, with a hint of fern green here and there. There's a large built-in drink cooler next to the refrigerator. I notice each shelf is filled with wine, except for the bottom two, which are filled with liquor. Someone likes their alcohol, but who am I to judge?

Isabella sets two mugs and two dessert plates down on the island and proceeds to pour coffee into my mug and then her own.

"How do you take it?" she asks.

"Sugar and cream, please."

"Same here." She spoons a teaspoon of sugar and a splash of creamer into both cups and then directs her attention toward me. "I don't mean to pry, but I was a little taken aback a couple of weeks ago when I saw you on the back patio. You looked … distressed."

I pause and try to think back. Two weeks seems like a lifetime ago; I've been so preoccupied with work … and Evangeline's journal. "I was probably stressing out over my workload. Did I see you? I don't even remember," I say, embarrassed. "Sometimes it's like I'm in a different world."

She studies me for a minute and then waves her hand in the air. "Oh, it's no big deal. I just wanted to make sure you were okay. You didn't quite seem yourself." She sips her coffee.

This is odd. "How did I seem?" She's piqued my curiosity.

"Your clothing … it seemed a bit … off. Not what I usually see you wearing."

I suddenly feel she's uncomfortable. "Off? In what way?"

"Forget it. You were probably just lounging around, and I'm used to seeing you dressed up, that's all." She sips her coffee again and reaches for a muffin. "So how are things going?"

Is she trying to change the subject? "Things are good. As I mentioned, work has been keeping me busy…"

She interrupts me. "I meant at home. How are things at home?"

I pause. "Wonderful. If you're asking about my marriage, things couldn't be better. How are things with Owen?" There's an edge to my voice.

She looks surprised, and I'm trying to figure out why. I feel as if she's trying to imply my marriage has problems when it's her marriage that is in shambles. Ah, yes, she's using a type of psychology on me. I've heard Jax speak of this before. A person will point out the faults of others—even invent them, if need be—in an attempt to cover up their own faults. There's a medical term for it, but I can't recall it right now. Isabella knows her marriage is falling apart, so she wants to try and make it look like mine is in trouble.

"Did I say something wrong?" She raises her brow as if she's genuinely confused.

I feel myself losing all emotional control. "Oh, please, Isabella. You don't think I've noticed what goes on in this house? Owen is so out of control, one can't help but to overhear his yelling, not to mention his erratic behavior. I saw him the night he chased you down the driveway and you sped away."

She immediately bursts into tears. I'm flabbergasted, but quickly reach out and touch her shoulder to comfort her. I'm completely disgusted with myself. *Me*, a person who helps abused women, acting in such a manner. What came over me?

"Oh, I'm so sorry, Isabella. I shouldn't have said those things. I'm so ashamed of myself. Please, forgive me," I say as I squeeze her shoulders, pulling her closer to me.

She's sitting with her hands covering her face. Her body shaking uncontrollably with each sob. I try to pull her hands down, but she fights me and pulls them back, not wanting to show herself. I could kick myself. Abused women are so low on self-esteem, even the slightest remark about their situation could make them feel like they aren't worth anything to anyone.

I see a box of tissues sitting on the desk in the corner of the kitchen and quickly grab several.

"Please, don't cry, Isabella. I can help you. I'm so sorry for what I said." I try to tuck a tissue into one of her hands and she takes it from me. She dabs at her eyes and nose and then buries her face again. "Please, talk to me. Let me be your friend. Let me help you." I rub her back with my hand and then give her a hug, trying to comfort her.

"I'm sorry for becoming hysterical." Her words come out choppy as she tries to speak between sobs.

"You have nothing to be sorry about," I quickly reassure her. "None of this is your fault. Please, let me help you."

"I need help, Greta. I need help so badly. I'm afraid he's going to kill me. You don't understand ... his temper ..."

"Yes, I do understand. I know he's threatened you, because that's what abusers do. But I promise you, there's a way out." I pull my stool closer to hers and sit on the edge, her hands in mine now. Her face is red and blotchy with jagged trails of mascara running down her cheeks.

"I'm scared. There's no way out. I've tried to figure out how I can get away from him, but I can't. I don't have any money, because only he can access the accounts."

"What about family?" I ask, hopeful.

"I'm an only child. My father is deceased and my mother is in an Alzheimer's treatment center. She doesn't even know who I am anymore. And it gets worse..." She looks at me with bulging eyes, filled with fear. "Owen pays for her medical expenses. She gets the best care money can buy. He uses it to trap me. To keep me from running away. I'm stuck, Greta. I don't know what to do anymore. I can barely function. He made me quit my job years ago so he could have control over me. He didn't want me to have my own career, my own money ... or friends. He wants to make sure I have nothing, and no one to run to."

My mind is racing as I take in every word Isabella is saying. Her story isn't much different than others I've heard over the years, but I've never seen a situation where the abuser has collateral. This is going to take some thinking before we're able to sort things out and figure out a way to break free from her abuser.

"You can stay with us anytime, hon. Don't worry about that. Jax will totally understand..."

"No! You can't tell him. No one can know. If it gets back to Owen, he'll cut off the funds for my mother's treatment. Please, you can't tell him."

"Jax is very good in situations like this. He knows how to handle them because he has years of experience in dealing with people like your husband. You can trust him. You can trust us, I promise."

"No, please! You mustn't tell him. I wouldn't be able to sleep knowing he could slip up in front of Owen. Only you and I can know. Promise me you won't tell Jax. Promise me."

I sigh deeply. I really want him to be a part of this. His input as a psychiatrist would be invaluable. Besides, he needs to know what's going on, as my husband, as a man, and as a neighbor. I'm not sure I can agree to not tell him. We don't keep secrets from each other, ever.

"He can help us, hon. I promise, you can trust him."

"No. Please. I'm begging you. I can't take the chance of Owen cutting off my mother's medical treatment. You must promise me. Give me your word."

She's so adamant, I'm forced to agree. I can see pure fear in her eyes. I nod my head. "Okay, I promise I won't tell a soul. This will be between only the two of us."

I don't feel right about it, but I agree to keep her secret anyway.

Chapter Fifteen
Evangeline

APRIL 12
WEDNESDAY AFTERNOON

I quietly peek in through the doorway of Jax's office before entering. He doesn't know I'm here, but it's Wednesday, three sharp, so he's expecting me any minute. I see him. He's pacing the floor like a caged animal. I feel a tinge of worry and fear shoot through my veins. It's an ugly feeling, but I know I can't hide forever. I have to face him sooner or later, and it's best to get it over with as quickly as possible. How bad can it be? It's not like he's going to kill me. I snicker as I head inside.

As soon as I set foot in the room, Jax rushes me. He shoves me against the wall with his hand wrapped tightly around my neck. I'm taken aback, and fear etches its way into my bones, but I keep telling myself he's not going to hurt me. I can't breathe. All I can see is Jax's eyes just inches from my own, aflame with fury. I can feel his body, rigid, up against mine.

"What have you done?" he says through gritted teeth. He

releases me and I fall to the floor. I reach my hands to my neck and cough, but I'm actually trying to cover up my laughter. I knew the journal would eventually make its way to him, so I'm prepared for this. This is my way of gaining some power in this relationship.

"Stop!" he yells.

"I can't help it. You just choked me!"

"Laughing. Stop laughing, you imbecile."

Oh, he noticed that. "Jax, my boy. When are you ever going to learn? If we're going to be partners, then you must give me equal power. Fifty-fifty."

"You idiot! How much have you written down? How many journals do you have? Tell me!" He reaches down and grabs my arms, forcefully pulling me to my feet. I almost lose my balance and he helps to steady me, but then raises his fist.

"Go ahead. Hit me," I taunt, but he grunts and turns away.

"How many journals, you lunatic?" he asks again.

"Just the one," I say and smile slyly.

"Liar!" He runs his fingers through his hair and sighs deeply. "You're going to get us sent to prison."

I shrug.

"Then you'll never get the life you want," he says.

"I'm not going to get it anyway, Jax. Don't talk to me like I'm a child."

"You *are* a child; at least you *act* like one." He's pacing the room, still shaking with anger. "I'm going to be sorry for asking this," he says, more to himself than me, "but why in the world would you leave that journal for Greta to find? And did you ever think it could fall into the hands of someone else?"

I shrug.

"Answer me," he yells. He faces me, folding his arms over his chest.

"I don't like the way you treat me … like I'm second best."

"That's because you *are* second best."

"You treat me like my feelings don't matter."

"Because they *don't*." He starts to pace again. "Sit down," he yells, pointing to a chair.

I take the seat across from his desk and he kneels in front of me, placing his hands on either arm of the chair.

"Evangeline, you're not even supposed to be here. You're a freak of nature."

I slap him across the face. He shakes it off and stands up. I guess he decided getting in my face is a bad idea. He rubs his cheek, which is already welting, walks around the desk, and takes a seat in his chair.

"When will you realize you're playing with fire?" I warn him.

He snorts sarcastically. "Do you even understand what you could have caused us by leaving that journal for Greta to find? She was getting ready to take it to the police, you idiot." He bangs his fist on the desk, but I don't flinch. I'm going to hold my ground.

"I didn't mention names. Only mine on the cover, and that could mean anything. Remember, I don't count. Isn't that what you always tell me? I don't matter."

"Any moron could figure out who we are, especially since the book was found in *my* house. Are you forgetting you'll go down too? There's no escaping that!" He laughs viciously, and

I kick his desk with my boot. "What do you want, Evangeline? What are you trying to accomplish?"

I tell the truth. "I want to be treated equally."

"Equally with Greta? Ha!"

"No. I know I'll never get *that*. I want you to treat me as a fifty-fifty partner in this instead of you getting to call all the shots."

"I call all the shots because I'm smarter. And here's the proof of that," he says as he opens his desk drawer and pulls out the journal. He tosses it onto the desk. I reach for it and he quickly slaps my hand. "Get real," he balks.

"Did you read the whole thing?" I ask.

"Why do you ask? Does it have a surprise ending?"

"It might." I smile crookedly, but he doesn't find me amusing in the slightest. He places the journal back into the drawer and then locks it, leaving the key in the lock. "Aren't you going to threaten me now and tell me how you can get rid of me with the snap of your fingers?" He doesn't speak. I take advantage of the opportunity and mosey over to the bottle of scotch sitting on the coffee table. I pick it up and roll it around in my hands a few times. Jax says nothing. I unscrew the cap and swig from the bottle. Still nothing. I take a seat on the suede sofa, prop my feet up, and swig from the bottle once more.

Within seconds he's making a beeline to me. He pulls me up by my arms, yanks the bottle from my hand, and shoves me toward the door. "Go," he yells.

"You're in no place to be telling me what to do." I remind him.

He gives me a wicked grin and then pushes me again. "See? *Child.*"

"If I act like a child it's because you won't let me be an adult." I head toward the door, knowing my time is up. I quickly turn to him, twist his shirt in my hand and pull him over to me. I plant a big smack on his lips and he pushes me away. "See you next Wednesday, doc, unless I see you sooner to clean up another crime scene." I glance over my shoulder at him.

If looks could kill, I'd be dead on the floor.

Chapter Sixteen
Greta

APRIL 14
FRIDAY EVENING

We pull up to the valet parking at L'Antica Trattoria. It's my favorite Italian restaurant, but we're not here to be wined and dined. On the contrary, we are entertaining some of Jax's friends this evening; his two business partners and their wives. We check in with the hostess at the door, but she knows who we are and promptly leads us to our table where we find our guests already seated.

"Are we late?" Jax asks as we approach the table.

"Someone's got to be last," Frank cracks. We all laugh and say our hellos, handshakes, hugs, and cheek kisses. "I just ordered a bottle of Tenuta San Guido Sassicaia. I mean, you're paying, right?" Frank says to Jax as he takes his seat. We all chuckle again. Jax pulls my chair out for me and I sit, lifting the hem of my dress to one side so that it doesn't drag on the floor.

Jax has known Frank and Ryan for many years. He went to college and then med school with Frank, so they go way back. He met Ryan during his internship. The three of them have been inseparable since, and now they own a practice together. It was Jax's idea to start a private practice, but I knew it was just a matter of time. Jax likes to be king. He likes to be in control and call the shots. Working for someone has never jived with him. He's strong willed, ambitious, and has his own ideas. He won't let anything stand in the way of what he wants in life.

I turn to Frank's wife. "Mia, you look beautiful. I'd never guess you had a baby five months ago. How's she doing anyway?" Mia is one of those women who can't put on a pound if she tries. *High metabolism*, she says. Must be nice. I wouldn't know; I have to work for mine. Mia is tall and slender with a smile that lights up a room, not to mention turns every head, male and female alike. Beautiful in a movie star kind of way. I'm sure she could have been a Victoria's Secret supermodel, if she'd traveled that road.

"Harper is a rambunctious one; that's for sure." She twirls a long strand of chestnut hair around her index finger and smiles proudly. She's got that first-time mother glow. I say give it a few years, and another baby or two, and let's see how she's looking. I giggle inside at the thought. She married well. Frank is no louse. Dark and exotic looking, like her; energetic, intelligent, a good businessman, and funny as hell. He keeps us all laughing, that's for sure. A noted psychiatrist—with a couple of APA awards sitting in his office—he is driven and loves what he does.

"Where have you been keeping yourself these days, Greta? Ryan said something about working from home?" Grace says, leaning in.

"Well, we just bought a new house in Mandeville. It's quite large with the perfect space for a home office. That way I'm not driving back and forth so much to New Orleans."

"How's that working for you? I bet it's quite peaceful."

"I love it. I feel like I get a lot more done now that I don't have an office to travel to. I notice I work later. I'm not sure if that's good or bad, but this one's always working," I wave my hand toward Jax, who is engrossed in conversation with the guys, "so it gives me more time to get things done. I've picked up some new clients recently who have been keeping me busy—some of the plantation owners," I say and take a sip from the glass of red wine the waiter just poured me. "I love being my own boss." Both Mia and Grace nod and smile.

They're both stay-at-home mothers with very little interest in careers. Grace and Ryan married as soon as they finished their undergraduate work. Grace started having babies—they have three now—while Ryan went to medical school. She is a bit paunchier than she was prebaby, but I guess most women are … except Mia. Something tells me Mia will always be slim and attractive.

Grace runs her fingers through her highlighted blonde hair and her blue eyes light up as if she's just had a revelation. "Let's do a spa day. Just the three of us. Heaven knows I need one. My little ones keep me so busy that I passed out in the bathtub last night. I feel like I never get to do anything. Every day is filled with diapers, bottles, and baby talk. If it weren't for my live-in nanny, I might have forgotten how to speak proper English." Mia and I laugh, although we can't quite relate at this point. I'm sure it won't be long before Mia will be feeling the same as Grace.

Not me, and not anytime soon. Jax has always been against having children too young because of our careers, but when do we decide it's time? He's thirty-five and I'm only a few years younger. I think we need to make a decision to start having kids in the next year or so. I don't want to be popping out babies in my forties. Every time we have the discussion, he blames our careers, but then he makes comments as if I'm the one who's not ready. He insinuates, psychologically, I can't handle motherhood. He denies this when I confront him about it, but I know I'm right. I know when he's psychoanalyzing me; I've seen him do it to others. And he does it to me every time we discuss children.

"I'm in! I need a hot stone massage. Those are my favorite. Nothing feels better than a massage," Mia says and sips from her glass of red wine.

"I need a detox mud wrap," I say, dreamily. Just the thought of being wrapped in hot mud makes me feel like I'm melting in my chair.

"I just need some peace and quiet," Grace says, wide-eyed. Both Mia and I laugh.

"What do you need to detox from, Greta?" Mia asks.

"Life!" I say bluntly.

The two of them exchange glances. "What's going on, hon?" Mia asks and they both lean in.

They're probably wanting to hear something juicy about

Jax and our marriage. Too bad I'm going to disappoint them. "Honestly, I think I'm in overload mode from spending so much time at the House of Ruth. I hate to say it; it actually makes me feel guilty, but I need a break."

They both lean back in their chairs. Mia pipes in, "Don't feel guilty. That's a lot to handle. It can be taxing mentally, not to mention physically. Whatever wears on us mentally will affect us physically as well. Anytime I'm under a lot of stress, I start experiencing stomach issues. Happens every time."

"I couldn't do it, Greta," Grace admits. "I'm too terrified that the abusers will find out where the women are being kept and come shoot us all. Do you ever worry about that?"

I shrug. "It's not what I'm thinking about when I'm there trying to help these ladies get their lives back, get their confidence back ... and get their courage back. They have to rediscover who they are as women, daughters, sisters, mothers, all while being hunted by madmen. It takes a lot of strength, courage, and just plain guts to start over under those circumstances. Most of them don't have families to help them out. An abusive man always makes sure they cut ties with the wife's family. That way he has full control over her." Mia and Grace nod, but I know they can't relate to the mind frame of an abused woman. Only another woman who's been through it can understand.

The face of my biological father flashes in my mind and I quickly shake it away.

The food arrives, breaking up our conversation. I'm quite relieved. I was starting to feel a bit emotional. Anytime I think about what these women go through, I experience numerous emotions: anger, hate, sadness, empathy. It brings out a desire for revenge in me.

Conversation is light during dinner, mainly monopolized by the men. The ladies and I set a date for our spa day. After our meal, I excuse myself to the restroom. We still have dessert and coffee coming. Jax is having a blast, laughing and joking with his best buds. He needs times like this in his life. I suppose we all do. A time to get away from the daily routines we're slaves to. These schedules we set ourselves, not realizing they're nothing more than homemade prisons. As a society, we're our own worst enemies.

Dessert is being served as I return to the table—*Cantucci di Prato e Vinsanto*. Almond-laced biscotti served with a sweet wine for dipping. Perfect after a heavy meal of pasta. Our friends are delighted, although probably not surprised. It's one of Jax's favorites after an Italian meal. He's predictable, because once he discovers something he likes, he sticks with it.

"Let's toast to a perfect evening of good friends and lots of laughs," Jax says and raises his wineglass in the air. The others join in, "*Salut!*" I raise my glass, but feeling a bit tipsy, I ask Jax to hand me one of the espressos the waiter set on the table. "Anyone else for an espresso?" He holds up a small coffee cup, not much larger than a shot glass. Mia and Grace both accept one.

The waiter leans over Jax, whispers in his ear and then slides him something under the table. He nonchalantly covers it with his hand. I watch him from the corner of my eye. He doesn't realize I noticed the sly exchange of words and discreet passing of an item. After several minutes of normal behavior and conversation, he peeks under the table to his hand. I also peek. It's a piece of paper, folded. Jax glances at it and his whole demeanor changes. He inconspicuously stuffs it into his pocket, waits a minute and then excuses himself. I watch as he heads toward the restrooms located to the back of the restaurant. Immediately tuning out the table talk, I try to figure out what's suddenly going on.

Evangeline

He's going to be furious with me. Jax will have my head for this, but I have to do it. I have no choice. I'm forced to interrupt his dinner. It's life and death. I'll try to make him understand. I see him. He's standing off to the side of the restrooms, in the corner, so as not to be seen. I can see the anger radiating off his face. His brow is lowered, lips tight, and jaw clinched forward.

Before I reach him, I say, "I had to. I have no choice."

"Quiet!" He pulls me over into the corner. "If you ever threaten me again …"

I interrupt him. "What, Jax …? What are you going to do to me? Stop it! I've heard it all before." He turns away, furious. I allow him a few deep breaths before continuing. "I had to threaten you because it would be the only way you'd agree to meet with me."

He snorts and shoots me an angry look. "Do you know how dangerous this is? What if someone sees us? This is weird. We shouldn't be here talking. It looks odd. And what if your presence causes a problem for Greta? You're playing with fire right now." He shakes his head in frustration. "Must you defy me on every single level?"

"That's not my intention."

"Tell me what it is that can't wait and then disappear." He leans in, putting his face up to mine so that he has my full attention. "You got it? Disappear!" I feel his hot breath on my neck, and I nod.

"Someone is following you," I say pointedly.

Jax groans and then punches the wall over my shoulder. "Evangeline!" He turns and starts to walk away. He's heated, and I've got to calm him down so he'll listen to me.

"Wait!" I yell out. A passing waiter turns in my direction, looking at me through narrowed eyes. Jax quickly returns to me.

"Keep your voice down. This isn't a game, Evangeline. You cause a scene and it will hurt us both. We won't be able to keep living as we are now, so watch yourself."

I know he's right, but I deserve respect and I won't accept anything less. "I chanced it tonight to do this. Show some appreciation."

His jaw clenches. "Okay, I'll play along. Who's following me, Evangeline?"

"I'm not sure. I just know you're being followed."

Jax groans again and breathes deeply, putting his fist to his mouth. He's upset. Not because he's worried, but because he doesn't believe me.

"It's a man. *That* I'm sure of, because I could see his silhouette in the driver's side."

"Is that all?"

"You don't believe me!" I say, unsatisfied.

"I do believe you. I do. Now we've got to break up this conversation. Do you understand?"

"Yes," I say.

"Do you?" he asks in a condescending tone. "Because I don't think you do."

I nod. My job here is done. If he gets his tail whipped because he angered somebody on the road, then that's his own fault. But if he's being followed because of something the two of us have done, this might be the beginning of something bad—really, really bad.

"I'll go first."

I nod, and Jax walks away from me.

Greta

"There she is! Greta, tell your husband he needs to get out more, and that if he keeps working like a madman he's going to end up with a heart attack at fifty-five," Ryan says, reaching over and slapping Jax on the back.

I laugh and return to my seat at the table. "I've been using that one for years. It doesn't faze him. He's too stubborn."

"Don't listen to them, they're just looking for a free meal every week." Laughter echoes around the table.

"Are you okay, love? You look a bit pale," Mia asks, studying me.

"I'm good, just a little lightheaded from too much wine, I

suppose." I smile and glance at Jax, who quickly drops his eyes when they meet mine.

I waited a minute after he left the table and then headed in the same direction. There was no sign of him. He must have been in the men's room … with his note. Somehow I missed him. This is driving me crazy. I can't concentrate on the conversation, because all I can think about is getting my hands on that note. A part of me wants to make a scene and just rip it from his pocket. This causes a horrible thought. What if he got rid of the note when he was in the restroom?

Suddenly, I'm aware of my chair being pulled out.

"Greta, darling, are you coming?" Jax says, smiling down at me.

I notice everyone has risen and is gathering their belongings, readying themselves to leave. I quickly hop up and grab my clutch, placing it under my arm. I can feel Jax's eyes on me, and when I meet his stare, he smiles warmly. He places his arm about my shoulders as we walk toward the door. We all stand outside, chatting while we wait for the valet to fetch our cars. The ladies and I confirm our spa date once more, just to make sure none of us tries to back out. We hug, kiss, and say goodnight.

I think about what a splendid evening we had as I slide into the passenger seat of Jax's BMW. I fasten my seat belt as he hurries in behind the wheel.

"We need to do this more often. It's always a great time," Jax says, still smiling from our goodbyes.

"Are you fine to drive?" I ask.

"How do you mean?" I hear some irritation in his voice.

"You drank quite a bit, no?"

"Oh. I'm good," he says shortly. "How're you feeling?"

"I feel great. As you mentioned, it was a nice time." I stare at his pants pocket, the one containing the note. Once again, I wonder if he's tossed it already. Where was he when he left the table? If he was in the restroom, he could have made a phone call. Yes, that's it. Someone wanted him to call. That doesn't make sense. They could have texted him, or left a voice mail themselves. Who has a waiter hand deliver a note? It hits me: someone in the restaurant. The author of the note was in the restaurant with us. They must have spotted him and wanted to have a secret word with him. Why so private? And why would he leave us to meet with someone who, apparently, feels as if they can't approach us?

Is it another woman? Is Jax having an affair? Never! I've already been through this before—suspicion, a million questions, secrets—and it always turns out to be a patient. He can't divulge information about his patients to me, or anyone, without a court order. I try to convince myself that's all this is, but there are too many oddities.

We ride in silence most of the way home, and I plan how I'm going to wait for Jax to fall asleep and then search his pockets for that note. Then I'll look at his phone to see if he's made any calls, or received any texts. I may even go through his emails. My scheming is interrupted as I notice Jax checking the rearview mirror every five seconds. His eyes are almost glued to the car behind us.

"What's the matter?" I ask.

"Huh?" he mumbles, distracted.

"What is it? Is something wrong with the car behind us?" I twist around in my seat to get a better look.

"Don't do that," Jax says, reaching out to push me back.

"What's going on?"

"This jerk keeps riding my tail. Don't worry about it."

"It doesn't look like he's tailgating," I argue. "Who is it?"

"It's fine, Greta. He's backed off now. Forget about it."

The rest of the ride home, I watch Jax out of the corner of my eye. He continues to glance into the rearview mirror. Are we being followed? If so, why?

Wake up, you imbecile. Jax is having an affair. His mistress is following you. Spying.

Go away. I'm not listening.

I keep telling you ... check up on him once in a while. There's a lot of secrets he's harboring.

"Stop it. Stop it!"

Jax jumps. "Are you all right?"

"Did I say that out loud?"

He giggles lightly. "Um, yeah ...you did." He puts his hand on my knee and squeezes.

"I'm tired." And confused. What in the heck is happening here? What am I missing? I know there's something going on right under my nose, but I can't seem to fit the pieces together. I turn in my seat again to check behind us.

"He's gone. He turned off." There is an edge to Jax's voice. I'm not sure he's being honest.

"It looks like the same car behind us, only they've backed off now," I argue.

"It's not the same one. I watched him turn a mile or so

back." He glances at me, and I see deception in his eyes.

We pull onto our street, and so does the car behind us. I notice Jax is white-knuckling the wheel. We're being followed. He's lying about it. He drives unusually slow to the edge of our driveway and stops the car.

"What're you doing?"

"Checking the mail," he says as he swings his door open and steps out.

"I got it earlier this afternoon. It was all junk."

He ignores me and walks over to the mailbox; the whole time his eyes are on the other car. It slowly cruises by us and into Isabella's driveway. It's Owen. Jax's eyes narrow as he watches him get out of his car and enter the house through the side door.

"What's that all about?" I ask when Jax returns and slides in behind the wheel. He puts the car in gear and proceeds down our driveway and into the garage.

"Odd timing, I guess," he tries to explain.

"Was Owen following us? And if so, for how long?"

"Following us? Why would Owen be following us?" He laughs, but I see concern on his face. He's not convinced it *wasn't* Owen.

Jax would be a lot more concerned if he knew what I knew. Owen is a wife beater. Does Owen know Isabella told me their deep dark secret? Is that why he's following us? He probably assumes Jax knows as well. I feel the strong urge to reveal the truth. What if I'm in danger now? It's one thing to be at risk working with the ladies at the House of Ruth. The men don't know who any of the volunteers are, or how to find us. But a neighbor has full access. He can watch me and find out when I'm home alone.

"Don't look so worried, Greta. Nobody was following us. Now come on. Let's go inside."

I fake a smile and step out of the car. Would Isabella tell Owen about our conversation? Certainly not. He'd be furious and she'd have to pay the price for doing something so disobedient. Does he have their house bugged? Did he overhear us talking the other day? I'll have to meet with her again, this time at my house, and see what's going on.

Once upstairs, Jax hits the shower. My eyes move to the dresser where he places his wallet and phone every night. I immediately reach for the phone and start searching through it.

'Atta girl!

No outgoing or incoming calls since we left for the restaurant. The only current text messages were to Ryan and Frank confirming our dinner plans earlier in the evening. Next, I search through his contacts, but find nothing out of the ordinary. I know everybody, but would he be foolish enough to place his mistress's name in his contact list? Certainly not. I return the phone to the dresser. I'm relieved and disappointed at the same time, which is crazy, I realize. I'm relieved to have found nothing, yet I know something secret is going on with him, so I'm disappointed I can't figure it out.

I go into the closet, where I spot his clothes thrown on top of the wicker laundry basket. I go straight for his pants, sticking my hand in his front left pocket. Empty. I reach into the right pocket and hear the rustling of paper. It's still here. My heartbeat speeds up and I can feel it thumping in the back of my throat. He never tossed it. With shaking hands, I open the folded piece of paper.

> JAX,
> MEET ME BY THE RESTROOMS RIGHT AWAY. DON'T IGNORE ME OR I'LL COME OUT AND MAKE A SCENE IN FRONT OF EVERYONE!!!
> I'M DEAD SERIOUS!!!
> EVANGELINE

I gasp as I read the signature. *Evangeline.* The author of the journal. Who the heck is this woman and what does she want with my husband? I reread the note several times. Jax had left the table to meet her in the restaurant. How long had he been gone? Was it long enough to ... to what? I had searched for him and couldn't find him anywhere. But I only remember going around the floor once. I wasn't gone long when I noticed he was seated back at the table. Had she been the one following us? Maybe Jax was telling the truth when he said the car had turned off. Maybe she took off once we got close to home. Maybe Owen pulling up at the same time we did was nothing more than a coincidence, and he doesn't know anything about my and Isabella's conversation.

My head is a jumbled mess of thoughts.

Is my husband having an affair?

That doesn't sound like Jax. He loves me more than anything. He's not the type.

That's what all women believe. Don't be a fool, Greta. You're holding the proof right there in your hand, silly girl.

She's been here. Evangeline. She's been in our house. That's how her journal got left behind. I breathe in deeply and then let it out slowly. She was in our bedroom. I found it in the closet. She purposely left it behind for me to find.

Is it starting to make sense now? Jax secretly bought the house some time ago so that he could have a clandestine rendezvous with his mistress. This house was meant for HER, *not you! They broke it off at some point, so rather than pay two mortgages—and risk you finding out about it—he tricked you into thinking moving was your idea, and then he made sure you'd find this house and fall in love with it. It was all a game. All part of a bigger plan. You were a pawn and you played right into his hands. Now Evangeline wants him back. She followed him to the restaurant and demanded he come back to her or she'd reveal the truth about their affair to you, and in front of all his friends. Am I getting through to you, Greta? Your husband is a cheat!*

I cover my mouth with my hand. I'm so stunned I can't breathe. I'm trying to inhale, but I can only make a whistling sound. I hear movement behind me, and I whirl around to find Jax watching me through narrowed eyes, which quickly widen when he sees the expression on my face. His demeanor rapidly changes, and I see concern wash over him as he reaches out to me. I discreetly shove the note behind a stack of folded shirts.

He's going to take care of me now. He's going to tell me everything's fine, and that I'm just having an *episode.* He's going to steal my reality and replace it with delusion so that I'm confused.

"Come on," he says as he steers me by the arms over to the bed. "You're allowing your thoughts to go crazy on you; making something out of nothing." He pushes me down gently on the bed, and I sit on the edge.

"How do you know what I'm doing?" I bark.

He raises his brow, surprised by my outburst. "Okay then, tell me what you were thinking."

I stare at him, but say nothing.

He sits down beside me. "I'm having an affair, aren't I? Maybe the car following us was her?"

My lips part in shock. How can he read my mind?

"I'll get your medication. Stay here," Jax says as he disappears into the bathroom. He's going to give me a pill so that I'll forget my revelation tonight. He does this to me every time I get wise to his deception. It's a memory loss pill, at least that's what I call it. The bottle has no label, so I can't look it up. He keeps it a secret from me so I won't know. So *no one* will know.

When he reappears he's holding the pill bottle along with a glass of water in one hand, and my pajamas in the other.

"I drank tonight," I remind him.

"Doesn't matter."

"I can't be popping pills with alcohol, Jax. Are you trying to kill me?" I freeze at my own words. *Is* he trying to kill me? I've never considered that before. Pills with no label, mixed with alcohol….

Jax shakes his head and chuckles softly. "Here," he says as he holds a pink oval pill out to me, "swallow this."

I pause. "I don't want to take the pill, Jax."

"I don't care what you want, or what you don't want. I'm the doctor and I demand you take this pill."

"You're going to force me to do something I don't want to do? Why? So I'll forget all this?" I can feel myself losing control, mentally and emotionally. It's almost as if something else, or someone else, is taking over.

"How many times have we been through this?" he says softly. "The pill doesn't make you forget things. In fact, it helps you to cope with your thoughts. To keep you from being delusional."

"How dare you refer to your affair as *my delusion*."

"Take the pill and then let's get you into your pajamas. Please, Greta, take it now."

"No! You take it. Then you can forget everything that happened tonight and wake up clueless in the morning."

He sits down next to me once more. I can hear him breathing heavily. I know he's out of patience, but he stays calm and speaks gently, just like any good therapist would. He's manipulating me. Gaslighting is what they call it … I think. He's manipulating me into questioning my own sanity. That's what he does every time I'm on to him.

He faces me and I can feel his eyes on me, but I don't look at him. I won't allow him to twist reality. He touches my cheek and turns my head toward him, but I keep my eyes low.

"Greta, you have a psychological condition. You already know this."

"You made it up so I'd be confused."

He smiles and lowers his head. "Please take this pill and let's move on." He holds it up in front of me and I knock his arm away. "You won't sleep tonight if you don't take it. Then I'll have to stay up with you to make sure you don't do anything crazy."

"Crazy? Did you just call me crazy?" I yell into his face. I've really lost it now.

"No, I didn't. I said your behavior will be crazy."

"You don't even have a name for my *craziness*, Jax. You're having an affair and sneaking around with this woman. And you're trying to tell me I'm the crazy one."

"It's called PPD. It makes you think ..."

I finish his sentence for him. "... you're having an affair when you're not. Yes, you've told me about a hundred times over the years."

"I never said *that*." He laughs. "It's Paranoid Personality Disorder. It's a Cluster A personality disorder. You already had it when we met—you were never diagnosed properly."

I fold my arms across my chest. Jax holds the pill in front of me.

"Where's the label?"

"There isn't one." He sighs.

"Why?"

"Because no one needs to know what these are except for you and me." He holds it closer to me.

"You act like I'm crazy."

"No, I don't, but you *are* eccentric, which sometimes causes you to experience paranoia at extreme levels. It's not crazy, but meds are good." He holds the pill to my lips, and I take it from him.

"Diazepam or Carisoprodol?"

"The latter."

"The stronger one."

"You need it," he says and hands me the glass of water.

I drink it down like a good little patient.

Chapter Seventeen
Greta

APRIL 15
SATURDAY MORNING

I awake groggy with a pounding headache and remind myself why I don't drink much. I groan as I roll over, clutching my head. Jax's side of the bed is empty. What time is it? I glance at the clock on his bedside table: 10:30. What? I fly up in a panic, causing shooting pains throughout my head, but then remember it's Saturday. I have nowhere to be. I sigh in relief and, slowly this time, flop back down until I feel capable of making my way downstairs.

I shuffle into the kitchen and spot Jax scrolling his phone at the table.

"You need to eat. Breakfast will be the best thing for you," he says, continuing to scroll.

"Wow. I feel like I could easily sleep another eight hours," I say putting my hand to my head. "What time did I fall asleep?"

"I'm not sure, love. It was late, though." Jax puts his phone away and walks over, giving me a tight hug and peck on the forehead.

"I don't remember much. It's quite foggy, actually." I chuckle, embarrassed.

"There's not much to remember. You drank too much, so I'm not surprised. Let's get some food and liquids in you. Rocio stopped in early and I asked her to cook up some breakfast for you."

"That's embarrassing. I'm too hungover to get out of bed and make my own breakfast?" I say, feeling ashamed.

Jax raises his brow in innocence. "I didn't tell her that. I just said you weren't feeling well and would need some help with breakfast." He holds my hand and leads me to the island, where a spread of food lies on the countertop.

"That's a lot of food." I giggle. "Did you tell her to whip all this up?"

"Oh, you know Rocio. It's in her nature to go overboard. Anyway, there's coffee, orange juice, and water. You need all three. Scrambled eggs, coffee cake, fresh berries, and some Greek yogurt." Jax points to each item as he names them and it reminds me of why he's a doctor. He has a knack for taking care of people.

I immediately flash to him handing me a pill and a glass of water. Was this last night?

"I'm sorry I have to leave you right now, but I have to run by the office and retrieve a couple of files for Ryan. I was supposed to fax some paperwork yesterday, but completely forgot about it," Jax explains.

"That's not like you," I comment and start piling some fruit on a plate.

"I think the dinner distracted me. I'll be back shortly." He leans down to kiss me before heading out the garage door. I'm disappointed, but used to it at the same time. I dollop some yogurt onto my plate and take a seat at the kitchen table with a large glass of juice. Feeling dehydrated, I gulp down half before I start to eat.

Another memory flashes through my mind. I'm swallowing a pill. Last night. Did Jax give me something? Why? I think back to the dinner. I remember arriving at the restaurant. Frank and Mia. Ryan and Grace. Spa date. Pasta. Wine. Dessert. Something pricks at me. I press myself to remember until it causes my head to ache. I stand and cross the kitchen, pulling out a drawer where we keep OTC medications. I grab the Naproxen, dumping two into the palm of my hand. I wash it down with my juice and continue to eat, even though I'm having to force myself at this point.

Think, Greta. Go back to the restaurant. Think!

Something's bothering me. Something happened at the restaurant. What is it?

Think, Greta.

The waiter. Jax. Whispering.

That's it! Keep going.

A note. Jax. Leaving. Sneaking. The car. Someone is behind us. Following. Owen.

Don't stop!

Jax. Shower. Closet. Pocket. The note. Evangeline. Pill.

I drop my fork. It's all coming back to me. Yes, there was

a note from Evangeline. How does Jax know Evangeline, and who the heck is this woman? I abruptly stand, running my fingers through my hair in despair. I want answers. I want answers right now, and Jax just left. He won't be back for hours. I feel the urgency for an explanation run through my veins. I want to get in my car and drive the thirty-six miles to his office and confront him. I can't do it over the phone. He'll cut me off saying something came up and he must call me back. I want answers. I want them right now.

'Atta girl!

I place my unfinished breakfast in the sink and head for the alarm panel by the garage door. We were being followed last night. I punch the code in, arming the system. I pour some black coffee and head for the shower, hoping the hot water and stimulant will help me to remember the details of the previous evening.

Jax is having an affair.

Yes, I remember. Jax and Evangeline.

This house was hers.

Rage roils through me and I can feel my heart in my throat. I remember everything.

The garage door opens and the alarm sounds. I don't flinch. I'm lying on the sofa in the great room, reading a book. I hear Jax fumbling with the buttons on the keypad. He sounds rattled.

"Greta," he yells out. "What's going on with the alarm?"

I continue to read. I hear his footsteps approaching.

"Greta! Did you hear me? The alarm. Why is it set?"

"Because we were being followed last night, Jax. Remember?" I take my nose out of the book so I can see his expression.

He stares at me a moment, not blinking. Surprised by my sudden memory?

"I remember everything, my dear, including Evangeline." His face becomes ashen with grief, and I can see his breathing increase as his chest rises and falls. I sit up to face him. "Care to explain, Jax?" I say as I dog-ear my page and place the book on the coffee table.

"Wh—What do you know about Evangeline? Or better yet, *how* do you know about her? Is this about the journal?" He joins me on the sofa, his movements slow and methodical, as if he's thinking carefully about each word he speaks, present and future. Every movement calculated.

"The note, Jax. Remember, or did you have a memory lapse, too?"

He pauses and pinches the bridge of his nose as if it will help him come up with a quick answer. "Don't look at me like that, Greta. You know I can't tell you everything. It's a violation of doctor-patient confidentiality."

"She's a patient?"

"Of course, she's a patient. What else would she be?" he says, throwing his hands in the air.

"I'm sorry, but I'm not going to accept *doctor-patient confidentiality* as an excuse for you to not give me answers about her. You're my husband *first*."

He nods. "I understand. Ask me whatever you wish, and I'll do my best to answer."

His words surprise me somewhat, but I'm pleased, to say the least. "Okay, how the heck did her journal get into our closet?"

"I must have left it there absentmindedly. When we moved, I had some files I wanted to keep in my home office, so I could refer to them at any time. I must have set it down to do something else, forgetting all about it."

I pause as I absorb his answer.

"My mind was on other things, Greta. If you had told me the name on that journal in the first place, I would've remembered it and stopped you from reading it."

"There's a *murder* in that journal, Jax!" I raise my voice and gasp.

"Calm down. Evangeline is a paranoid schizophrenic. She's as crazy and delusional as they come," he blurts out and then lowers his head as if he's said too much. "It's unethical for me to talk about her to you. Why can't you understand this?"

"I do understand." My voice softens.

"After you gave me that journal, I glanced through it and found that it's full of gibberish, fantasies, and paranoia. Her thinking is unpredictable. Her behavior is erratic. She can be a danger to herself, but not others. She'd never hurt anyone, but she has these delusions that she confuses with reality. She has trouble discerning what's real and what's not." Jax sighs deeply. "Schizophrenics hallucinate. They need to be on heavy narcotics, which can be dangerous, and with serious side effects. Evangeline is one of the most extreme cases I've ever encountered, and she has to be handled with care."

I feel the tenseness in my body ease as Jax continues to

explain. I feel empathetic toward him and what he must go through as a doctor dealing with severely mentally ill patients.

"When I received her note last night from the waiter, I knew I couldn't ignore it. Can you imagine the ruckus it would have caused if one of my patients approached our table delusional and confused? It could have gotten us banned from the restaurant, not to mention be a huge embarrassment." Jax snorts and shakes his head.

"Why did she say it was a life and death situation in the note? What happened?" As long as I'm receiving answers from him, I'm going to continue to ask questions.

"She told me someone is following me."

"That's why you kept watching the car behind us," I add, putting the pieces together. "Was it Owen?" I remember the way Jax stared him down when he pulled into the driveway and went inside.

Jax chuckles. "No. Owen's got nothing to do with anything."

As far as Jax knows, but I know something he doesn't. A twinge of guilt shoots through me and I feel like a hypocrite. Here I am, forcing forbidden doctor-patient information from my husband while I'm keeping secrets from him. I promised Isabella I wouldn't tell Jax anything because she swore if Owen found out, he'd hurt her, maybe even kill her.

"Who was it then? Following us?"

"I think it was Evangeline. Schizophrenics love to stir up drama; it's what they do. They thrive on it. It would be just like her to dramatically warn me about someone during dinner with my wife and friends and then follow me to try and worry me. They use scare tactics. You wouldn't understand, hon."

"I agree with you there." I nod and go over everything Jax has revealed to me about Evangeline. "Did you turn the journal over to the police?"

"No, I didn't. I explained that to you. It's all fabricated. In fact, I wouldn't put it past her to have created that journal for no other reason than to try and rile me up. I didn't even know she kept a journal until she brought it with her to a session one day. She kept referring to it, waiting for me to bite, and when I didn't she started reading passages out of it. I finally couldn't stand it anymore, so I took it from her, agreeing to read it. I knew it would be nothing but delusional ramblings, so I put it aside and ended up forgetting about it."

"There's a man she keeps referring to. What if they really are involved in someone's murder?" I feel chills move through my body at the thought of being so out of control mentally.

"He's a figment of her imagination. She's talked about him before; always making up new stories about him. She even changes his name on occasion. She can never keep her lies straight." Jax breathes deeply and then says, "Can we stop now? Have I said enough to make you understand there's nothing going on behind your back except craziness with a patient?"

"Yes, we can stop. Thank you for being so patient with me. One of the reasons I married you." I chuckle.

Jax leans over and pulls me into him. "I'll never let you down, Greta; I'll protect you at all costs. No one will ever harm you, whether it's one of my patients or a stranger. You don't have to worry about it. And you don't have to worry about my safety. I'm a psychiatrist and know how to handle patients like Evangeline."

I hold on to Jax tightly, absorbing every word.

I've never felt safer than I do right now.

Chapter Eighteen
Greta

MONDAY AFTERNOON

I made sure to get my work done early today so I could have lunch with Isabella. I waited to text her till early this morning, after I saw Owen leave. I invited her over and she accepted right away. I didn't want to take the chance of him seeing the text and accusing her of something shady. This way he'll never know she came over.

I asked Rocio to prepare lunch for us and then gave her the rest of the day off. I don't want her to bear witness to anything we may say. Sometimes even knowing someone is an abuser can put one in danger. Now I stand over the spread of food in the kitchen, admiring Rocio's ability to make tea sandwiches look so beautiful. The layout includes carrot and raisin, cucumber with brie, and smoked salmon with avocado tea sandwiches; scones with clotted cream; cinnamon plum jam; miniature pistachio cakes; toasted teacakes with apricot compote; and some Earl Grey to wash it down. I love this woman. A true miracle maker, she is.

The bell rings and I head toward the front door with a smile on my face. Isabella and I will be having a wonderful lunch; I can already feel it. I fling open the door to a bright-eyed, glowing Isabella. Her smile consumes her face, and I immediately feel a twinge of pain in my heart realizing she doesn't have anyone to spend time with. No interaction with the outside world because of her controlling, abusive husband. We hug and I notice she holds on unusually long. Again, she's dressed to the nines; flowing silk multi-colored sundress with Louboutin heels. Her hair and makeup look like she just came from the salon. I'm wearing a white tank top with blue capri pants and sandals. I'm no match for this supermodel look-alike. She pulls a bottle of red wine from the Chanel tote slung over her shoulder. I tilt my head to one side, allowing a devious giggle to escape me.

"One can't have lunch without wine, can they?" She winks at me.

"It's actually more of a tea party inspired menu. So tea would be more appropriate," I say.

"Do you have a liquor cabinet?" she asks with raised brows.

"Er, yes."

"Wonderful! It goes great with tea."

"What does?"

"Liquor, of course." She makes her way to the kitchen, and I follow along, noting it's going to be an adventurous time with this one. "I don't get to do anything, Greta. I've got to let loose when I can. Understand?" She smiles brightly.

I nod. I do understand, wholeheartedly.

We move the food to the living room, set it between us on

the coffee table and then sit opposite each other on gold silk Victorian sofas. We sample everything, numerous times. Isabella downs almost the whole bottle of wine on her own. She poured me a glass before we started eating, but I've only sipped from it once.

"Are you going to drink it?" she asks, tilting her head toward my glass.

I slide it over to her. "You can have it."

"I don't want it. I want *you* to drink it. Drink with me, Greta. Loosen up and have some fun," she says and twirls her glass, inhaling deeply before taking a sip.

"I don't need alcohol to have fun, thank you," I insist.

She laughs. "Me neither, but it makes me forget what my life is like." Her expression turns solemn. "Even if it's just for a few hours, it eases my pain. I'll take whatever I can get."

I lower my head. My heart breaks for her. I pick up my glass of wine to toast. "To new beginnings," I say. Isabella furrows her brow, looking at me as if I'm crazy.

"Give me a new beginning and I'll toast to it."

"One is *never* stuck, my dear," I inform her.

"Then you haven't met my husband."

"But I *have* met him, and I know your situation. Again, one is *never* stuck." I toast the air and take a sip from my glass. "Let me ask you something."

"Shoot," she says and downs the last of her wine.

"Do you think Owen may have your house bugged?"

She pauses. "It's possible, I suppose, but I really don't believe so. I know every square inch of my home and I've never come across anything suspicious looking. We have outside cameras, which have sound, I believe, but that's it. Honestly, I don't think Owen pays much attention to the security system. He trusts I never go anywhere because he knows I'm too afraid to lose the medical support he supplies for my mother. He knows I'd never do anything to risk that. And he's right, I won't, hence the fact I *am* stuck."

I smile crookedly and sigh. "I stand by what I said, but let me ask you this ... where was Owen Friday evening around ten-ish?"

She tilts her head upward in thought. "He was in a meeting with clients that ran late. He rushed home to change and then met a few of them for dinner and drinks. He said it was to seal the deal. Why are you asking such strange questions about him?"

"Jax and I were out to dinner Friday evening and on the way home we thought someone was following us. We pulled up at the mailbox and Jax got out, but the car pulled into your driveway. It was Owen. I thought maybe we were mistaken that he was behind us the entire time, but then my paranoia got the best of me. I worried he might have your house bugged and heard our conversation, where you told me about your situation." I lift my glass to take a drink and discover I've finished it.

Isabella perks up in her seat and leans in as if she has a secret. "He was at Orleans Wine Bar. Where were you?"

"L'Antica Trattoria."

"That's the opposite direction. There's no way he could have known where you were unless he was there, too, and he wasn't. I guess he could have followed you guys when you left your house, which means he would have lied to me about meeting clients, but that's nothing new. He lies all the time. What time did you go out that night?"

"Eight. What time did Owen leave?"

"Eight," she says and puckers her lips. "But why would he follow you guys? It makes no sense."

"Intimidation. If it was him, he purposely made it obvious so we'd know. As if he was warning us, or threatening us to not interfere in his business. Trust me, I know how abusers work."

"Now, that *does* sound just like him. He's a bully."

We go back and forth, discussing whether Owen could have been the one following us, never able to decide one way or the other. I think her house could be bugged, but she swears it's not. Deep inside, though, I know it's him. He followed us to make a statement. It was a warning that if we mess in his business, he has the ability to pop up when least expected. This is how abusers operate. They do things to intimate others so that they live in fear. This way, they always feel they have to watch their backs. Owen followed us so we'd fear him.

"You know what's good with pastries?" Isabella asks, taking a bite of pistachio cake.

I shrug. "What?"

"Liquor." She laughs. "Do you mind?"

"Go ahead," I say and wave my hand toward the bar.

"There's only one way I could ever be free of Owen," Isabella says as she pours amaretto into her teacup. "I'd have to kill him."

"See? I told you no one is ever truly stuck in a situation.

There's always a way out." I smile and gesture for her to hand me the bottle. She pauses, raising an eyebrow, and then slowly passes me the amaretto. In her eyes, I can see a mountain of thoughts building within her.

"You're not serious," she says incredulously.

"I *am* serious. There are plenty of women who regain their freedom in life from the deaths of their abusers."

"And the courts just let them off the hook? Just like that?"

I chuckle at her innocence. "No, no, my dear. Courts aren't involved in what I'm talking about."

"Then you're talking about cold-blooded murder."

"Who's the cold-blooded one?"

She stares at me, jaw dropped in surprise, yet taking in every word.

"I—I don't know …"

I interject before negative thoughts have a chance to flood her mind. "When are you going to be done kowtowing to Owen?"

She lowers her eyes and shrugs.

"How much money do you stand to gain from Owen's death? It would, most likely, pay for top notch healthcare for your mother for the remainder of her life. You'd never have to worry about him hurting, or even killing, you again. You could stop drowning your sorrows and your miserable existence in a bottle. You could go back to work, do whatever you want, even date. You'd have a new life with a butt load of cash. Your own little paradise." I smile, but Isabella is looking right through me …

… imagining what life without Owen would be like.

Chapter Nineteen
Evangeline

APRIL 19
WEDNESDAY MORNING

I sit at my usual table on the coffeehouse patio, sipping my chai latte when Jax comes barreling into his parking space. I watch as he hurries through the door and places his order. I can hear him in my head: grande, quad, nonfat, one-pump, no-whip mocha, with almond milk. I chuckle and the guy at the table to my right shoots me a curious glance. Jax looks sharp in his navy pinstripe suit today. Red silk tie. It looks like Ralph Lauren; same with the shoes, black calfskin oxford. I love to observe him in a situation where he's not studying me, analyzing me. Because he refuses to acknowledge me in public, Wednesday mornings are my best opportunity to give him a little taste of what it feels like to be watched, every move being scrutinized.

I see him run his fingers through his hair a couple of times while waiting on his coffee. Curious. That's something he does when he's on edge. I wonder what's got him worked up this morning. Greta, maybe? Is he worrying about her … again … still? He's such a sap. So madly in love with her. The chick has got problems. She always has, and he's always known. I think when they met, as a psychiatrist—and a pretty fresh one at that—he viewed her as a challenge. A project, maybe. Over the years he's come to the realization that she's not going to change. Nothing is ever going to get better. It is what it is, and no amount of therapy in the world can help this broad. I chuckle again at his naivety. This time the guy next to me doesn't look.

I watch as Jax picks up his snobby coffee and heads toward the door. He holds it open for a young couple and then hurries through before getting stuck playing doorman. He stops abruptly on the sidewalk and then turns in my direction. What's this? Holy smokes, he's coming my way, his eyes set on me like a man with a mission. Should I be worried? My body tenses and I can feel my heart rate increase as my blood pressure rises. He's never done this before. I shift uncomfortably in my chair. He's never acknowledged me in public. I'm not sure how to react. I breathe in deeply.

He stops in front of me, staring down into my eyes. I look away.

"Come and take a ride with me," he says casually.

I'm not sure I should. "Why?"

"Because I want you to. Come on." He tilts his head toward his car.

"So there can't be any witnesses?" I notice the guy to my right shoots us a startled look.

Jax reaches down and grabs my arm, tugging on me to stand. I follow his lead. He holds my arm firmly all the way to his car, where he opens the passenger door and waits for me to get in, closing it behind me. I watch him closely as he walks around the front of the car and slides in behind the wheel. He places his coffee in the cup holder and starts the engine.

"Where're we going?" I ask nervously.

He turns to look at me, but says nothing and backs out of the parking space. He shifts gears and we're off. My body is trembling, but I try to act calm. Unafraid. Unmoved by his bizarre behavior. For years I've watched him at the coffee shop and he's never so much as looked at me, and now we're driving away in his car.

"Are we going to your office?' I ask.

This makes him laugh, but it's hollow sounding. "My office? You are so terrified of my office."

"That's because bad things happen there."

"Bad things don't happen there. That's in your head. My office is a place for healing and that's what takes place there. I heal people's minds, their emotions. I make sense of their thoughts, their behavior. You don't like it because you know you're not supposed to be here."

"Stop it!" I can't bear to listen to him tell me how I don't matter, how insignificant my life is. "I'm a person. I have feelings."

"Evangeline! I'm not going through this with you again. You don't count, and you know it. Deep down you know you don't matter. Nobody cares about you but you. Admit it!"

"That's not true. I have my own life to think about," I snap.

"No you don't! There's nothing significant about you or your life. You're here to do what I say … period. You have no life of your own and you never will. Do you think I can't see what you're trying to do?"

I shake my head. "I don't know what you mean."

He recklessly pulls into the lot of a dilapidated warehouse and speeds around to the backside. My heart is thumping so hard I feel like it's going to explode. I struggle to breathe and put my hand to my neck. He slams on the brakes and turns the ignition off. In a flash, he's out of the car and flinging open my door, yanking me out. He slams it shut and then shoves me up against the car. He presses his finger to my cheek, his face in mine.

"I know what you're doing and this stops here. Do you understand me?"

"I'm completely clueless, Jax. I have no idea what you're talking about." I look around at my surroundings. There's no one in sight. In fact, there's no one for at least a mile. We're at a warehouse out in no man's land, and I wonder how he even knows about this place.

"Okay, play dumb and let's see how far that gets you." He takes a step back, and relief washes over me. "You're trying to destroy my marriage," he barks.

I immediately laugh, but it's more out of hysterics than humor. "That's ridiculous. I've kept your secrets for years, and even Greta's, for that matter. Why would I want to betray you now?"

"For the same reason you've always wanted to … so you can have a *new life* … go *live your dreams*."

He's right about that.

"You don't get to have dreams, Evangeline. Get it through your delusional head. No one owes you anything. And if you really want to get technical, you're trespassing!"

I gasp and he lifts his brow in surprise.

"Do you want me to leave, Jax? Do you want me to disappear and never come back?"

"Yes!"

My jaw drops. "Who's going to help you, Jax? You can't get by without me. Who's going to call you in the middle of the night and tell you what's going on? I'm your spy. I'm your lifeline, you idiot."

"You're also the one filling Greta's head with lies, hoping you can turn her against me."

"I'm flabbergasted at your allegations."

"Save it!" he shouts, throwing up his hands. "First, you plant that journal full of details about what we've done. That could get us sent to prison. You do realize if I go down, you go down?" He shakes his head. "Then, you write that stupid note in the restaurant, knowing it would cause Greta to be suspicious."

"It was an emergency," I say, defending myself.

"You're planting seeds, Evangeline," he yells, causing every vein in his neck to tighten. "Then she woke up the next morning and remembered everything." He looks deep into my eyes. "*Everything!*"

"How's that my fault?" I say coolly and shrug in innocence. Even though I'm pretending I'm not intimidated, I'm scared out of my wits.

"She asked all kinds of questions about you, and I had to cover my tracks by claiming doctor-patient confidentiality. I pretended like I was being unethical by discussing you with her. Of course, there was nothing unethical about it. You're not my patient, and I'm not your doctor, so there was no harm in answering her questions."

"I'm not your patient?"

"Get real," Jax sniffs.

"You're not my doctor? Then what are we to each other?"

"Think about what you're saying, Evangeline. Think! Why would I counsel you? Does that make sense to you? What good would it do to counsel you? You're nobody!"

I feel a pang in my heart. We stand in silence, and I watch Jax closely, facing away from me now, arms crossed over his chest, thinking. About what? Probably how he doesn't need me anymore and wants to get rid of me.

"Let's just agree that we need each other…"

He snorts.

"I'm sorry for the way I've been acting lately, Jax. I just wanted you to care about me. I just wanted you to feel something for me … to treat me like a real person with feelings."

"Evangeline…" he turns and meets my eyes, "I'm so sick of hearing about all your needs. You're wearing me out. You have a job to do. If you can't do it, then I've got to move on."

"Which means getting rid of me," I bark.

"Which means getting rid of you," he confirms.

"Give me another chance, Jax. I'll be good. I'll make things right. I'll help with Greta, I promise." I step toward him and he steps away from me. "I'm sorry for the trouble I've caused. I'll put my feelings on the backburner, I promise. I'll make you both my priority, I will. Please, trust me," I say and reach out to touch his arms. He quickly pushes me away, repulsed.

"Don't touch me. Get in the car," he orders.

I open my mouth to protest, but think twice. I can't take the chance of angering him more. "I'm scared," I admit, hoping to play on his sympathy, if he has any.

"You should be. Now get in," he says as he opens the car door and gestures with his hand.

I step one foot into the car and then pause. "Please, admit right now that you need me," I beg. He grabs my arm and pushes me down into the car seat, slamming the door closed. I watch him walk around and slide in behind the wheel. He starts the engine and we leave the warehouse parking lot.

I slowly let the air out of my lungs. "Where are we going?" I get no answer. "Are we going to your office?"

He looks over at me, and I see a slight curve form on the corners of his mouth. There's evil in his eyes as he contemplates getting rid of me. I shouldn't have been playing tough the past few weeks. I've made things worse for myself. I should have left Greta alone. I shouldn't have interfered. It's all backfired in my face.

Jax pulls up to the coffee shop and stops. I breathe a sigh of relief, and he hits the button unlocking the doors. He doesn't look at me. I start to say something and then stop myself.

As I open the door he says, "Don't show up today." I pause. He traces the BMW emblem on his steering wheel with his fingertip, never looking up.

I come to grips with the cold hard truth as I watch him drive away. If I have any chance at all at freedom, Jax will have to die. The thing is, I'm not the killing kind.

But I know someone who is.

Chapter Twenty
Greta

MAY 1
MONDAY MORNING

I follow the hostess to the table where I find Isabella already seated, scrolling through her phone. As soon as she sees me, a grin spreads across her face and she quickly hops up and hugs me. I settle into my seat and, as nonchalantly as possible, I give her the once-over. She looks good. Beautiful, in fact. Her face is glowing and I see a sincere happiness in her eyes. I would think her life is fantastic, if I didn't know the truth.

"I bet you were surprised to get a text from me this morning, weren't you?" she asks, twirling the straw in her drink.

"Actually, I was. Pleasantly surprised. I needed a little break, so meeting for brunch is a perfect plan for me." I smile graciously at her and wonder how long it will take her to bring up Owen. "What's their specialty?" I ask, glancing over the menu.

"I love the crawfish ètouffèe with a side of boudin."

"Sold," I say and place the menu to the side.

"How are things with your business? Keeping you busy?"

"Like you wouldn't believe, but I'm not complaining. Busy is good. It means a bigger paycheck." I smile and give her a wink.

The waitress shows up and asks for my drink order. Isabella quickly interjects. "She'll have what I'm having, and I'll have another." The waitress nods and leaves us.

"What am I drinking?" I ask curiously, although I suspect it to be strong and alcoholic.

"Roffignac," she answers with a sly grin. "It's like a brandy highball with raspberry shrub."

"I can't drink that right now. It's too early and I have to go back to work today," I explain.

"You are such a prude, Greta. Let loose once in a while," she says, stirring her drink and then sipping from it.

"I'm a prude because I don't like to drink much?"

What's the matter? Jax doesn't allow you to day-drink, or what? He seems like he's the controlling type. Strong personality, set in his ways, calls all the shots." She stares at me intently, waiting for an answer.

"Actually, you just described him perfectly." I chuckle. "If you really must know, bad things happen when I drink, so I keep it to a minimum."

"Bad things happen when everybody drinks," she chortles.

Our beverages come and we toast to *bad things*, and then have a good laugh.

She shoots me a devilish grin. "Shall we get down to business?"

I had the feeling it wouldn't take long. She's had a couple of weeks to mull over what I said about getting rid of her abuser in order to live the highlife, and she wants to take me up on it. What abused woman wouldn't?

"What do you have in mind, dear?" My eyes meet hers, letting her know we're on the same page.

"How would we do it?" she asks. I can hear both fear and excitement in her voice.

"It's so easy, you'll be shocked. In fact, you'll wonder why you didn't do it a long time ago," I say, flashing her a wicked grin.

"Do tell."

"You drug him, of course. He's a pharmaceutical rep and my husband's a doctor. We've got narcotics at our fingertips just waiting to be used." I throw my head back in laughter.

"You have to be with me when I do it. I can't do this alone," she says worriedly. She glances around the restaurant to make sure we can't be overheard, paranoia already setting in.

"Of course, I'll be there, hon. I wouldn't have it any other way."

She raises her brow. "You sound as if you've done this before."

I see the waitress approaching and put my finger to my lips to shush Isabella. The waitress sets my drink in front of me and suddenly I feel like it's the right choice. As soon as she's out of earshot, I resume our conversation.

"I've never killed anyone, but that doesn't mean I haven't thought about it. For years, I've taken care of women who've been bloodied and bruised, broken bones, broken spirits;

thinking they're worth nothing because some psychopath beats them down, physically and mentally. It makes me sick. Some of these women go back to their abusers because they're convinced they can't do any better. It's just a matter of time before they end up being killed." Isabella puckers her lips and shakes her head. "So, yes, I've thought about it, even planning it out in my head at times. I can't bear to see these women left scared, homeless, and penniless."

"That's what'll happen to me, Greta. If I don't find a way out, Owen will eventually kill me. And if I die before my mother…" Her lips quiver and she quickly turns away.

I reach across the table and squeeze her hand reassuringly. "We won't let that happen. We can do this and then you'll never have to worry about your, or your mother's, well-being again."

"Tell me how," Isabella says between sobs. "I've got to break free from this existence. This is no way to live. There's no joy in my life, Greta. The only thing that makes me happy is when Owen allows me to visit Mom, and even then she doesn't know who I am anymore. Please, help me."

I take a long sip of my drink. "I will stop by with a wonderful bottle of wine. I'll inject the bottle with a syringe, so the drugs will already be in it. All we have to do is get him to drink it. I'll make up something celebratory so he'll feel obligated to toast with us."

"I don't think that'll be a problem. He drinks a lot anyway." She pauses. "What about Jax? What are you going to tell him? How will you keep him from coming with you?"

"Don't worry about that. I'm a good liar. I'll think of

something." We stare at each other for a minute and then bust out laughing.

The waitress strolls up asking for our order. Isabella lets her know what we want and I tune them both out, thinking about how clever I am, and how easy it's going to be to knock off Owen. He'll never even know what hit him. He'll drink and then die. It can't get any easier than that. Of course, there are details that still need to be worked out.

Isabella waits for the waitress to get out of earshot and then says, "They'll do an autopsy to figure out why a young healthy guy suddenly keeled over. We have to find a drug that leaves no metabolite trace. Tranquilizers are out because they can be detected in the blood."

"I haven't gotten that far, dear. Give me some time to research it," I say.

"No need. I already have." She glances over the room before continuing in a low voice. "Potassium chloride. Doctors use it for patients with low levels of potassium. When administered, the drug is simply metabolized into potassium and chloride, both of which are normally found in the body. Yes, there will be elevated blood levels of these components, but ..." She pauses long enough to take a swig of her drink. "A potassium chloride overdose causes severe heart arrhythmias, mimicking a heart attack. Within minutes, the heart will spasm and then stop functioning. It's called sudden cardiac death, or SCD. Blood levels will show an elevation of potassium, but no fear, whenever any muscle tissue is damaged, such as the heart tissue, unusually large amounts of potassium are released into the bloodstream. So a medical examiner would chalk it up to be normal and list the cause of death as a fatal heart attack."

I'm dumbfounded. My jaw drops open in shock. I try to speak, but my voice fails me. Only a small squeak escapes my throat.

Isabella watches me for a minute and then softly giggles. "Yes, I've been thinking about this for a very long time. I've never had the guts to do it." She folds her napkin neatly across her lap and smiles. "Great! Our food is coming. I'm famished!"

I sit back in my chair and try my hardest to act normal considering our psychotic table talk, smiling at the waitress as she places our plates of food on the table. I'm aware she's talking, but I don't hear what she's saying. I feel as if I'm in another world. We're really going to do this. We're going to kill Owen.

Isabella brings me back. "Greta? She's asking if you want another drink, hon."

"Keep them coming." I smile up at her. I divert my attention back to Isabella, who is cutting into her boudin. "How do we get this potassium …"

"Chloride," she finishes. "That's where you come in. You'll have to steal a prescription pad from Jax. You don't mind, do you?"

"Um … no. I suppose not." I slowly unroll the silverware from the black cloth napkin, placing the fork and knife alongside my plate and smoothing the napkin in my lap. "Outside of the prescription pad, you really don't need my help, Isabella. You've thought it all through."

"Oh, but I *do* need your help. I need moral support. I'm

scared to death. I can't go through with it alone. I'm too weak. I may sound determined right now, but that's all it is … determination. I'm full of fear, though." Her eyes are darting wildly about the restaurant as she speaks. "I feel like Owen can hear us. Like, somehow, he's going to know we had this conversation."

I felt the same way the other week when Jax and I thought Owen was following us. Was he? Did he know Isabella had confided in me somehow? I watch as she scarfs down her plate of food and orders another drink. I eat more slowly, pep talking myself. We can do this. The fact Isabella has done all the research has set my mind at ease. We just need the drug and we're ready.

"Sooooo, when can you get the prescription pad? Don't worry about forging the prescription. I'll do all that so nothing can ever be traced back to you." She takes a bite of her ètouffèe. "Mmm, so good," she says, closing her eyes for full effect.

"It's a wonderful choice. I'm glad I ordered it, too. I'll have to bring Jax here sometime." I take a bite and smile, taking in the food, the scenery, the drinks, and our conversation of murder. Even though I'm a bit taken aback by the fact Isabella has worked out all the details, I'm pleased just the same. Less for me to do. She's smart and on the ball. She knows what she wants and how to get it, she only needs someone to hold her hand. I'll be her hand-holder. "I'll get it today. I'll stop by Jax's office and surprise him."

I check my watch and see it's still early enough to take him lunch. I wave down the waitress and order the same plate of food with an unsweetened iced tea to go, and then I smile at

Isabella. We finish our meal and then hug goodbye. We'll meet again tomorrow morning so that I can give her the prescription pad. A life of freedom isn't far off for Isabella.

I enter the lobby of Jax's practice and wave to Amelia, his office administrator. She's on the phone and holds a finger up, telling me to wait. I glance around the waiting room. It's emptying out since it's close to lunch. Jax will be surprised to see me and delighted to get lunch brought to him, although it's not as healthy as he'd normally choose.

Amelia sets the phone down and lets me know Jax is with a patient, but will be finished up in about five minutes. I take a seat and dig my phone out from my handbag. This will give me a couple of minutes to check my emails. I've received two from potential clients asking for quotes. They left their numbers, so I'll call them when I'm finished up here. I can't allow murder to interfere with business. I giggle at the thought and notice Amelia glance my way. Oops. Was that out loud?

A middle-aged woman emerges from the direction of Jax's office, eyes bloodshot and swollen. I wonder if she feels any better after unloading her deepest secrets to a stranger. That's what shrinks are, strangers with a medical degree, giving advice based on medical findings instead of personal knowledge of a certain person and situation. Patients could paint any kind of picture of themselves. They could be honest about who they are, or hide their true inner thoughts out of shame, or psychosis. Does one *really* know if they're crazy or not? A crazy person probably assumes he or she is sane and it's everyone else who's crazy.

My thoughts are interrupted as I become aware of Amelia talking on the phone with Jax. She tells him his wife is waiting for him.

I jump up from my chair, tossing my purse over my shoulder and grabbing the bag of food. "I'll go back," I say as I round the corner toward Jax's office.

"He's coming out," Amelia yells after me.

"No problem. Thank you." I always feel like she tries to keep me from his office. I know it may seem irrational. Call it woman's intuition, but I get this same feeling every time I visit. She tries to keep me occupied in the lobby while Jax comes out to meet me. Then he steers me outside to one of the park benches where he can walk around and stretch his legs. Because he sits the majority of the day, he runs five to seven miles every morning and likes to walk around when he has a small break.

I rush around the corner of Jax's office just as he's coming out and we bump into each other.

"Whoa! Are you okay? I didn't see you. Why the rush?" Jax asks as he leans over and kisses me.

"No rush, dear. I just got tired of the waiting room. Look!" I say, and hold up the bag from the restaurant for him to see. "I brought you lunch today."

"Best wife ever!" He laughs and hugs me tight, lifting my feet several inches off the floor.

"Save that remark until you see what it is." I chuckle.

He sets me down. "Let's eat outside …"

I interrupt him. "No, let's not. I don't want to go outside. Let's stay in your office." I smile and he narrows his eyes. "Allergies," I explain.

"Okay … fair enough."

"Come over here and sit on the sofa. I'll sit at your desk. We'll change places today. You're my patient and I'm your shrink." I laugh as I lead him to the sofa and set his food down on the coffee table. I pop the straw into his tea and set the napkins and fork next to the plastic container, which I then open so that he can see the deliciousness I brought him. "Smell that," I say as I wave my hand in front of my nose as if to magnify the aroma of Cajun bliss.

"I smell alcohol." He places his hands on his hips, wearing a look of disappointment.

"Oh, Jax." I shake my head. "Don't be such a prude."

His jaw drops. "Wh—What did you just say? Did you just call me a prude?"

I laugh and turn on my heel. I've got work to do. I've got to distract him with this food in order to steal his prescription pad. "Sit. Eat."

"What have you been doing all morning?" he asks and slowly takes a seat on the sofa, eyes clouded with suspicion.

"I met Isabella for brunch."

"Did you drink … or eat?" he asks, furrowing his brow.

"We did both, Jax. Relax." I take a seat in the chair behind his desk and drop my purse to the floor.

"I don't remember you mentioning a lunch date with Isabella."

"That's because I didn't. It was a last-minute decision." I

decide to act a bit tipsier than I am, because it seems to be distracting him quite well. He's not paying much attention to my behavior, chalking it up to alcohol. I get right to work, opening his top desk drawer to peek inside. *BINGO!* There it is! The prescription pad. That was too easy.

"What're you doing? Stop going through my desk, woman," he says as he takes a bite of boudin.

"I need a pen," I explain, pulling one out of the drawer, which I leave open several inches.

"This is delicious. Where'd you get this again?" he asks, practically inhaling his food. I mentally pat myself on the back.

"It's a Cajun restaurant Isabella turned me on to. I'll have to take you there one weekend." I smile. I watch him closely, and when he leans over to take a bite I nonchalantly stick my hand into the open drawer and feel around for the pad. The tips of my fingers touch it, and I quietly pull it out and let it drop into my purse sitting on the floor. I wait a few minutes and then discreetly pick up my bag, placing it into my lap where I shove the pad down into it and zip it shut. Jax never notices a thing. He's too distracted by his lunch and the fact I drank so early in the day.

We kiss goodbye, ten minutes before his next client is to arrive. He's none the wiser his wife is about to commit a mortal sin.

I can't wait to get home and tell Isabella I've got the pad!

MONDAY EVENING

I pull up to our mailbox and notice Jax standing with Owen in his driveway. What's going on here? Could Jax be confronting Owen about the night we were followed? Certainly not. I get out of the car to check the mail, the whole time keeping an eye on them. Jax laughs and I notice Owen pat him on the back. You've got to be kidding me. Best friends? Why's he being so buddy-buddy with Owen?

Why wouldn't he be?

Because he thinks Owen was following us the other night. Or maybe I'm the only one who believes that.

I quickly jump back into my car and pull into the garage. I head over to Jax and Owen.

"There she is. Hi, babe. We were just talking about you," Jax says as I approach the two of them. Out of the corner of my eye, I notice Owen staring me down. Jax grabs hold of my hand and gives it a gentle squeeze.

"Talking about me? What for?" I fake a smile.

"I was just telling Owen about the big account you snagged with Southern Oaks, and how you did some work for Oak Alley last year. And what's that new one you just landed? Can't think of the name."

Crap! Jax is ruining everything right now. My new account was going to be the reason I use to take a bottle of laced wine to Isabella's. It's supposed to be a celebratory drink. I'll have to make up a lie now. I guess no harm done.

"It's the Ormond Plantation," I say, smiling proudly. I feel anger rising in my chest the longer I stand here listening to these two chatting back and forth. I excuse myself to say hello to Isabella. I notice Owen watches me as I walk to the front door. I crack it open large enough to stick my head in. "Isabella. It's me, Greta."

She comes rushing to the door and gestures with a wave for me to enter. She grabs my arm and pulls me over in front of the living room window. This way we can keep an eye on Jax and Owen as we chat about Owen's demise.

"Get a load of this," she says, gesturing toward the window. "I almost fell over when I saw the two of them out there chatting it up," Isabella says and breathes in deeply.

"How did this happen?" I ask.

"Owen pulled up and then Jax called out to him."

"Jax initiated the conversation?" I pucker my lips in thought.

"Is that odd?"

"Well, it seemed to me he believed Owen had been following us, even though he tried to tell me it was someone else. I know when he lies." I scrunch my face. What is Jax up to?

"Were you able to get the prescription pad?" she asks nervously.

"Yes. Hide it good," I say as I pull it out of my purse and hand it to her. "After you're finished with it, burn it."

"Don't worry. I'll be careful," she assures me.

"How are you going to cover up his name?" I point to the top of the pad where Jax's practice is listed.

"Oh, that's nothing. I can change that with a simple trick on the computer and then reprint it, watermarks and all."

I raise an eyebrow at her. "Really?"

"You learn to do all kinds of things when you're at home all day, especially if you live with a lunatic," she sniffs, and we both bust out laughing.

"Once you get the prescription, bring it to me and I'll put it in the wine. Then we'll pick a night for me to come over. I'll have to make up a reason for a celebratory drink, so just go with it."

Isabella grabs my arm. "Here comes Owen. I've got to run upstairs and hide this," she says, holding the prescription pad to her chest.

"Go. I'll let myself out, and I'll try to delay him a minute." I quickly make my way out the front door, thinking up a reason to gab with Owen, but once I lay eyes on him, I can see there's no need. He's coming straight for me, and he's got something to say; I can see it in his eyes.

"You and my wife seem to be hitting it off," he says, but there's no smile on his face. There's no pleasure to his tone.

"I could say the same about you and Jax, no?"

"I like him. He seems to be a hard worker. He knows what he wants and doesn't seem to be the type to let anything stand in his way." Owen smiles crookedly.

"I think we all deserve to go after our dreams, don't you? I mean, if husbands and wives don't allow each other to flourish and grow, then marriages would become stale and unloving."

"I hope you're not filling my wife's head with this kind of crap," he says and laughs as if he's joking, but we both know he's dead serious.

"Does this bother you, Owen? Knowing that I might be

filling Isabella's head with the truth about what a beautiful person she is? She's smart, intelligent, talented, driven, loving, and compassionate. Is it a crime for me to tell her these things? You're her husband. You should be the first person she can run to when she's in trouble. You should be her strength when she's weak—her protector. The one person in this world who makes her feel safe."

Owen's face changes; his jaw tightens, his eyes narrow, his brow scrunches, and I wonder if this is how he looks when he's about to send a blow to Isabella's face. Is this what she sees when he raises his hand to her? It's ugly.

"Are you insinuating I'm not any of those things to my wife?" he says through clinched teeth.

"Are you, Owen? If something tragic happened, would you be the first person she'd run to, or would it be the neighbor she just met a few months ago? Who would she feel safer with? Who could she trust more?" I smile and stare deeply into his eyes, letting him know I'm aware of his secrets. I see his rage emerging, but it doesn't scare me. I almost wish him to lay a finger on me. Jax would snap his neck in a heartbeat.

"You think you know it all because you work with battered women. What a hero you must be in your own eyes. Don't try to play one here, Greta. It will cause you problems so great you'll wish you were dead."

"Oh, Owen, threats don't scare me. I'm not some little fragile woman who's scared of the big mean man." I laugh sarcastically and his brown eyes flash with rage. "Bring it on, big boy. Bring. It. On!" I turn on my heel and start down the driveway. I don't look back, but I can feel Owen staring me down, as if his eyes are penetrating my flesh. I keep walking, head held high.

Then I spot Jax.

Crap! He's standing just inside of the garage ... watching. His lips part as I approach him and I know it's coming. Twenty million questions.

"What the heck was *that*?" he asks suspiciously.

"What do you mean?"

"C'mon, Greta. For a moment, it looked like the two of you were going to start throwing punches."

I laugh and start toward my car. I click the trunk open, lean over and grab a bag of groceries. Jax is hot on my trail, so I turn and plop the bag into his arms, forcing him to take it. I take the other bag out, slam the trunk closed, and head toward the door.

"Are you going to tell me what's going on, or do we have to play the game where I pry it out of you, hounding you until you eventually spill it?"

I step inside and then stop abruptly, causing Jax to bump into me. "Owen is an abuser," I say under my breath and continue into the kitchen.

Jax quickly follows me inside and shuts the door. "Say what? How do you know this?"

"Isabella confided in me. She also told me not to tell anyone, including you, so don't say anything. You'll have to act normal when you're around him." I start unloading the groceries. Jax is standing by the island, still holding his bag. I take it from him and empty it onto the counter, giving him a few minutes to compute what I've just revealed.

"He knows you know about it?" he asks, concerned.

"He does now. Honestly, I think he wondered if I knew, but wasn't sure, so he was testing me. I pretty much let him know he's not going to bully me like he does her." Jax leans onto the island and buries his head in his hands. I'm a bit alarmed at his reaction. "What's wrong with you?" I ask, giving him my full attention. I hear him groan into his shirt sleeve. "Jax!"

He straightens and pulls me over to him, cupping my face in both hands. I've never seen him so serious. "Greta, promise me … promise me you'll stay out of it. Please, please, please, stay out of it."

My jaw drops in shock. "I will do no such thing. I'm an advocate for battered women, and you're asking me to allow one of my friends to be abused without helping her?"

Jax groans again and drops his head down as if defeated. "We moved out here for some peace and quiet, and now you're going to go and screw it all up trying to save the world."

I watch as Jax grabs a wine bottle sitting on the counter and a glass from the cabinet and then heads toward the great room. I hear another groan escape him on his way out.

His behavior is utterly bizarre. Could this be about Owen's friendship? From what I've witnessed, Jax hasn't seemed too interested in him up to this point. Why on earth is he so concerned about me getting involved? He's always been so proud about the work I do, helping battered women at the shelter. I decide to leave him alone with his thoughts while I get dinner ready.

Once I've plated the salmon with green beans and laid it out on the table, I set out to find Jax. I check the great room first and find the French doors ajar. He must be on the lanai enjoying a cigar with his wine, although he usually waits until after dinner to smoke. I step through the open doors and take a look around. The outside lights are off, but I spot him standing quietly behind the hedge in the shadows. He hears me and quickly places his finger to his lips, motioning for me to be quiet.

I tiptoe over and he whispers in my ear, "Listen."

I hold my breath, but hear nothing. I open my mouth to speak, but Jax places his finger to my lips, silencing me. That's when I hear it. Owen is yelling at the top of his lungs. We're too far away to make out what he's saying, but we can hear his voice. We stare at each other, wide-eyed, as we listen. We hear glass shatter, and I grab Jax's arm in alarm.

"We have to do something," I say anxiously.

"I know. Let's call the police," he says and pulls his phone from his pants pocket.

"He could kill her in the time it will take for them to get here. We have to go over there," I plead.

Jax pauses. "Listen, I think it's stopped."

We stay quiet for a minute, but hear nothing. Jax turns his phone on and starts to dial. I grab his hand to stop him. "What are you doing?"

"I'm calling the police," he says, pulling his hand away.

"Wait! I think it's over."

"So what? We need to call the police," he says strongly.

"You just said in the kitchen to stay out of it."

"That's before I heard him beating her. They won't know we did it. It could be any neighbor."

"The other neighbors are too far away to hear."

Jax looks askance at me, alarm in his eyes. "What's *really* going on here, Greta? Why don't you want me to call the police?"

"I know Isabella enough to know she'd never want the police showing up at her house because of a domestic dispute. Just let it go. She's humiliated enough. Find a reason to go over there and make sure she's okay." Calling the police on a domestic dispute and then finding the husband dead days later would draw way too much suspicion.

Jax scratches his head in thought. "I told him I'd give him one of my Cuban cigars. Of course, I didn't mean tonight, but I could run one over there."

"Perfect! I'll sneak around by the garage so I can see better. That way I can make sure you're okay."

Jax rushes into his study to fetch the cigar. After a minute, he emerges, tucking a handgun into the back of his waistband and covering it with his shirttail. He holds up the cigar for me to see. He places it in his shirt pocket and gives me a thumbs-up. I hurry back onto the lanai and quietly sneak around the garage, where I can duck down in the shadows of our crepe myrtle.

I see Jax ring the bell and then he turns toward me. The door opens and Owen emerges. After a moment, Jax pulls the cigar out of his shirt pocket. My heart is beating fast, but I quickly remind myself he has a gun. They seem to be joking around, and I suddenly feel sick. I know what sparked Owen's temper tonight. It was the short exchange of words I had with him as I was leaving earlier. That's all it took for him to erupt into a madman. Poor

Isabella paid the price for my uncontrollable tongue. I should have kept my mouth shut.

After a few more minutes, Owen steps inside, and Jax heads home. I stay low as I sneak back to the lanai and into the house.

"What happened?" I ask anxiously, as Jax comes through the front door.

"Nothing. I told him I'd forget about the cigar if I didn't bring it to him tonight, and he laughed. He was totally normal, Greta. He didn't have any marks on him. He was smiling and joking around with me. He left the door open like he didn't have anything to hide. When I first got there, I could see in through the sidelights, he was watching TV with his feet propped up like he didn't have a care in the world."

"Not like a person who'd just beaten his wife," I say, shaking my head.

Jax reaches out and pulls me over to him. "I'm sorry we had to witness that, and I'm sorry you deal with this sort of thing on a regular basis. I know it must be hard, but it's also dangerous. Best left in the hands of the police, okay?"

I wrap my arms around his waist and my right hand lands on the handle of his gun. "You better put this away." I chuckle. As Jax heads into his study, I think how it won't be long and Isabella will never have to deal with Owen again.

She'll be free to do as she pleases.

Chapter Twenty-one
Evangeline

MAY 3
WEDNESDAY AFTERNOON

I haven't seen Jax since the coffee shop incident. I don't know what else to call it. He's so hot and cold when it comes to me. I wish he'd see me for who I *really* am, but he only cares for Greta. Nothing else in his life matters. I wonder, does she even know how important she is in his life? Personally, I think she takes advantage of him. Yes, Jax is headstrong and sets the ground rules, but he also caters to her, and she's no fool. She knows his sweet spots, how to push his buttons just enough to break him—to make him give in. Then she rewards him for allowing her to walk all over him, by giving him anything he wants. It's quite sick, if you ask me.

I haven't shown up at the coffee shop or my Wednesday session in two weeks. I wonder if he's missed me at all? I know he pretends he can do without me, and it wouldn't faze him in the least, but is that *really* true? I think deep down he has a soft spot for me, or I would've been gone a long time ago. Jax has the ability to get rid of me, and even though he threatens it at times, he hasn't done it. Sometimes he even thanks me for my hard work in keeping his marriage together. One could say I'm a bit of a spy when it comes to Greta. I keep an eye on her, make sure she doesn't do something crazy. I chuckle at my choice of words. Oh, what am I saying? She's as psychotic as they come. That's why I'm here. I make sure she doesn't make any horrible mistakes during one of her psychotic episodes. Jax *needs* me. Without me, he'd never know what she's up to.

I'm sitting outside his house right now, making myself comfortable out on the lanai. I can't stay away forever. He wouldn't want me to anyway. I bet he's been a little worried about me, wondering if I'm going to come back. It might even keep him up some nights, I'm hoping. He needs to see my value, something he's blinded to quite often. I came early today so I can hang out for a while before he gets here. I needed a drink so I popped into his kitchen, helping myself to a bottle of wine, and then got comfy in a lounging chair on the lanai. There's always a door unlocked. I believe he leaves it for me.

I lie back, allowing the sun to soak into my pale skin. I'm getting my daily dose of vitamin D. Apparently, Greta has been out here this morning. There's a mug half full of coffee sitting on the table with pink lipstick coloring the rim. Pink, ugh. It's a far cry from my Kat Von D lip color. Today I'm wearing *Exorcism*. I had to laugh when I was applying the blood black paint to my lips. It's so appropriate. I wonder if

Jax will think it's as funny as I do? I'll have to ask him. He'd love to *exorcise* me one day.

"Greta."

I jump up from my chair, bumping the bottle of wine, which topples over, but I catch it just in time. Not a drop spilled. I marvel at my quick reflexes.

"Greta. There you are." The voice is closer now.

Crap! Who the heck is this coming over?

I sit back down, carefully setting the wine bottle on the table. I watch as a tall redhead comes into view. Uh-oh.

"Greta," she says again.

Stop calling me Greta, you nosy witch!

"Greta's not in at the moment," I answer. I don't smile. I don't offer my hand. I don't get up, and I don't make eye contact. I want her to go away. I'm here to see Jax and I want to be alone with him.

"I beg your pardon?" she says and casually strolls over to me.

I wince at the sight of her face. "My, my. What happened to your face? Did you get into a bar fight?" I chuckle, closely looking her over. Black eye, swollen lip, cut above her brow. "It looks painful. Did you fall down the stairs or does your man have a temper that shows its ugly face when he drinks?"

The redhead stares at me in bewilderment, lips parted, but no sound comes out.

"Would you like for me to tell her you came by?" I ask slowly. My tone lets her know I don't feel like company. She glances around our surroundings and then back at me. Her eyes make their way up my body, starting at my combat boots, black fishnet stockings, black skirt, black jacket, black lace fingerless gloves, black nails, blood black lips, black eyeshadow, and, finally, my long, straight black hair. It's a wig, but she doesn't know that. Jax won't let me dye my hair black. He totally forbids it.

"Your makeup …" She pauses.

"Do you like it? I just bought a new lipstick today. It's called *Exorcism*, because that's what Jax wants to do to me. Exorcise me. Oops, I've said too much."

She looks startled. "Where is he?" she asks, looking toward the French doors.

"No one's here, lady. Jax doesn't like to see me when anyone is around, so he gets rid of them every Wednesday at appointment time. Greta, Rocio, and anyone else who likes to come around. I guess he didn't count on any busybodies coming by, though."

She continues to stare at me as if I'm a creature from the black lagoon. Come on, I know my dress is a bit gothic and my makeup looks as though it should be on Vampira, but I'm not some freak for everyone to gawk at.

"Look …" I raise my brow and wave my hand in anticipation of her name.

"Isabella," she says slowly, as if I have an IQ of thirty.

"Isabella, I'll tell them you came by." I grab ahold of the bottle of wine and lift it to my lips, taking a swig. Not the most ladylike thing, but I forgot to grab a glass when I was inside.

"Are you her sister?" she asks.

"Sister? Uh, no." I laugh sarcastically. "We couldn't be more different."

"But you look like you could be related. What's your name?"

"Evangeline. Have you ever heard of me?" I chuckle. "I've never been told I resemble Greta in any way, shape, or form," I snort. "Have you ever met Greta? She looks nothing like me." I'm almost insulted by the comparison.

"Maybe not in style, but the facial structure looks identical," she says, leaning in to get a better look.

She's making me nervous now. "Look …" I pause.

"Isabella," she says.

"Isabella, I'll be honest with you. If Jax shows up and finds me out here talking with you, he'll take a whip to me. He's already upset with me, so things will truly get rough if he catches us both out here. I *really* don't want to go inside. I still have fifteen minutes before he arrives, and I'd like to sit out here and drink in peace."

"Owen was angry with me the other night. That's how this happened." She points to her black eye and then carefully runs the tip of her finger over her puffy lip.

"Owen? Is that supposed to mean something to me?" I raise my brow. "Look, I'm sorry that your man is a creep, but I'm not the one to talk to about this. I'm sure Greta will be more than happy to listen to your sob story when she gets home, but I've got my own problems, lady. I can't help you." I raise up and grab my bottle of wine. "See ya," I say as I go through the French doors. Talk about dense. Take the hint, sugar, I don't want company. I'm not in the chattiest of moods. I've got bigger fish to fry. Here's some advice, *leeeaaave him!*

I'm sitting on the barstool at the kitchen island when I hear

Jax arrive. Garage door raises, car pulls in, door lowers. He enters the kitchen, stopping abruptly when he lays eyes on me. The corners of his mouth curve upward slightly, but it's not quite a smile. Is he happy to see me? He drops the mail on the table and slowly makes his way to the opposite side of the island. He stretches his arms out at his sides, holding on to the edge of the granite countertop. He stands, not speaking, not moving, just staring at me.

I'm nervous. I don't know what to say, but I manage something anyway. "Are you ready to talk?" I ask, but have no idea what it really means.

"That depends." He sighs deeply, eyes never leaving mine. "Are you done trying to wreck my life? Are you finished trying to destroy my marriage?" He tilts his head to the side. Not like he's anticipating my answer, more along the lines of making a statement. He's saying he holds all the power. He's saying there's no way I can make it without him, so I have no choice but to oblige.

"I am," I say shortly.

"Ah, so you admit it now." He licks his lips as if he can taste his victory.

"I do." Again, I'm keeping it short. I'll let him do all the talking so I can't screw anything up, as usual.

He remains still, watching me, analyzing my every move, my every breath. His eyes so heavy upon me I feel each movement I make is forced and comes out awkward. He chuckles and looks away. I exhale.

"Come on." He turns and heads toward his study. I follow. I'm relaxed from the wine, but still nervous—not sure what to expect, but in a good enough state of mind to accept it. "Sit," he says, not looking at me, and gestures to the chair across from his desk. I do as I'm told. "Did you get a phone?"

My heart skips a beat, and I don't answer.

Jax's eyes meet mine. "Did. You. Get. A. Phone?"

"Why are you asking me this?" I can hear the anxiety in my voice.

"Because there's a charge for an extra phone on Greta's bill."

I shrug, puckering my lips as if I have no idea what he's talking about.

"Hand it over," he says and puts his hand out in front of me.

"I need it. In fact, it's vital that I have it. It's my lifeline, Jax."

"Give it to me." He raises his voice.

"What if I need to call you and I can't find a way?" I argue.

"You'll find a way. Now, hand it over before I get up and take it from you forcefully."

I groan as I take the phone from the inside of my left boot and toss it on his desk. I wait as he goes through it, searching calls, searching texts, checking emails. It doesn't take long because I have no life. No friends, no *real* ones anyway. He doesn't allow me to have contact with the outside world. I thought maybe a phone would help ease my loneliness.

Jax opens the locked drawer with a key he pulls from his front pants pocket, and drops the phone inside. "Do you have anything for me this week?" he asks. I can see hate in his eyes. He truly despises me for who I am … an invasion to his marriage. It angers him that he needs me.

"Evangeline!"

His voice startles me as it shakes me from my thoughts. "There's nothing," I say, depressed.

"Good. Then take all that crap off." He waves his hand over the length of my body.

"Take what off?" I ask, appalled.

"That awful ensemble. Your black nails, your black lips, your black eyes, that wig. I can't look at it anymore."

I stroll through the kitchen on my way to the bathroom and grab the bottle of wine I left sitting on the counter earlier, giggling at my sneakiness. I scrub my face, taking drinks in between. It's the only thing that keeps me going. I'm drunk now. Jax will be furious. I take a detour when I leave the bathroom, crashing on the couch in the great room.

I'll deal with the repercussions later.

Chapter Twenty-two
Greta

MAY 5
FRIDAY EVENING

Isabella came by briefly last Tuesday and dropped off the potassium chloride. We've set up the dirty deed for Friday. Jax has dinner planned with some investors he's been speaking with about expanding his practice. It's been in the works for some time, and they're discussing details to see about moving forward.

I hold up the bottle of a mid-range French red wine (I don't want to waste an expensive bottle of wine, but it can't be too cheap or Owen won't want to drink it) and peer in through the glass. I search for anything floating around that shouldn't be. It would be disastrous if Owen popped the cork, poured a glass, and found something floating in it. We'd be caught! This morning, I ground the pills in our coffee grinder. It worked quite well. It left them with a consistency similar to baking soda. I poured the powder into a syringe—mixed with a small amount of red wine—and then injected it into the bottle through the cork. I wasn't sure it would work, but with small short thrusts, I was able to eventually get in all into the bottle. I let it sit all day, giving it a good shake every now and then to make sure it dissolved completely.

I throw on a pair of black cotton slacks with a cream silk top and my nude Chanel heels, as if I've just come from work. My body is rigid with nerves. My heartbeat is speeded up, which means my breathing is as well. I take several deep breaths to calm myself before heading out.

When I get to Isabella's front door, I pause again to catch my breath. I need to seem normal. Perfectly normal. She's supposed to answer the door to make sure Owen doesn't have a chance to shoo me away. One more deep breath, and I ring the bell. I hear someone fumbling with the lock on the other side. Isabella cracks the door open abruptly, panic in her eyes. Has she changed her mind? I raise my fingers to my lips and gasp.

"We can't do this. Something has happened," she whispers through the crack, and I see fear in her bright green eyes.

"What do you mean? What do I do? Go Home? What if we don't get another chance?"

The door swings open, ripping it from Isabella's grasp. "Another chance to do what?" Owen stands in the doorway with a wry smile and narrowed eyes. He looks from Isabella to me and then back. "Well, what is it? What in the world are you two whispering about?"

"Greta got a raise," Isabella blurts out.

"A raise?" Owen scratches his head. "How does one get a

raise when they're self-employed?" He raises his brow, staring me down, waiting for an answer.

I force a laugh. "Wh—What she means is, I've just landed a new account." I lock eyes with Isabella and nod.

She also forces a laugh and then corrects herself. "That's what I meant."

"A new account? Where?" Owen smiles, but it's not out of joy or congratulations for me. No, it's pure evil, and it radiates off him like the cloud of stench that follows Pig-Pen around.

"Ho-Homous House," I stammer. Crap! That's wrong. That's not the right place we'd rehearsed. Isabella's panic has thrown me off my game. I want to run, fast, in the opposite direction. I think of excusing myself. Telling them I forgot to make an important call, and I'll have to come back some other time. I raise my hand to my chest and attempt to take in a breath. I turn toward my house and wish I'd never left.

"Is this for a celebratory toast?" Owen yanks the wine bottle from my hand.

I lock eyes with Isabella, waiting for her to respond. She doesn't.

"Y—Yes, it is. Jax is out with investors tonight again, so I thought maybe the two of you would like to celebrate with me. You know, toast to my new job … account."

"Well, come in, then. I never turn down a drink. Let me pop the cork on this and we'll toast." Owen disappears around the corner, leaving Isabella and me to chat out of earshot.

She grabs my hands, fear in her eyes.

"What's happening?" I whisper. "You're supposed to pour the wine so that you can give us a different drink. He's going to pour us the drugged wine. Go!" I step through the doorway and push her in the direction of the kitchen.

"I can't," she argues.

"It's too late now. It's done. Now, get in there before he drugs us all." I shove her again, but she still doesn't budge.

"You don't understand. There's something ... strange going on."

"Owen's acting strange?" I'm completely clueless.

"No, you are." Her eyes widen, lips trembling.

"I don't understand," I say, flabbergasted. "I messed the script up a little, but no big..."

"No, not that. I met a woman the other day outside your house. She looked just like you except ... different. I left confused and it bothered me for several days. I thought about saying something to you, but I felt it might cause problems between Jax and his patient."

Owen calls out to us from the kitchen. "Let's toast."

"Patient?" I say in bewilderment.

"Yes, he was seeing a patient at home."

"Jax doesn't see patients at home," I correct her. "What are you talking about?"

"There was a woman out on the lanai waiting for him. She told me you weren't home and that Jax sees her every Wednesday."

"No one comes over on Wednesdays. What's her name? Did you get a name?"

"Evangeline, but..."

I don't hear anything else that comes out of Isabella's mouth. My mind stopped absorbing the moment she spoke the name Evangeline. I feel dizzy and lightheaded. I look around for a place to sit, but we're still standing in the foyer. "Why didn't you tell me about this?"

"I just thought it was a patient, but something kept bothering me about it. Her appearance."

"What about it?" The words barely roll off my tongue.

"She … she's …" Isabella hesitates and leans her head back.

I grab both her shoulders, turning her toward me. "What is it? She's what?"

She looks me in the eye. "Evangeline is you, Greta. You're Evangeline!"

"What in the world are you talking about? You've lost your mind." I feel myself start to hyperventilate.

"This is the wrong time to be discussing this. We've got to get that bottle away from Owen." Isabella steps away from me just as we hear a loud thump. We both pause long enough to look at each other and then we run toward the kitchen. Owen is slumped over on the floor. His wineglass is on the counter, just a swallow left. There are two more glasses, filled with wine, sitting close by.

"Oh, my gosh. It works that quick? Oh, my gosh. How much did you put in the wine?"

I shrug. "The whole bottle."

Isabella stares at me, eyes full of fear. "What do we do? I'm scared. I can't do this," she screams.

"It's done. Calm down." I stand over Owen. We need to check his pulse to make sure he's dead, but I feel if I bend over I'll pass out. My head is still reeling from everything Isabella just told me about Evangeline. I have a million questions, but we have to deal with this mess first. We've got to make sure Owen is deceased and then call an ambulance. This seemed so cut and dry in the planning stages. So easy. Put the drug in the wine, he dies, get rid of the evidence, and then call an ambulance. Why do I feel so disconnected? My mind can't compute what to do next. I glance at Isabella and she's as pale as if she's just given a pint of blood. Her eyes are locked on Owen's lifeless body lying on the floor.

The room starts to shrink, closing in on me. Everything turns black.

And I'm out!

Chapter Twenty-three
Evangeline

TEN MINUTES LATER

"Greta. Greta, please. Wake up! I need you. Wake up."

I hear Isabella's voice calling out to me. She sounds so far away, like she's yelling through a tunnel. That's when I feel the palm of her hand against my cheek. I blink my eyes open. I think she just slapped me in the face. Everything is blurry, and I'm seeing stars. I make out a figure hovering over me. I rub my eyes, trying to get them to focus. Slowly, Isabella's blurred face becomes crystal clear.

"What happened?" I squeak.

"I'm not sure. You just fell over. I guess you fainted. It took me a while to wake you up. You really scared me." She glances around the room. "We've got to do something about Owen. You've got to pull yourself together. Can you stand?"

"I guess so," I say groggily.

"Let me help you." Isabella grabs on to both my arms and pulls me up, helping to steady me as I land on my feet.

"Better?" she asks, looking hopeful.

"Yeah, I guess." Where am I? What am I doing here? How did I get here?"

"You have to check his pulse. I don't have it in me to touch him," Isabella says as her focus shifts to the other side of the room.

I glance in the same direction and jump back, horrified at what I see. "What's happened? Who's that on the floor? What have you done?" My voice is hoarse, coming out in a loud whisper.

"What are you talking about, Greta? We did this together. What's happening to you? Are you okay?"

"Did this together? What're you talking about? I just found myself on the floor next to a dead man. I didn't do a darned thing," I say, putting both my hands to my chest in innocence.

Isabella abruptly grabs my arms and shakes me. "What are you trying to pull here, Greta? This was *your* idea. What kind of game are you playing with me?" she says hysterically. Her eyes are wild and her mouth twisted as she gapes at me, waiting for me to respond.

"Stop calling me Greta, you imbecile." I shove her away and press down my disheveled clothing, trying to collect my thoughts. She watches me, shock on her face, trying to figure out who I am. I glance back over to the poor sap's lifeless body lying on the floor. "We did this?"

Isabella nods madly.

I carefully look over the room. There are three wineglasses sitting on the counter. One is almost empty, the other two are full. "We poisoned him?" I ask in surprise.

"Drug overdose," she corrects me. "We, well … you, injected the bottle with potassium …"

"Save it," I say, raising my hand to her. I feel around in my pockets. I pull the phone out of my front pants pocket and speak into it. "Call Jax."

"Are you out of your mind?" Isabella yells and rushes me, grabbing at my phone. "We didn't agree to this. It's only supposed to be us in this together. Don't you dare involve your husband. You promised!" Her face is red with rage, eyes bulging, and spittle peppering me as she yells.

"You had that deal with Greta, not me," I say sternly and turn away from her.

Jax answers almost immediately. "Hi, babe."

"No, sugar plum! Guess again." There's silence on the line. "So sorry to disappoint you."

Jax pauses. "Why are you calling me?"

"Your goody-two-shoes wife has done it again. Apparently, she was doing more than having small talk over coffee with the neighbor next door." I glance at Isabella and roll my eyes. "They were plotting to kill her husband, which they've done, by the way. I'm looking at a dead guy lying on the kitchen floor. He's been poisoned." Isabella gasps, covering her mouth with the back of her hand. "Oops, my bad … he's been drugged to the point of overdose."

Jax falls silent a beat. "Owen is … *dead*?"

"Looks that way, honey bun!"

"Where's Isabella?"

"Standing in front of me shooting daggers at me," I say, giving her a wink.

More silence. "So, she knows who you are now." It was more of a statement than a question.

"No kidding, Sherlock. How soon can you be here?"

"Fifteen minutes." The line goes dead.

I take in a breath and then slowly let it out.

Isabella finally speaks, voice trembling. "What the heck is going on here?"

"Don't worry about a thing, sugar. Jax will fix everything once he gets here," I explain confidently.

She examines me for a few minutes, watching my every move. "Who ... are you?"

"Hi. My name is Evangeline, I'm the scapegoat. Glad to meet ya. Is that a formal enough introduction?" She stares at me, her eyes a torturous mixture of confusion and fear. I almost feel sorry for her. She's just an innocent pawn in Greta's deadly game. Or is she? Actually, she doesn't seem to be too devastated over her husband's demise. "You and Greta planned this together?" I ask, narrowing my eyes.

Her lips part, but only a moan escapes her.

"Look, I know you're confused right now. It's best we wait for Jax and then he'll fill you in on anything he feels you should know."

"Greta's done this before?" she asks weakly. I check the time on my phone. Ten more minutes until Jax arrives. "She kills and then passes out, and *you* wake up?" Her face contorts with disgust.

"Do you have a bottled water?" I ask.

"Fridge." She half points across the kitchen.

I step over Owen's body and open the refrigerator's large

stainless steel door. I grab a bottle from the top shelf, twist open the cap, and suck down half. I can feel Isabella's eyes watching my every move. She's amazed with me. She's wondering who I am, and how I exist. How can I be a person inside another person? Her head is a twisted mess of confusion as she tries to piece it together, yet she can't because it's too bizarre for the average human mind to comprehend.

"You've got a split personality, or what?"

"I don't. Greta does. My mind is fine. I'm sane, but she's completely off her rocker," I answer, her eyes still heavy on me.

"What part does Jax play in all this?"

"He comes when I call. He … takes care of whatever mess Greta leaves behind. He's really good at covering things up. That's how she's gotten away with it all these years."

"All these years?" she says, alarmed. "How long has she been killing?" Her face is pale, causing her makeup to look heavy. I check the time once more. A single minute feels like an eternity. "Look, I know you don't, er, know me, but I'm not going to tell anyone anything about what's going on. I mean," she waves her hand toward her dead husband, "I'm in no position to be telling someone else's secrets when I have my own."

We both sit at the kitchen table in silence, me picking at my cuticles just so I don't have to make eye contact. "Greta is not who she pretends to be. She does horrible things and then pushes them off on me, leaving me to clean up her mess, which I would never do if it weren't for Jax. He makes me do these things. If it were up to me, she'd be in prison."

Isabella scrunches her face in confusion. "But if she goes to prison, don't you go to prison? It's not like you can switch bodies."

I sigh. "If I could, I would have a long time ago. And yes, whatever happens to Greta, unfortunately, happens to me as well."

"So Jax or no Jax, you'd be cleaning up Greta's mess regardless," she says and purses her lips.

It's not like I'm not aware of this tiny significant detail. I am. I just need to blame Greta for anything and everything I can. "She ruins my life. Jax ruins my life. I want to escape them both," I say, feeling anger rise in the back of my throat.

"Let me ask you … where did you come from? I mean, from where I sit, *you* don't have a life. Aren't you piggybacking on Greta's life?"

This chick is starting to get under my skin. She sounds like Jax.

She scratches her head in confusion. "Help me to understand. You're a split of Greta's personality. You're actually *part* of her, just a different part, right? Like an alternate ego?"

"Are you an expert on DID?" I bark.

"I'm just trying to understand what's happening here. I apologize if I offend you. I don't mean to." She looks up toward the ceiling, eyes filled with curiosity. "Multiple personality disorder usually stems from childhood abuse. Is that what happened to Greta? She was abused by a man as a child. That's why she's so passionate about helping other battered women. Am I right?"

I watch her, intrigued, as she puts the pieces together, but I don't speak a word. She seems to be able to read my thoughts because she continues as if I've validated her speculations.

"So something horrible happened to Greta, and that's how you were born. You emerge whenever she's experiencing something traumatic." Her eyes light up as she paints a picture of our lives in her head.

"It's called Dissociative Identity Disorder, or DID. And I can *emerge* anytime I want, but Jax doesn't allow me to. He says I'm trespassing. He tells me that he didn't marry me, he married Greta, and that I have no right to be here." Jax will kill me if he finds out I'm confiding in this wackadoodle.

Isabella tilts her head and puckers her lips. "He does have a point." She shrugs.

"I was here long before he was," I snap.

"As a psychiatrist, I'd imagine it wouldn't be too tough for Jax to get rid of you, eh?"

"He needs me too much," I say confidently, although I'm not sure if I wholeheartedly believe this.

"He *needs* you? Ah, I see. She kills, and then you and Jax come to the rescue and clean up the crime scene to keep her from getting caught. Does she have any recollection of what she's doing?"

I shake my head. "None. She kills and passes out and then I wake up and call Jax. He shows up, we fix it and then we don't speak of it again."

Isabella gasps. "This is the most bizarre thing I've ever heard. You're nothing like her," she says with excitement in her voice. "The complete opposite. When I saw you, the other day, I could barely recognize you as the same person. You're much more uncouth … unrefined. Oh, no offense," she quickly adds, the corners of her mouth slightly curving upward.

"I'm only twenty-one, give me a break."

She straightens in her chair and claps her hands together. "Oh, my gosh, you even have a different age. It really *is* like you're a totally different person. Someone with her own identity."

I throw my hands in the air. "That's what I've been trying to explain to Jax all this time."

"He hates you?" she asks, tapping her chin with her index finger.

"He's only interested in me when I'm helping him; when I can be beneficial to him. Other than that, he can't stand me."

"What about Greta? How does she feel about you?" she asks curiously.

I laugh. "She has no idea I even exist. She gets to go on her merry way, living life in her happy little delusional world, while I'm kept prisoner, cleaning up her messes. It's not fair, I tell you." My rage has surfaced and it feels extraordinary to unload on someone. I have to be honest, I hated this broad from the second I first laid eyes on her, but now I'm beginning to think she's the only person in this world who understands me. She, like, totally gets me. She feels bad for the way I have to live; trapped in someone else's life, being controlled by other people. It's a living freakin' nightmare, and this chick totally gets it! I want to hug her.

The doorbell rings repeatedly, and I'm almost disappointed I have to discontinue my therapy session with Isabella.

"I better handle this," I say and, reluctantly, stroll to the door. Jax rings the bell several more times, and I yell out that

I'm coming. I swing the door open to find him with a look of horror on his face. He pushes through the door and quickly closes it behind him.

"Where is he?" Jax says hoarsely. I know he's nervous because his mouth always goes dry when he's having anxiety.

"Follow me," I say and lead the way. I can feel Jax's breath down my back as he follows close behind. We enter the kitchen and his eyes freeze on the dead man sprawled on the floor. A full minute goes by before his gaze darts around the room, searching for Isabella. Once he spots her, he shakes his head.

"Are you out of your friggin' mind? What were the two of you thinking?"

Isabella's eyes fill with shame, but she says nothing.

"The two of you got together over lunch and decided this would be a good idea? This sounded logical to you? Killing your husband?" Jax throws his hands in the air and starts to pace.

"Um, Jax, darling, we don't have time for your lecture. Do we dump the body or call the police?"

"Call the police?" Jax says in exasperation.

"You might want to listen to the plan they've worked out before making a judgment call." I direct my attention to Isabella. "What's the name of that drug you used?"

Isabella slowly raises herself up from the chair, holding on to the edge of the table to steady herself. She seems a bit wobbly. "It's called potassium chloride. An overdose mimics a heart attack. The coroner will rule it a heart attack. We planned to call the police and say …"

"It will be in his blood. The coroner will find it," Jax quickly shoots back.

"Actually, blood levels will show an elevation of potassium, but that's normal after a heart attack. So, a medical examiner won't think anything of it."

Jax scratches his head and sighs loudly. "Are you sure about this?"

"I'm positive. Trust me. I know what I'm doing."

After a minute, Jax sighs again and says, "Let's call an ambulance. But first, let's get our story straight. I had just arrived home when I received your phone call. I immediately rushed over here and started CPR. After they examine the body, they'll discover he laid here a good half hour before you called for help. Here's what you tell them …" Jax speaks every word slowly while Isabella and I attempt to absorb our roles. "You were both outside, having a drink on the patio. When you came in for a refill, you found him on the floor and immediately called 911. You don't know how long he'd been like that. He had complained about indigestion after dinner, but was fine and watching TV when the two of you went outside."

Jax glances over the kitchen and waves me toward the bottle of wine sitting on the counter.

"Dump that down the sink along with what's in the glasses. Put the bottle in a bag and we'll place it in my trunk so I can get rid of it tomorrow." He directs his attention to Isabella. "Do you have another bottle of red wine?" She nods her head. "The autopsy will reveal he drank red wine. Open another bottle, pour a splash into his glass and then you and

Evangeline chug down a glass. If you were out on the patio drinking, it will need to be on your breath." He turns to Isabella. "Where's the potassium chloride?"

She starts to point toward me and then catches herself. "Greta has it, but she used the whole thing. She's the one who injected the bottle."

"Of course she is," Jax says.

We quickly go to work, doing as we're told, while Jax rolls Owen's body over and starts fake CPR.

Once we're done changing out the wine bottle and chugging down a glass, which I needed oh, so badly, Jax orders us to unlock the patio door and turn the outside lights on.

He looks at Isabella. "Call."

She doesn't hesitate. She picks up the landline in the kitchen and dials 911.

"Something is wrong with my husband," she cries hysterically, "he's collapsed on the floor and I don't think he's breathing."

I pucker my lips, tilting my head to the side … not bad. We've got quite an actress on our hands.

She hangs up, wipes away the fake tears streaming down her face, and takes a drink of her wine, cool as a cucumber.

"Call my cell," Jax tells me. "Just in case they check our phone records, they'll see where Isabella called an ambulance, and you called me for help."

I do as I'm told and we let our call connect for about fifteen seconds. Just enough time for me to tell him what's happened and to come over.

The ambulance arrives in just shy of ten minutes, although

every minute felt like an eternity. My palms are sweaty as I stand to the side and observe. The paramedics are already transporting Owen by stretcher out the door and to the ambulance, while a few stay behind asking questions. Jax does most of the talking. Isabella's fake hysteria doesn't allow her to give many details, not that there are any: we were outside, we came in for a drink, we found him lying on the floor, we called 911, Jax came over to help. It's pretty cut and dry.

As soon as Jax and I were no longer needed, we moseyed back home, where we sat on the lanai drinking scotch for what seemed like hours. We mostly drank in silence. I could tell he was livid at his precious little killing machine of a wife. I asked him how long he was going to keep up the charade, but he never answered. He just sipped his glass and smoked his cigar. I think his heart ached for Owen. Jax liked him. They had things in common and maybe Jax thought they'd be good friends one day. Of course, he probably hadn't known he was abusive to his wife.

On the other hand, I could be completely wrong. I could be mistaking his sad demeanor for pure disgust. He could be thinking about how much of a burden Greta is and trying to come up with ways to get rid of her. I chuckle. Only in my dreams.

I leave him on the lanai and crash in his bedroom, as I always do after a killing, wondering what I'll be facing when I return.

It's dark. I'm surrounded by blackness. Where am I? Oh, no, what's happened? I sit bolt upright, my heartbeat increasing, my body starting to tremble, fear rising in the back of my throat. Am I safe? I feel around until I find a lamp on the bedside table. This seems vaguely familiar to me. I click the lamp on and immediately breathe a sigh of relief. I'm in Jax's bedroom. But why? I mean, I know how I got here, but what am I still doing here? I check the digital clock sitting next to the lamp; it's four in the morning. I should have gone dormant and Greta should have come out by now. We should have switched already. What's happening? I turn to Jax's side of the bed to find it empty. That's odd—he's not much of a night owl. He probably passed out on the sofa.

I tiptoe down the stairs and into the great room. Nothing, but I notice the French doors are still sitting open. Did he fall asleep outside? I cross to the lanai and find him sitting in the same lounging chair from earlier this evening, smoking a cigar.

"Oh, my gosh. You're still out here?" I circle around to face him, and I take a seat in the chair next to him.

"Greta, what're you doin' awake?" He slurs his words and I can barely understand him. He attempts to prop his elbow on the arm of the chair, but it slips off, causing him to lurch forward.

"No, it's Evangeline," I say slowly. Jax is not fond of drunkenness. In fact, it disgusts him, so I'm a bit taken aback by his condition.

"'Vangeline." He cocks his head in my direction, and I get a glimpse of his glassy blue eyes. "What're you doing here? You shouldn't be here." He attempts an angry tone, but fails as his words run together.

"Come on," I say as I grab him by the arms and pull upward. "We've got to get you upstairs."

"Where's Greta?"

"That's what I'm wondering." I don't think there's ever been a time when I wanted her to show up more than anything else. Jax is hard enough to handle sober. Drunk ... I'm not sure what he's capable of, but at least he's so sloshed right now he couldn't harm me if he tried. I chuckle at the thought of him trying to exorcise me out of Greta's body.

I yank him up out of the chair, but he falls right back. "Help me, Jax. You're too heavy for me to pull you up."

"Then just leave me here. I'm fine," he says as he slumps into the chair, head nodding, and closes his eyes.

"You can't sleep outside on the lanai. You'll wake up in shame in the morning."

"How could I feel more shame than I do right now?"

I tilt my head to the side and purse my lips. "You have a good point." I've never seen the sap in this condition before. I'm used to the Jax who holds his head high, proud, confident, intelligent, and strong. Drunk Jax is quite pathetic, weak, and whiney. I guess we all have different sides to us. Multifaceted personalities. Some we show, some we don't. We're all vulnerable deep down. Maybe it's the people who act the strongest on the exterior who are really the weakest.

Greta displays a hard exterior, someone who's cool in all situations. Deep down she's so weak she can't control her urge to get revenge, so she gives in to it. Whereas, I'm a person who's outwardly weak when it comes to my emotions, yet deep down I'm like a lion. I can attack when need be, but my intentions and actions are always well thought out.

I grab on to Jax's arms and try to hoist him up once more. He groans and falls through my grasp like Jell-O. I slap him across the face and he lurches forward, placing his hand on his cheek. I take a step back, although I have no fear of him in this condition and even wish he'd drink more often. Life would be easier for me if he did.

"Woman, I'm going to hurt you in a minute," he spits.

"Yeah, I don't think so. At least not tonight, Jax. Come on before I slap you again. I admit, it really felt good, and I wouldn't mind doing it again." I chuckle.

"Do it again and see what that gets you," he says as he attempts to hoist himself up using the arms of the chair. Once he's halfway in a standing position, I grab on to him and pull him up the rest of the way. "Don't touch me," he says and tries to push my hands away, but I keep a firm grip on him and start to edge him toward the French doors.

We finally make it up the stairs and into his room. I let him fall on his back into bed. I manage to get his clothes off, leaving only his T-shirt and boxers. He won't like this in the morning, if he even remembers how he got undressed.

I chuckle at the thought.

Chapter Twenty-four
Evangeline

MAY 6
SATURDAY MORNING

Jax stumbles into the kitchen around noon. I watch him from my seat at the table where I'm having coffee. I ate hours ago. He's had a shower and shaved. He's combed his wet hair back; it's still dripping slightly onto the collar of his shirt. Our eyes meet when he enters the kitchen, but he quickly turns away. I've made breakfast. All his favorites. I even soft poached the eggs, exactly how he likes them. He lifts the pitcher of orange juice and pours some into a glass and then chugs it down, sighing loudly afterwards.

"I'm sorry I slept late," he says from a dry throat. He walks over to me and bends down, kissing me on the lips. He strokes my hair, waiting, no doubt, for me to speak. I can't hold it in any longer and I bust out in laughter. The tender look on his face turns to confusion, causing me to laugh harder.

"It's me, you doofus," I manage to choke out in gasps.

He steps back, appalled. "What're you talking about?"

"It's me, Evangeline." I'm still laughing, but start to calm myself as his expression turns grave.

"Get out of here, Evangeline. You're skating on thin ice already. Do you think it's wise to start breaking rules?" he says, lips tight in anger.

"Oh, I'd leave if I could. Trust me," I say and sip my coffee.

"What in the world are you talking about now? Get out!" Jax turns away and crosses to the island, where he starts making a plate of food. "Why're you here?" he asks as he butters a piece of toast.

I correct him. "You mean, why am I *still* here?"

He stops buttering and meets my eyes. "What does that mean?" he asks slowly.

"I never left. I'm still here. I even went to sleep and still woke up like this."

Jax looks alarmed. "Well … do something. Switch."

"I can't. I've already tried."

"Well, try again." He raises his voice.

"I don't know how," I insist.

"What do you mean? Just do what you always do and get Greta back." He puts the toast down. I now have his full attention.

"Aren't you listening? I can't. It's not working."

He blinks. "Not working? What does that mean? What is it you normally do to switch?"

"Nothing, really. I just kind of … think about it, I guess, and then it happens. This time it didn't." I shrug and take a sip of my coffee. Ooh, the look on his face is hysterical, and it's all I can do to keep from laughing.

"Then think about it harder," he yells, slamming his palm on the counter.

I bust out in laughter once more, and his eyes flash with rage. "I'm sorry, I'm sorry," I say and hold my hand to my chest, trying to get my laughter under control. "But you should see your face right now. You look like someone just punched you in the nose."

His lips part in shock. "Are you insane?" He walks over, towering above me. "This isn't a joke. It's my life!"

"And according to you, your life sucks," I say mockingly.

"What are you talking about?"

"I'm talking about your little drunken pity party last night. *Oh, woe is me, I'm so sad. I'm tired. I can't do this anymore.* Remember that?"

Jax turns away and runs his fingers through his damp hair. "Get out!" he says through gritted teeth.

"Really?" I ask unbelievingly. "I can go?"

"I don't care, just get out of my sight." Jax walks back to the island and resumes putting his breakfast together.

I slowly rise and reach for Greta's purse, sitting on the small table inside the garage door, then unhook her keys from the key rack. I back out the door, watching Jax the whole time. He never turns around.

And I'm off.

I arrive home after dinner. I'm not sure what kind of greeting to expect, but I'm prepared for anything. The house is dark. I can hear the TV on in the great room as I slowly make my way to it. Jax is lying on the sofa, remote in hand, but when he hears me, he raises up, looking me over.

"She hasn't come back," I say.

He sighs heavily, tilting his head back. "Come over here." He sits up and pats the sofa cushion next to him.

I take a seat and he mutes the television. The room is dark except for the flickering of the TV, casting shadows over the furniture and walls.

"Take your shoes off," Jax says and bends down to help me slip them off. "Now lean back and relax. Get comfortable." I do as I'm told, adjusting the throw pillow behind my neck. Jax pulls my legs onto the sofa, and scoots up next to me. "I want you to breathe in deeply, hold it for a count of five, and then breathe out slowly for a count of five." I sit up and he grabs my shoulders and pushes me back down. "Take it easy," he says softly.

"What's going on here? What are you doing?"

"It's a relaxation technique that may help you to switch."

"Is that all it does?" I fake a laugh.

"What else? Has there ever been a time when you couldn't trust me?"

"Ha," I answer.

"Don't be smart. Seriously, haven't I always kept my word?"

He's got me there. He *has* been a man of his word. "Yes."

"Then close your eyes and trust me."

"I have to close my eyes, too?" I sigh and do as I'm told.

He waits a minute before continuing. "Picture yourself in a safe place. It's quiet. Peaceful. You feel secure there, because no matter what, no harm can come to you. You feel warmth and love, making you want to stay there."

Jax's voice trails off and I feel myself being lifted to a place of peace. Almost as if I've left the present realm and entered another. Everything is black; even the flickering of the TV has ceased. I'm floating around in darkness, but I like it. I feel safe. I feel at home.

I hear a faint voice. Is that Jax calling out to me? No, it's a female. A small voice of a girl.

"Mommy. I'm looking for my mommy. Can you help me? Can you help me find her?" she calls out.

What's your name?

"My name is Daisy, and I'm lost."

How old are you, Daisy?

"Five. Can you help me?"

I can try. When did you last talk to her?

Daisy's voice fades away as another one takes over. This is a man. He's angry.

"I want to know why she gets all the special treatment. It burns me up. I want to hurt her. Why can't we switch like we used to? And why does she still get to do what she wants?"

A female answers. "He's imprisoned us. That's what he's done. It's not fair. When do we get a turn?" She has a British accent.

I hear Daisy again, calling out. "Mommy."

"Oh, shut up, you little brat," barks the British woman. "Can someone please take this snot-nosed brat to her mother?"

"She's gone. Somehow she's escaped like the others." It's the voice of a teenage boy. "I don't think she's coming back here. At least, she won't if she's smart."

"If the others escaped, then the rest of us can," says the angry man. "We need to figure out how they're doing it."

"It's so stifling in here. I can't live the rest of my life with a bunch of morons. Someone help me," yells the Brit.

"Trust me, I don't want to live with you guys, either," says the teenage boy. It dawns on me his name is Josh.

"Mommy."

"Shut up, kid."

Who are you people?

"Well, well, the teacher's pet has returned." "It's about time." "We wondered if you were ever coming back?" "She's a privileged pig." Numerous voices are coming at me all at once.

Where am I?

Laughter erupts between them. "Did you hear her?" "She's forgotten who we are." "She's living so privileged out in the real world, she's forgotten what it's like to be one of us."

"The doctor's in love with her," the Brit says, laughing. "That's why she gets to do what she wants. Isn't that right, Queen Evangeline?"

"We need to kill the doctor so we can get the heck out of here," yells the angry man, and I suddenly know his name is Stephen.

"We need to join forces. I'm telling you," Josh says. "If we join together, we'll be stronger and we can overpower Greta and then kill the doctor. Why doesn't anyone ever listen to me?"

"Because you're immature and your ideas suck." This is a new voice. It's gruff, the way an older gentleman would sound.

"I don't hear you coming up with any better ideas. If you're so mature and smart, then let's hear what *you* have to say. What's your plan?" Josh says defensively.

"We have to play head games with the doc, just like he's doing with us. We have to manipulate him the way he manipulates us. The problem is, you idiots fall for his tricks," says the older gentleman, and I recall his name as well. It's Henry.

"If your plan is so great, then why're you still here?"

"Yes, I'd like to know, too. How do we go about manipulating the doctor? He shuts us down every time we try to come against him," says the Brit, and I realize her name is Annabel.

"You people mess it up every time he comes around because you fight over him like children. Everyone wants a voice. Haven't you figured it out yet? He's not listening to you! He's never listened to you, because all he cares about is Greta," says Henry.

Josh chimes in, "That's why we need to kill her, but noooo, no one will listen to me because I'm too immature. We'd be outta here already if you'd let me have my way."

"You can't kill her, you buffoon. It would be a sure death for the rest of us," Annabel balks.

"Mommy!"

"SHUT UP!" everyone yells in unison. I hear Daisy start to cry.

"What kind of a mother leaves her kid behind?" asks Annabel.

"The one who wants to get out of here more than anything," remarks Stephen. "I'd do the same."

Where did you people come from? Why are you in my head? Get out! Get out! Get out!

They all erupt in laughter.

"The privileged fool has lost her mind. She doesn't even know who she is anymore?" says Annabel.

"What's wrong, Evangeline? Is the doc erasing your memories, or are you just too good for us?" Josh asks sarcastically.

"She wants it to be just the two of them. She wants to take the place of Greta," taunts Stephen. "She wants a life playing the rich wife of a successful doctor."

"She's in love with him. Aren't you, Evangeline?" "No, she's more like his personal assistant." "He certainly doesn't care about her." "Most definitely not." "He'll never set her free. He's too busy using her." "She likes doing his dirty work." "That's because she doesn't know any better." "Moommyy!" "SHUT UP!"

I open my eyes, arms flailing in the air. I grab hold of Jax's T-shirt, twisting it in my hands. He jumps, startled, and grabs hold of my wrists. "Don't send me back there. Please don't send me back there. I don't belong there. Help me, Jax. Help me."

"Calm down, woman. Take a deep breath. You're okay now." I'm trying to sit up, but he's holding me down, not allowing me to move. "Breathe, Evangeline. You're here with me, in my house. Look around. See?"

I try to break free from his grasp, but can't. He's too strong and has completely overpowered me. I want to run away. I want to jump into Greta's car, no, *my* car now, and drive and never stop. Just keep driving far, far away. I squirm and wiggle, but I can't break free.

"Stop! Evangeline, stop. I'll let you go, but you have to stay calm. You can't move. Got it?"

I nod, wildly.

"There you are. See? You're fine. Everything is fine." He watches me for a minute and then takes my wrist in his hand, looks at his watch, and checks my pulse. He strokes my hair in an attempt to calm me, and to gain my trust. "Breathe in deeply."

I fill my lungs with air, causing my chest to expand.

"Hold it. One, two, three, four, five. And then let it out, for one, two, three, four, five."

I breathe this way three times, Jax watching me closely.

"Tell me what happened," he says softly, continuing to stroke my hair.

"I heard voices. Mean, angry voices."

"Tell me what they said."

"They hate me. They want to hurt me because they're jealous. They hate you, too. They're trying to figure out a way to kill you." Jax remains imperturbable. His eyes stay calm as if he's not fazed by this news.

"How many are there?"

I rack my brain trying to remember their terrifying voices. "Five ... there are five of them. Who are they, Jax? Who are they?" I grab on to his arm and feel my nails dig into his flesh.

"You're fine. They can't hurt you. Stay focused. What are their names?" Jax stares into my eyes so intensely I have to look away.

"Josh. Um, Stephen. Annabel. Daisy."

"That's four. Who else?"

I groan in frustration. "I can't remember. I don't know."

"Is it Henry?"

My eyes widen. "Yes! That's it. Henry. How do you know that?"

"Tell me what they were saying," Jax says.

"They said the others have escaped, but that you're holding them captive. They said you're manipulating them and tricking them into captivity. They think if they kill you they can break free. That's what they said." I nod my head excitedly.

"Is it Stephen … the one who wants to kill me?"

"He started it, but they all agree. How do you know them?"

"Did they say anything about Greta?"

"Not really. They're more interested in you and me. Why, Jax? Tell me why."

He ignores my questions. "You said Daisy, but what about her mother, Pricilla?"

"She escaped and left her behind. Who is she? They were mean to her. They don't care about her." I see an anxiousness in Jax's eyes. "What's going on? Please don't ever send me there again."

"You don't have to go back right now, but you will soon. I'll let you stay tonight, but you're to be gone in the morning."

"NO!" I yell out. "I can't go back." I dig my nails deeper into his arm, causing him to wince in pain and break free.

"Not this again. You don't belong here, Evangeline. This isn't your home," he says sternly.

"Well, *that's* certainly not my home. It was like the black pits of hell."

"Actually, yes, it *is* your home. You're just having trouble remembering it, that's all." He shifts his weight, but stays seated on the edge of the sofa next to me, and I know it's to keep me from getting up.

"What are you talking about?" I feel my heart beating hard in my chest. I want to know the truth, yet I fear it at the same time.

"Never mind. Don't worry about anything, okay?" He turns away long enough to take a sip of water from his glass sitting on the coffee table.

"You can't put me through something like that and then not tell me what's going on. What do you mean I don't remember? You're scaring me, Jax. Tell me," I demand.

He faces me once more and scoots deeper onto the cushion, causing me to be tightly wedged between him and the back of the sofa. I feel my chest become tight with anxiety.

He pauses. "Do you think you're the only one?"

What does he mean *only one*? "The only ... *one*?" I ask, slowly.

"The only personality. Do you think it's just you and Greta?"

I stare into his eyes, not sure what to make of this, not knowing how to answer. *Yes, it's just me.*

He chuckles and looks down into his lap. After a minute he meets my eyes and asks again, "Do you think it's only *you*?"

I know exactly what he means. "Yes," I answer firmly.

"There's where you're wrong, Evangeline. There's more of you. There's always been more of you, but you're the strongest, and you're my favorite, so I've always given you priority while stifling the others as best I could."

I try to sit up, but when I do I feel Jax tighten against me, and I'm unable to move. "I just want to sit up and breathe."

"No."

I roll my eyes in annoyance, but it's really fear I feel. If he believes I need to be restrained for what he's about to tell me…

I don't finish my thought. "What happened to the others? How did they escape?"

"They didn't *escape*."

"Then what happened to them?"

"I got rid of them."

I raise my brow. "I don't understand."

"Yes, you do. They've integrated. They just don't realize it. It's done under hypnosis, so nobody remembers anything, including you and Greta."

I gasp for air, putting my hand to my chest. "You said you weren't going to do this. You promised."

"No, I said I wouldn't do it to you anytime soon. I never said anything else about the others."

"You're manipulating me … and them. You're trying to trick me."

"No, I'm not. I've always been upfront with you. You're losing some of your memory as the different personalities integrate. It causes memory loss. You forget some things, that's all."

I don't believe him. He's a liar. Even the others said the same thing. He lies and manipulates. He's sneaky and conniving. I feel panic spread over my body. He's going to kill me.

"How many have integrated? How are you doing this?"

The corners of his mouth curve upward slightly, and I try to read his thoughts through his eyes. He has no respect for me. He doesn't care about me. He has no love for me. He thinks I'm not real. He thinks I'm some alternate personality, and that's not true, I'm *somebody*. I have a life. I have dreams, goals, and feelings. I want to travel, get married, and grow old with the man I love. I want to see the world! "Tell me," I yell out. "Tell me how you're doing this." He's sneaky, evil, and cruel. He's tricked us all and we're now dying one by one.

"There were over twenty." He reaches for his water glass and drinks again. I try to wiggle free when his weight shifts, but he quickly restrains me again. "Now there's six of you. I do it through psychotherapy and hypnosis. I know each and every one of you. I know your names, your backgrounds, your thoughts. I'm aware of your hate for me and the threats. I've been listening to threats for over four years."

"Four years? You've been doing this for four years?"

"It's a long process. The more you integrate, the less you remember about each other. In the beginning, the personalities used to switch almost constantly. It drove me crazy. But about two years in, it slowed down. That's the result of the psychotherapy."

I try to stay clear minded as I take in everything he says. "Have any of them ever hurt you?"

He half-smiles. "Yes, they have."

"Who?" I'm not sure why I ask him this.

"Stephen's never been fond of me."

"Greta?"

"She doesn't know anything."

I pause. "So why did you send me back just now? What were you trying to accomplish?"

"I was trying to send you away so I could have my wife back."

"Why didn't it work?" I ask, slowly.

He shrugs. "I guess you got scared and came back."

"You said a minute ago you only allow me to come out because I'm your favorite. Did you mean that?" I ask, sheepishly.

"Honestly? Yes, I meant it. You're the only one I can tolerate, really, and even then, you work my last nerve." He chuckles, and I'm glad to see his face light up, even if it's only for a few seconds. "Even though you've always hated me, too."

For a fleeting moment, I'm shocked to know he realizes I'm resentful toward him, and then I remind myself who I'm dealing with. He's a darn good psychiatrist. The awards lining his bookshelves didn't come from mediocrity. "You hate everyone else?"

"It has nothing to do with hate, Evangeline. I just want to get rid of you all so I can have my wife to myself. Something I've never experienced."

"So, you've always known about us, even before you married Greta?"

"You used to know the answers to these questions. You're losing your memories as you integrate. You don't have long." He looks deep into my eyes, and I almost feel as if he's searching my soul. He wants to read me so badly right now. He wants me to show him how I'm feeling. I can't give him the satisfaction, but deep inside I feel like I want to explode in panic. I have to hide my emotions.

"Answer me," I demand, trying my hardest to remember.

"I met Greta in the rain at the French Quarter. She'd been stood up by a blind date. She caught my eye as she strolled down the sidewalk toward the street. I could tell she was angry. I thought she was too beautiful to be angry. It started pouring down rain and she had no umbrella. With caution, I approached her and covered her with mine. She wasn't amused, and in no mood to chat with a stranger, especially a man, but I asked her out anyway. I was charming enough, and she, a bit reluctantly, gave me her number. I set up a date with her for the following weekend."

Jax turns away and takes a drink of his water, swallowing it slowly. "But she didn't show up." He looks back into my eyes. "You did."

My lips part in surprise. "Wh—What?" I try my hardest to remember, but none of Jax's story sounds familiar to me.

"You waltzed up to me with this huge grin on your face, stuck out your hand and said, 'Hi! I'm Evangeline.'" Jax smiles as he recalls our meeting. "I knew then I was in love. I thought, *this one will be a true challenge.* And I was up for it, so here we are today."

"Most men would have hightailed it in the opposite direction."

"I'm not most men."

"Why'd you wait so long to treat her?" I ask curiously.

"That's enough questions," he says, and I can see his hard exterior taking over now.

"This is the last one, I promise. Just tell me."

He rolls his eyes. "Okay, but then I'm going to bed. I was

still in school. I didn't get my medical degree until I was twenty-nine. I spent some time studying her and Dissociative Identity Disorder. Once I really felt comfortable treating her, I did, and it's been going good. She had more than twenty personalities and now I've got it down to six."

"You mean five," I correct him.

"I mean six. You forgot to count yourself."

I feel a twinge of pain in my heart.

He stands and stretches. "I'm going up to bed," he says as he heads toward the staircase. "You can sleep in the downstairs guest room. Be gone in the morning," he says without ever turning around.

I watch as he disappears up the staircase and wonder what it would be like to be his wife. I try to imagine how it would feel to be loved by him.

To hold his heart in the palm of my hand.

Chapter Twenty-five
Greta

MAY 7
SUNDAY MORNING

I step out of the shower, wrap my wet hair in a towel, and throw on my softest, fluffiest robe. I'm tired, which is odd, because I feel like I've done nothing but sleep all weekend. I could keep sleeping, though. I hear the bathroom door creak open and Jax pokes his head around the corner.

"Hey, there," I say, smiling. "Good morning."

"Greta?" he says with raised brows.

"What, dear?"

He smiles and enters the bathroom, wraps his arms around me tightly and lifts me up. "Ah, it feels good to hug you," he says, burying his face in my robe.

I chuckle. "What are you talking about?"

"Nothing. It just feels good to have you here with me now." He sets me down.

"So good that I ended up sleeping in the guest room last

night?" I woke up this morning confused and can't for the life of me figure out how I got in the guest room. "Did I drink and act crazy? Did I black out? I mean, that's why I don't drink anymore, so what happened? I was really scared I had upset you, and that you'd be angry with me this morning. So, when you came in here happy…"

Jax gently places his finger to my lips to quiet me. "You didn't do anything wrong. You didn't drink, so stop worrying. I have a vague memory of you waking me up in the middle of the night because I was snoring something fierce. I guess you decided the guest room would be your best chance at sleep." He chuckles.

I place my hand to my chest and breathe a sigh of relief. Jax hugs me again and gives me a peck on the cheek. "How about breakfast on the lanai?" he asks.

"I'd love it, but I just woke up. I haven't cooked anything yet. I feel so tired … and confused. Remember, years ago, my blackouts when I'd drink? I know it hasn't happened in a long time, but I swear I feel the same way. Like I've lost some time somewhere. A significant amount. This weekend feels like a blur to me." My lips quiver. I can feel myself becoming emotional, and I fight it off.

Jax blinks. "You … seemed … normal …"

"Did you give me one of those pills? Maybe on Friday night?" He's watching me closely, the way he does when he's psychoanalyzing me; when he's playing doctor instead of husband. "Maybe I had a drink on Friday …" Anxiety is building in my chest. "… and you gave me a pill when you got home, or something, not realizing I'd had a drink. I'm good with only one or two drinks, you know that. This shouldn't have happened." I'm feeling stifled, so I squeeze past him into the bedroom. I tug on the belt of my robe, mainly because I need something to do with my hands.

Jax follows me and gently squeezes my arms from behind. "I don't think anything like that happened," he says softly.

"You like to give me those pills, ya know, even though they make me forget things." My body is trembling now.

"They don't make you forget, Greta. They relax you so your mind doesn't get overloaded with too many thoughts."

I swing around to face him. "Don't talk to me like I'm an idiot. You and I both know they erase my memory." I twist the towel on my head tighter.

Jax grabs my hands in his and places them on his chest. "I know you're not an idiot, babe. You just need to trust me as a doctor. I know what's best for you. I wish you'd just…" Jax leans over my shoulder and peers out the window. "Oh, crap!"

"What's going on?" I spin around and see two policemen coming up the sidewalk.

"Stay here," Jax says and quickly grabs a pair of jeans from the closet and pulls them on.

"What's wrong? What's happened? Why are the police here?" Questions are flying as I follow him to the top of the stairs.

"Just stay in the bedroom. Don't come down here," Jax says as he hurries down the staircase.

I rush back to the window to watch. After a few seconds, I see him on the sidewalk by the porch. He shakes hands with both officers and then crosses his arms over his chest. One of the cops takes a small pad and pen from his pocket. He writes every time Jax speaks. I lean into the window to see if I can hear what they're saying, but I can't make it out. I glance at Isabella's house and notice a figure standing in one the windows. It looks like her. She's probably wondering why the police are at our house. After a few minutes, the officers turn and head back to their cruiser parked at the end of the driveway.

Jax comes back in and I can hear him thumping up the staircase. I sit on the chaise at the foot of our bed, feeling as though I need to brace myself for what comes next.

"What's going on?" I ask when he appears in the doorway.

"Good, I'm glad you're sitting. I have some tragic news," Jax says and sits next to me. My heart skips a beat. "Owen had a fatal heart attack Friday night."

"Wh—What? Oh, my gosh. Poor Isabella. I've got to go over there." I feel frantic inside and I grab on to Jax's hands, pulling him closer to me. He wraps his arm around my shoulders. "He's so young. I don't understand," I say, confused. "Did the police just tell you? Wait! Why were the police here?"

"Greta." Jax pulls away from me now and stares at the floor. "You're asking a lot of questions that you probably won't understand the answers to. Why don't we wait a couple of days and then we can go over and give Isabella our condolences together, okay?"

I can't believe Jax's response. I feel like he's keeping secrets from me. "Did you already know about this? Did I? Is that why you gave me the pills? To calm me down … and now I don't even remember what's happened?" I jump to my feet and Jax immediately pulls me down beside him.

"Calm down. You were really torn up about it. I had no choice but to give you the medication."

"I knew it," I yell out. "The moment I woke up I knew, because the weekend seemed like a blur to me. You think I can't tell, but I can. You can't trick me. I always know, Jax. I always know."

He sighs heavily.

"Why in the world were the cops here? And don't lie. I want the truth," I demand.

"They needed more of my personal information, that's all."

"Your information? Why would they want that?"

"Because I was there that night. I performed CPR on Owen." Jax gets up and crosses into the closet. He removes his undershirt, replacing it with a blue polo. "It's time for breakfast. Let's focus on that right now," he says, straightening his shirt. "Let's give it some time to sink in and then we'll go talk to Isabella in a few days, okay?"

I stare Jax down, trying to figure out his game. What's he trying to pull here? "Okay," I agree, but only to appease him. I have every intention of paying a visit to Isabella today as soon as he turns his back.

We have breakfast on the lanai, taking full advantage of the cool Louisiana weather while we can. I found leftover eggs, hash browns, and fresh fruit in the fridge. I toasted some bagels, made coffee, and we had a wonderful meal. Now we're sitting, sipping coffee, and listening to the leaves rustle about the yard as the wind tosses them around. I love the cool morning air, accompanied by strong coffee, and the sound of birds chirping. It's my favorite time of the day.

I can't stop thinking about Isabella. Poor thing, to lose her husband so suddenly. Then I think back to what she shared with me in confidence that day in the kitchen. She'd said Owen had her trapped because he was taking care of her mother. I can't help but wonder, in all her grief, if there's not a small part of her that's glad he's gone. If I was in that same situation, I might be glad to be rid of him. In Isabella's situation, death would be better than divorce.

"Maybe Isabella's not grieving as much as we think she is," I say and turn toward Jax. He's sitting in the lounge chair next to me, head back, eyes closed. There's a sunray peeking through the treetops painted across his forehead.

He tilts his head toward me and narrows his eyes. "What do you mean?"

"Remember, I told you Owen was abusive?" I shrug. "Maybe she's glad he's gone. This could be a lucky break for her."

Jax purses his lips, eyes frozen to mine. Does he think I'm terrible for saying that? After a minute he says, "Did you ever talk to her about him dying?"

"Him dying?" I laugh. "It never occurred to me he could have a heart attack and be dead in a few days. I mean, as a counselor, I suggested some ways in which she could leave him, but it wouldn't have worked out for her. He was paying for her mother's medical expenses. Remember? I told you all this." I take a sip of my coffee and notice Jax is still eyeing me. "What is it?"

"You went over there that night," Jax says slowly. "You went over there with a bottle of wine. Do you recall doing that?"

I'm taken aback. "I went over there with wine? Are you sure about this?"

Jax nods. He's playing doctor now, not husband. This puts me on guard.

"Is this what she told you? Because I know I wouldn't go over there to drink. I mean, she likes to drink, I admit. And she's always trying to get me to do it." I make it a point to look into Jax's eyes. "I don't do it, though. I don't drink with her. I know that's how bad things happen, and I've explained that to her."

"When you two have gotten together, eaten lunch, shopped, whatever you're doing ... have you had anything to drink with her? Think hard, Greta."

Jax's questions are starting to worry me. Did I drink? I rack my brain thinking about each time we've gotten together. They're vague recollections. Why can't I remember better? Why do I have to fight just to remember something from a week ago, or a month?

It's the pills, you fool. Jax drugs you so you won't know what he's doing.

I shake my head. "I don't drink."

Jax looks away.

"Why are you asking me these questions? Tell me what happened."

"Honestly, Greta, I'm not really sure. You called me from there. I was almost home. I arrived a few minutes later and found him on the kitchen floor. I performed CPR the best I could, then the EMS showed up."

"The police came and I talked to them, right?"

Jax nods.

"And because I can't remember anything, you don't want me talking with them again, right?"

"Pretty much," Jax confirms.

"You shouldn't have given me that pill," I snap.

"YOU shouldn't have been drinking." His eyes flare with anger, and I look away. I don't remember. I don't drink, unless it's just one, and Jax is usually with me.

Those pills are stealing your life. Jax is stealing your life.

"So, you *did* give me one of those pills."

He glances at me and then leans his head back and closes his eyes. The ray of sun has moved further up now, crossing the chair just above his head.

I quietly wait a while to see if Jax is going to fall asleep, and he does. I step inside the house to change shoes and make myself presentable, and then I slip over to Isabella's.

I ring the bell and she answers almost immediately.

"Greta," she says breathily and then pauses, "right?"

I raise my brow and she tugs me by the arm, pulling me inside the foyer and shutting the door behind me. For a grieving widow, she looks superb. Full face of makeup, hair nicely curled with her bangs clipped back away from her face, satiny leopard print top, and flowing black slacks.

"Did you just get back from somewhere?" I ask curiously.

"No, actually, I'm getting ready to leave. I'm going to visit my mom." She half smiles.

"Look, I won't keep you. I just wanted to give my condolences." I notice the confused look on her face and I try to explain. "I mean, I know I was here when Owen had a heart attack, at least, that's what Jax tells me. I just don't remember." I have her full attention. "You see, he gives me these pills anytime I feel a bit stressed out, and they cause me to have ... well, sort of a memory lapse, I suppose," I say, embarrassed.

She scrunches her face in confusion, but nods as though she understands. We share an awkward moment of silence, before she finally speaks.

"So, you don't remember ... anything?" She puckers her lips to one side.

I shake my head. "Not really. Honestly, I don't even remember coming over here."

She glances down at her watch. "I've got to run. Visiting hours are short on Sunday."

"Of course. I just wanted to stop by and see how you're doing," I say, concerned.

Isabella opens the door for me, and I step out onto the porch. "Oh," I turn to face her, "before I go, did I have anything alcoholic to drink while I was here?"

"It happened so fast, we didn't get a chance to," she says as she smiles and shuts the door.

She rushed me out of there, but I totally understand why she doesn't want company. I wouldn't either.

Jax said you were drinking, That was a lie. He gave you the pill so he can control you. Wake up, Greta! Jax is a louse!

Chapter Twenty-six
Evangeline

MAY 10
WEDNESDAY AFTERNOON

I've been sitting on Jax's lanai for over an hour, enjoying some free time. I happened to find a deck of cards in the chest in the great room and spread them over the table outside. I've been playing solitaire and sipping some brandy. Jax won't care. He won't mind the missing brandy or that I've been hanging out here for a while. All that's a lie. He won't like either. That's why I'll cover my tracks before he gets here.

I spread out the cards over the table for another hand of solitaire when I hear leaves crunching under someone's shoes. I look up to see Isabella, and I smile wryly.

"Greta?" she calls out, but I don't answer. I go back to playing cards. "Hi! I saw you out here, and thought I'd come chat for a minute."

"Greta's not here," I say without looking away from my game.

"Okay, well, I … I mean, you're the one I really want to talk with anyway."

This piques my curiosity, and I set the deck down. "What do you want with me?"

"Answers," she says and takes the seat across from me, uninvited. She's dressed to the hilt.

"Oh, no. I'm not playing twenty questions with you again." I wave her away.

"Oh? I think you kind of liked it the other night. It seemed like you were getting things off your chest. It felt like a release, didn't it?"

I sigh heavily. She does have a point. "Tell me what you want to know, and I'll do my best to answer." I may or may not be telling the truth.

"Greta came over the other day and she didn't seem to remember anything," Isabella starts, but I quickly intervene.

"Yeah, that's how it works. She kills and then blacks out and doesn't remember a thing."

"That's not true!"

Isabella and I both jump, startled. I turn around to find Jax standing in the doorway of the French doors.

"Don't ask her. She doesn't know anything. Besides that, she's losing her memory by the minute."

"Pfft." I roll my eyes.

Isabella shifts uneasily in her chair. "Hi, Jax. I'm sorry, I didn't mean to intrude. I'm just trying to understand."

Jax crosses to me, picks up my glass of brandy and pours it on the ground. He caps the bottle and sets it aside. "What can I help you with?" He directs his attention to Isabella. She glances at me and then back at Jax.

"That's fine. You can talk in front of her," Jax says and takes a seat on the wicker couch. He crosses his legs and rests his arm along the back, cool as a cucumber. Isabella slightly pulls her chair in toward him, as if she's discounting me now that he's here.

"Greta came by the other day and she didn't seem to remember anything. I mean, *anything*, if you get my drift."

"I'm not sure that I do." Jax narrows his eyes.

Isabella shifts in her chair again. "Well, like the conversations leading up to the night of Owen's passing. She seemed clueless about them. If that wasn't her I was talking to, then who was it?" She nods at me. "Was it you?" Jax immediately puts his hand up to shush me.

"What is said today is kept between the two of us, deal?"

"See? I told you he doesn't treat me like a real person," I snap.

"If you speak again, you're going inside." Jax gives me a stern look. "Greta doesn't remember anything once a switch is made. She thinks she suffers from blackouts that are caused by the medication I give her. She thinks I'm trying to harm her, or trick her for some reason."

Isabella's brow raises in surprise, but she quickly puts on a poker face.

"It's the others. They tell her bad things about me so she'll leave me. That way they can have control over what she does and what they get to do. As long as I'm around, they don't have control. In fact, they know I'm helping her, that I'm curing her, so they want me gone." Jax scratches his head. "Let me ask you this, was she drinking any of the days you got together?"

"Every time."

"Every time?" he asks, surprised. "That explains a lot. Greta isn't supposed to drink because it causes her to switch. You could have been speaking with one of the others if she has no recollection of your conversations, but I was already aware of this."

"Do you mind me asking how you knew?" Isabella says softly.

"The other night, when you said you and Greta had planned to off your husband ..." Isabella's eyes move to the ground as if she feels a pang of guilt, but I know better than to believe that. This broad wanted her old man dead so badly, she could taste it. I chuckle inside. "... Greta would never have that conversation with you. It's not her."

Isabella scrunches her face. "If it's not her, then who is it?" She doesn't look at me this time.

"I don't know. I've been trying to figure it out for a long time now. She had over twenty personalities at one point, one being quite sinister. Through extensive psychotherapy, I've integrated all but six." He sighs. "I was hoping to find out which one is menacing, but I can't figure out who it is."

"It's Stephen. I keep telling him it's Stephen, because he's trying to kill Jax," I blurt out.

Jax drops his head forward and sighs heavily, and I notice the alarmed look on Isabella's face.

"One of them is trying to ... *kill* you?" she says, horrified.

I bust out laughing. "Not one, all of them."

"Excuse her. She's like a child I have to babysit," Jax says, clinching his jaw. "Look, I know you feel worried about what you and ..." he waves his hand in my direction, "... *someone* did. I don't care about that, okay? I just care about keeping Greta safe." He fiddles with his wedding band, spinning it on his finger.

"She gave a statement to the police. What if they question her again and she tells them something different or says she can't remember? That will surely draw suspicion." There's worry in Isabella's voice.

"I've already talked to her about it, so don't worry. But here's the thing, her mental issues are severe. Dissociative Identity Disorder is a very real and serious mental disorder, not to mention the narcotics she's on. If I ever had to defend her, all I'd have to do is produce her medical records. One look and no judge or jury would treat her as a reliable witness. In other words, her word would be worthless."

I see relief, as well as sympathy, wash over Isabella's face. We all sit in silence for a moment.

"How often does this happen?" Isabella asks cautiously, sounding as if she's not sure she really wants to know.

"Like, all the time. Jax and I are constantly cleaning up Greta's messes."

"Evangeline is a pathological liar. You can't believe a word that comes out of her mouth." Jax shoots me an angry look. "It's happened a handful of times. It didn't take me long to realize the men all have something in common."

"What's that?" Isabella asks curiously.

"They beat their wives."

"She, I mean, the killer chooses victims from the women's shelter, or what?"

"No, thankfully. That would probably lead the police to us, eventually. The victims are different people Greta meets. I don't know, it's like abused women are attracted to her. They immediately know they can trust her just by casual conversation in the grocery store line, or while getting a facial, or getting her hair done. It doesn't seem to matter. She meets a new friend and then within weeks … it happens. It's not Greta. It's someone else. I've been trying to get rid of him, or her. It won't be long now. I've almost accomplished complete integration through psychotherapy sessions."

"How many people know about this?"

"Now? The three of us. The killer has never involved another person. He, or she, has always worked alone."

"So I'm the first one?" Isabella raises her brow in surprise.

"And the last," Jax assures her.

She glances my way and then slowly stands. "Jax, I want you to know I'll take all this to the grave. You don't have to worry about me."

"I know I don't. I know you'd never jeopardize your own freedom, or leave your poor sick mother behind." Jax leans forward. "Greta can beat the system because of her mental illness, but you … you'd go to prison for the rest of your life." He stares into her eyes, letting her know he's not playing around.

"Understood." She nods and turns to leave. We sit in silence until we no longer hear the leaves rustling beneath her feet.

"Are you worried?" I ask.

"Not in the slightest. She's going to be too busy

rediscovering freedom and life to care about anything else. Besides, if she wanted her *own* abusive husband dead, do you really think she's concerned about anyone else's?"

I shrug.

Jax hops up and starts inside. "Come on," he says, beckoning to me with a wave of his hand.

"Come on? What for?" I ask, surprised.

"Session," he says, as he disappears into the house.

"We're actually going to do something today?" I lag along behind him.

He chuckles. "We do something every Wednesday, Evangeline."

"Yeah, we hang out and argue, but that's the extent of it."

"Not true. You just never remember."

I round the corner into his study and he closes the door behind me.

"Why are you shutting the door? There's no one here except for us."

"So you can't leave. You get distracted if I leave it open."

"Do you mind telling me what's going on?" I say, annoyed with his mysterious behavior.

"Sit," he says as he grabs hold of my arms and guides me to the sofa.

"This is making me nervous, Jax. Please tell me what we're doing."

"The same thing we do every week."

"That's not an answer," I argue.

He pushes me down on the sofa and then takes a seat across from me. "Lie back and get comfortable," he orders.

For some reason this feels oddly familiar to me, and my chest tightens with anxiety. Is he trying to pull a fast one on me? He's trying to trick me.

He's trying to get rid of you, Evangeline. I hear Stephen's voice. *Let me at him. I'll choke the life out of him. Get out of there, Evangeline. Someone stronger needs to take over. You're letting your feelings for him cloud your judgment.*

And her Barbie-sized brain. It's Annabel. I hear laughter.

My eyes close.

And I'm out.

I hear Stephen. His voice is angry. I'm in darkness again. Pitch black. I know this place, and I loathe it. I long to be set free. That's what Jax is going to do ... set me free, so I can get out of this hellhole.

I hear Stephen again. His voice is faint.

I speak out into the darkness. "What's happening?"

"Shh, quiet. I'm listening," Annabel says.

"To what?" I ask.

"Your lover boy and Stephen. He's going to kill him this time." She laughs wickedly.

I hear Jax ... his voice is soft. "Why are you angry right now, Stephen?"

Something ... something ... "prisoners," Stephen says. I can't make it out. I feel like I'm fading into nothingness. It's like I have no substance. I don't feel like myself; I feel like I've stepped out of my own skin, and for the first time, I question my reality.

Who am I?

Where am I?

How did I get here?

Where did I come from?

Why do I feel so disconnected? Almost like I don't belong here. I've got to get out of this dark pit. I need to escape. I need to get back to Jax. This place is frightening me. It wants to swallow me up. I feel it wanting to submerge me into its nothingness. "Help me," I scream out. "Jax, help me!"

"Shut up, Evangeline! Have you lost your mind? What's wrong with you lately?"

"She misses her boyfriend. *Help me, Jax, my darling. You're my Prince Charming. Muah, muah,*" Josh says and laughs, cruelly.

"Both of you zip it. I'm trying to hear what they're saying," Annabel shouts.

I strain to listen, knowing as soon as Stephen's conversation with Jax is over, he'll call for me. Jax will want me to come back. I've only gotten to spend a few minutes with him today. He'll want to see me longer.

I hear Stephen now. "Tell me how the others escaped, and I'll give you want you want," he says coolly.

"I'm not bargaining with you, Stephen. I'm telling you how to get out of here. The problem is you won't trust me." Jax! That's Jax's voice! He's trying to get rid of Stephen so I can come back.

"Why would I trust you? You never keep your word."

"I always keep my word, Stephen," Jax shoots back quickly. "You create these delusions in your own mind and then believe they're real. You can trust me. You've always been able to trust me, you just choose not to."

"That's not true," Stephen yells, and I hear a loud thump, like he's pounded the table with his fist.

"Calm down. Your temper will get you nowhere with me," Jax says flatly.

"I'm not leaving until you tell me how the others escaped," Stephen threatens.

"Why are you so upset? What's happened to you that has caused such anger?" Jax's voice is calm.

"Stop asking me stupid questions. I'm not buying into your psychobabble. It's just a way to manipulate others so you can control them."

"Why would I want to control anyone? I just want to help you, that's all. Why don't you give me the chance? Put your trust in me and see if that doesn't lead you to the same place as the others," Jax explains.

"So, you're telling me that your psychobabble crap is what helped the others to escape?" Stephen asks, sounding doubtful.

"That's exactly what I'm telling you."

"I don't believe you."

"Why would I lie?"

Stephen laughs sarcastically. "So you can manipulate us. Control us, like you do Evangeline. She's your right hand. If you tell her to *jump*, she asks you *how high*."

"How would you know what goes on between Evangeline and me?"

"Because I hear things."

"You don't hear everything," Jax says sternly. "So you're

really *not* sure what goes on, you're just guessing, and you're guessing wrong. This is the difference between you and the others."

"What do you mean … the difference between me and them?"

"You're delusional. You create scenarios in your head, believing they've actually occurred when they haven't."

I hear Stephen growl with rage. "I'm done playing your games, Doc. Tell me how to get out of here, or I'll kill you in your sleep. You hear me?"

"Threatening me will get you nowhere. In fact, it only hurts *you*, Stephen. It causes you to hang on, emotionally, to a place that's harmful. If you can't face your demons, if you can't handle your pain, then you can't grow. You'll never *escape* to the same place as the others, because you won't allow yourself to do what they've done."

"What did they do?" Stephen growls.

"They went to a place of acceptance. They faced their fears head-on, and because of that they found the freedom they were searching for."

"Is that why Daisy got left behind by her mother? Because she doesn't understand how to *tune in* to her own pain, but Pricilla did? Because of that she got to move on, but Daisy got left behind?"

It's silent for a minute. Jax must have answered with a nod, because I no longer hear him. Stephen continues, "If I allow you to dig deeper, you're telling me I'll be free of this captivity?"

"That's what I've been telling you from the start, Stephen.

You trusted everyone else, didn't you? Well, they all trusted me. Now look who's been set free, and look who's still in captivity. You are, along with a handful of other doubters. You all trust each other, but you don't trust me. I'm the doctor. I'm the only one who knows what's going on here. I'm qualified to help you, but you won't let me."

"That's because you and Evangeline have something going on," Stephen barks.

"And what's that?"

"Secret things that you don't talk about. Things you've forbidden her to talk about. When we ask her, she denies it. The only reason you have control over her is because she's in love with you."

"She's not *in love* with me. She *trusts* me. There's a difference." There's an edge to Jax's voice I know all too well. He's getting worn out, losing his patience.

"Tell me how to get out of here, to get away from these creeps, or I'm coming after you. We all will. We'll take you down, Doc. Don't think we won't."

"Let me help you, Stephen. Let go and allow yourself to feel the pain of the past. Nothing was ever your fault. Quit blaming yourself and quit running from it. You didn't do anything wrong. Your father was an abusive man; you were just a child..."

I hear Stephen yell out in anger. "I'm going to kill you!" There's a loud thump, then another, and another. What's going on? I'm scared ... for Jax ... for myself.

"Stop it, Stephen," I scream wildly. "Leave him alone."

"Shut up, Evangeline, you idiot! Let him be. Let him get

rid of the doctor, then we can all escape like the others," Annabel says.

"Jax! Jax!" I scream, but get no answer. I hear grunting and thumping, and I picture the worst. I can hear furniture being knocked over. "What's happening?"

"I'll tell you what's happening," Josh chimes in, "Stephen is following through with our plan. He's going to finally do away with this arrogant jerk so we can live in peace." He laughs wickedly.

"Mommy! Please, I'm scared. Somebody hold me; I'm scared," Daisy cries out.

"It's okay, sweetheart. You hear that sound?" Annabel asks, and everyone is quiet long enough to listen to the struggling going on outside of this darkness. "That's our ticket to freedom, dear. We'll soon be living the high life." She raises her voice, "Go, Stephen! Get him! Kill him!"

I'm completely frantic on the inside. My head fills with Daisy's cries, Stephen's yelling, Annabel's and Josh's cheering, and an occasional grunting sound made by Jax.

Then everything goes quiet.

Chapter Twenty-seven
Evangeline

What's happening? Where am I? Where's Jax?

Jax is dead. They've killed Jax. No! This can't be happening.

There's pain radiating from the side of my head. I blink my eyes open, letting them adjust to the light. I touch my temple and wince in pain.

Have we killed again?

It's coming back to me now. The struggle between Jax and Stephen.

I raise myself up. I'm in Jax's study, on the sofa. Alone.

"Jax," I scream out. I stumble to my feet and head for the kitchen. Empty. The house is quiet except for my heavy breathing. I check the great room next. He's not there, but I hear something. I hold my breath and quiet myself so I can listen. It's water. I follow the sound. Someone is running water in the half bath down the hall from the living room. I slowly make my way to the door, which is standing open. I see someone leaning over the sink, face in the water. It's Jax.

"Oh, thank God, you're okay," I cry out. He jumps at my

voice and quickly spins around, facing me with wild eyes. "It's me, Jax. It's Evangeline."

"Don't sneak up on me," he yells out, startled.

Oh, my gosh … his face. "Are you okay?" I ask softly.

"Look at me! Do I look okay?" Jax points to the left side of his face.

His eye is black and purple, his lip is bruised and bleeding, and his cheek is swollen. "Oh, Jax, I'm so sorry. I tried to stop it, but I couldn't. They all ganged up on me. They're in it together. They want you out of the way."

"No kidding! I kinda got that impression." Jax turns the water off, wrings out a wet washcloth, and places it to his face. "I need an ice pack." He turns from me and heads toward the kitchen.

"Let me help you, please," I say, and follow along behind him.

"I don't need your help," he grumbles.

"Please. I feel responsible. They did this because of me. They're jealous about my relationship with you."

"We don't have a relationship." He enters the kitchen and heads for the furthest cabinet on the right, but I grab his arm and steer him toward the bar seat at the island. He allows it without putting up a fight. I assume he's had enough fights for the day. He sits, scooting his stool in and resting his elbows on the counter.

I cross to the cabinet, where I see some medical supplies: aspirin, ice pack, cold medicine, nasal spray, vitamins, and a few more bottles I don't pay attention to. I grab the aspirin and the ice pack. I quickly fill the pack with ice from the freezer and then check the fridge for a beer. I grab a bottle from the second shelf and pop the cap off. I set it down on the counter in front of Jax along with two aspirins.

"Take these," I order and then gently press the ice pack to his face. He winces in pain and pulls away from me, taking the pack from my hand.

He exhales loudly and then presses it against his eye.

I ask, in my gentlest voice, "What in the world happened?"

"You don't know?" He looks shocked.

"I heard everything, but it took me by surprise…"

"It took *you* by surprise? I wasn't ready for *that!* One minute we're talking—and I actually thought we were making some headway—then the next minute he's pounding my face."

"I think he was trying to kill you, Jax. Everyone was cheering him on."

"That's nice to know." He adjusts the ice pack and frowns. "Yeah, he was trying to kill me. Look at my neck." He pulls back his collar and I can see a faint hand mark on his neck. "The madman was trying to choke me, that is, after he finished wrecking my face. One minute, we're talking calmly, and the next minute he's jumping on top of me. He came right over the coffee table. It sent me flying back in my chair and then he started whaling on me." Jax shakes his head in disbelief. "He got some good punches in because he caught me off guard, but it didn't take me long to subdue him, naturally. Five-four, a hundred and fifteen pounds isn't much of a challenge for me."

"I can see you fought back," I say and rub the large bump on the side of my head.

"Oh, well, I had to. I had no choice. I couldn't let him, or them, kill me, could I?" He pauses. "I guess you haven't looked in the mirror," he says and his eyes move to the floor.

I raise my hand to my cheekbone and immediately feel a sting of pain shoot through my face.

"The bump on the head was an accident. I had to backhand Stephen. It was either that, or die. It sent him flying backwards where he hit his head on the coffee table, but it accomplished what I needed. … unconsciousness." He looks me over and then reaches out his hand. "Let me see. Come here." I move closer to him, but I'm aware it's not me he's concerned for.

He sets the ice pack on the counter and places his hand on my cheek, causing my head to tilt to the opposite side. "It's bruising. Does it hurt much?"

I nod.

He moves his hand to the side of my head, finding the knot. "Crap! That's not good." He shakes his head and his eyes flash with worry. "How am I going to explain this?" he mumbles under his breath. The question isn't meant for me, so I don't attempt to answer it.

He gently pulls me down onto the barstool beside him and places the ice pack on my cheek. He holds it there for a few minutes and we sit in silence. He moves it to the knot on the side of my head. I take it from him because I'm not Greta. I wish it was me he was concerned for. I wish it was me he longed for, but I know the only thought going on in his head right now is how I'm not Greta.

"What are you going to tell her?" I finally ask.

He shrugs. "I haven't figured that out yet. Whatever I decide, I'll still get accused of giving her a pill that caused her to black out, stealing her memory."

I see a deep sadness in his eyes, and I feel a pang of sympathy. I've always given him trouble because I could never have my way. I could never have him, and I could never have the life I longed for. It made me resentful. I had plotted with the others to do away with Jax. I was going to help them kill him so we could all escape him. But that only makes sense when I'm trapped in that dark hole. Once I'm on the outside, living, I can see he'll never let me go, because he'll never let Greta go. The others don't have a chance to get away, but they don't understand why. They're thinking as individuals, when in reality they're all one unit, one consciousness, one person. I'm different because Jax allows for me to be different, and I need to be grateful for the time he allows *me* to be *me*.

The problem is, I want to stay with him.

Chapter Twenty-eight
Greta

MAY 11
THURSDAY MORNING

"I just don't understand how this could happen. I don't sleepwalk," I say, turning away from the mirror to face Jax. I'm in the half bath off the kitchen. He's leaning against the doorframe next to me.

He shrugs. "It happened. And you *do* sleepwalk. Remember right after we were married? You used to do it every week and you'd wake up in the oddest places. Once you even woke up outside in a patio chair, remember that? You never recall what happens in between. Most sleepwalkers don't. It's quite normal."

I giggle at the memory. "I'd forgotten about that. How bizarre. So tell me again, I was coming down the stairs?"

"I heard a thump that woke me up. I noticed you weren't in bed, so I was a bit alarmed. I found you wandering around the hallway, heading for the staircase. I called out to you, but it didn't faze you. You just kept going. I realized you must be sleepwalking, so I went after you to keep you from falling down the stairs. I pulled you back, and I guess it startled you. You swung around and started punching me, hence my bruised face." Jax rubs his black eye and continues. "Then you started to back away in fear and stepped right off the first step. I was able to catch you to keep you from falling all the way down, but you managed to bump into the banister a few times anyway."

I listen as Jax explains why we both awoke with injuries. Although his story is curious, and a bit alarming, I can't help to find a little humor in it all. I guess because it looks like I did a number on his face. I feel awful, but he honestly doesn't seem to mind a bit. He's not angry or upset with me; in fact, quite the contrary.

He leans down and puts his arms around me, hugging me and lifting me in the air. "Now, let's get some breakfast, shall we?" He kisses me and carries me to the kitchen.

I laugh at his silliness. "You're going to be late to work."

"Actually, I called Amelia and had her reschedule my appointments for today and tomorrow. I'm not going in," he says, taking two juice glasses out of the cabinet and setting them on the island.

"Not going in? That's not like my workaholic husband. What gives?"

"Well, I didn't get much sleep after the sleepwalking incident because I wanted to stay awake to make sure you didn't try it again. Plus, darling, I can't go into work looking like this." He points to the marks on his face. "I'm black and blue, for Pete's sake." Jax smiles good naturedly, and I feel relieved he takes things so lightly. I know it's the psychiatrist in him. "Anyway, your family is coming in a few days, and I thought I'd help you get ready for them. You know, make myself available to you."

"What did I do to get so lucky? I've married the most fabulous man in all the land."

"I've told you that for years, my love. Have you only just now started to hear me?" We both chuckle and I give Jax a quick hug before starting breakfast.

"I can't wait for my parents to see our house. I'm so excited. It's been a while since they've been here."

"Yes, it has. They always want us to come to them, which gets under my skin because they're retired with an open schedule. Whereas, we have work to contend with."

"I've tried to explain it to them numerous times, but you know how self-absorbed my family is. My mom and stepdad only have one thing on their minds—planning their next vacation."

"Truth. Okay, Hannah and Aiden will be here tomorrow afternoon, correct?"

I nod. "And they're going back Tuesday. But Mom and Paul leave on Monday afternoon, so we can expect them to be busy hitting the French Quarter, eating, shopping, and doing all those things they love to do. Oh, and she said to have the beignets and boudin waiting for them when they arrive."

"Are you kidding me?" Jax laughs sarcastically. "We're not doing that. If they want beignets and boudin, they can go downtown and get some. They know where everything is.

They're from New Orleans." Jax throws his hands in the air in frustration.

"Didn't you just say you were going to help me get ready for them? They're our guests, we need to treat them special." I try to make light of my mother's demands, but Jax knows all too well that she's a royal pain in the rear end every time she visits. That's one of the reasons I don't mind so much when they insist we come to Seattle. Then we're the ones who receive the pampering.

"Everyone knows when you visit New Orleans, you go to Café Du Monde for beignets, and you have to eat them right then and there while they're hot and fresh. You can't bring them home and save them for later." Jax shakes his head with annoyance.

"If you'll do those two things for me tomorrow, I'll be more than grateful." I bat my lashes, causing him to break into a smile. "Rocio will be here tomorrow to clean. My parents can take the bedroom suite downstairs and we'll give Hannah and Aiden the guest room upstairs."

Jax breaks four eggs into a mixing bowl and starts to whisk. I notice he's clinching his jaw.

"Don't tell me the beignets and boudin have got your tutu in a twirl?"

He stops whisking and scrunches his face. "My what in my what? Greta, speak English."

I laugh as I mentally pat myself on the back. I know how to get under Jax's skin, but even more, I know how to make him laugh. "Your tutu in a twirl." I smile.

"Never mind, I don't even want to know what you're

talking about. If you're asking me if I have any concerns about this visit from your family, the answer is yes, I do."

"Care to explain?" I ask curiously.

"For starters, look at our faces. What are they going to think when they show up here and both of us are sporting battle scars?"

"Nothing a little makeup can't cover," I say assuredly.

Jax tilts his head to the side. "Seriously?"

I move on. "What else?"

"Well, the neighbor's husband was just ki…"

He stops in midsentence. "Say what?"

"I mean that he's dead."

"He had a heart attack, Jax. People have heart attacks all the time and most of them are at home. Everything will be fine. Ya know, you sure do carry around a lot of anxiety for a psychiatrist."

"That's not true." Jax purses his lips and then we both bust out laughing. "Okay, I admit it. I need to take some of my own advice, don't I?"

"Big time, Doctor. Take a chill pill and then call me in the morning."

"Okay, that's enough," Jax says, trying to stifle his laughter. "I just meant we have a lot on our plates right now."

"It's nothing we can't set aside for a few days," I say as convincingly as possible.

"You're right. You're absolutely right."

"Did I just hear you correctly? Did you say *I'm* right?" I tease.

He shoots me a smile and then pours the beaten eggs into the skillet sitting on the stove.

"I admit my family visits can get a bit tense at times, but we all love each other and things always get worked out, right?"

"With a little therapy, yes." Jax chuckles as he stirs the eggs.

I grab a bag of bagels from the pantry, toss a couple into the toaster and then head to the fridge for the cream cheese. "This will be a fun visit because we have this new house," I say with a smile.

"I agree," Jax answers, but I see concern in his eyes.

I'm determined to make this the best family visit we've had in years!

Chapter Twenty-nine
Greta

MAY 12
FRIDAY MORNING

I catch Jax at his desk, file open in front of him.

"What're you doing?" I ask, somewhat perturbed he's chosen this time to work. "You're supposed to be picking up the beignets and boudin."

"If you say that one more time … nobody gets anything."

"Jax, come on. You promised."

He laughs, lightly. "I know. I'm teasing. I just wanted to look over a few things from a patient's record. I'm done." He quickly closes the file and places it in the bottom desk drawer.

"Don't forget to take my car and get air in the tires, please," I remind him.

"I haven't forgotten. I'm outta here," he says as he stands and presses down his white polo shirt and blue jeans, smoothing them out. He looks good. Even his casual wear is nice. Jax has always been one to dress up for any occasion;

whether he's lounging at home or running errands, he'll look put together, which is sometimes challenging for a man. "Are your keys on the key rack?"

"Yes, and I also made a small grocery list of a few items I forgot to pick up yesterday."

"No problem. Looks like I'll be gone a while," he says and pecks me on the cheek. "Call if you think of anything else, dear."

I check both guest rooms, fluff pillows, put out my best toiletries, and set fragrant candles around. I want everything to be perfect for my family. After making a few more adjustments to the décor, I do a final walk-through of the house and everything looks perfect. "Rocio," I call out as I head toward the kitchen. "Rocio."

"In here, miss," she calls from Jax's study.

"What are you doing in here?" I ask as I enter the room.

"Mr. Jax tell me to dust his study," she explains and continues to sweep her feather duster across his desk. "I just have the bookshelf left, and I be finished."

"That's fine. Then I need you to clean the glass on the French doors leading to the lanai."

"Yes, Miss Greta."

"Thank you." I turn to leave, but notice Jax has left his desk a mess. I scoot around to the other side so I can throw the loose paperwork into a drawer. I notice his keys sticking out of the lock in the bottom drawer. I eyeball them for a minute and then glance at Rocio, who has moved on to dusting the bookshelf. "That will be all for this room, Rocio. Thank you."

"Yes, Miss Greta," she says and hurries out of the room.

I pull the desk chair out and take a seat. Every ounce of my being knows I shouldn't be doing this, yet it doesn't stop me. It doesn't even slow me down. I turn the key and pull the drawer out. The first thing that jumps out at me is Evangeline's journal. He's got it under lock and key, and I realize that's what a responsible therapist would do. It's nobody's business but the author's, and I guess Jax's. Feeling no conviction, I take the journal from the drawer and set it on my lap. My eyes fall on numerous files with handwritten names across the top of each. Why is Jax keeping patient files in his home office? He doesn't see patients here.

I finger through the files. First names only. That's curious, no last names? Stephen, Annabel, Daisy, Josh, Pricilla, Henry, Sammie, Kevin, Lana, Nathan, Gabby, Brenda, Frankie, Veronica. There's more, but one in particular catches my eye: **EVANGELINE**. I immediately pull this one out. It seems to be tucked away, almost as if it's been hidden behind the others. I hear my cell ringing from the kitchen and I quickly close the drawer, lock it, and place the journal, along with the file, under my arm.

I race to the kitchen and grab my phone. It's Trish from Bocage Plantation. "Hi, Trish," I say, out of breath. I sent her an email this morning with my ideas and sketches for the new ballroom they're adding on next month. I assume that's the purpose of her call, and I'm right. She wants to make a few color adjustments. I try to concentrate on what she's saying, but all I can think about is the folder tucked under my arm. I fight the urge to open it and instead focus on my call. I sit at the desk in the kitchen, grab a pad and pen from the drawer, and start jotting down notes as Trish talks.

"Uh-huh. Right. I see," I answer as she speaks, showing her she has my full attention, but I can't wait to get off the phone. I don't have much time to read the file and return it before Jax gets home.

After another ten minutes, I'm able to end the call. I've taken plenty of notes I can refer to later to refresh my memory. I head upstairs so I can read in private with no interruptions. I run, skipping every other step, and hurry into the bedroom, shutting the door behind me. I slip the journal between the mattresses on my side of the bed and then sit on the chaise at the foot.

I stare at the closed folder for a minute, almost scared of what I might find inside. Her name is crudely written in Jax's hand at the top left corner. I slowly flip it open and find numerous pages of notes dating back over seven years. Some are handwritten using single words at times, such as *confusion, delusional, angry, intense, hysterical.* Then there are typed notes which are more detailed. I grab a typed page without paying much attention to their order and start to read:

Evangeline has major mood swings, leading to erratic behavior. She'll confess her love for me and then in the same breath will tell me how much she despises me. She seems to hate the others, yet she goes along with anything they say. They have a strong influence over her while she's with them, but once she separates from them, she does her own thing. She exhibits strong traits of Borderline

Personality Disorder. She demonstrates a recurring pattern of instability in our relationship, as well as others she's formed over the years.

Sometimes, how I feel about her determines how she'll feel about me instead of making up her own mind. She pushes me away and then does everything she can in a desperate attempt to keep me. She experiences identity disturbance. One day she'll refer to herself as a princess and then the next she'll tell me she's evil with a black heart.

Everything she does is impulsive. Her actions are never thought out, and she has no regard for how they will affect others. She's discontented every second of the day, never satisfied, and is obsessed with having "her own life." She is completely self-absorbed. She demonstrates a pervasive pattern of instability in interpersonal relationships, self-image, and emotions. If I wasn't around to guide her and set limitations, she'd probably be dead by now.

She dresses in gothic clothing and dark makeup attempting to get a rise out of me. In fact, most of her actions are an attempt to get a reaction from me. I downplay her shocking behavior and then explain it has repercussions which will drive a wedge between us. This usually sets her back on track.

She never has anything nice to say about Greta. She hates her, but never reveals a logical explanation for her feelings. I receive answers such as, "Because I do" and "I don't know, I just do." She has a lot of jealousy toward Greta and will put down her lifestyle, her career choice, her appearance, and will then tell me she'd make me a better wife. I think she just wants to be front and center, believing if I allowed her to take Greta's place, she'd have the "life" she obsesses over.

With my jaw agape, I stick the paper back into the folder. Anger radiates through my body, and I feel my flesh turn hot. How dare Jax talk about me with his clients! He has no right, no reason. Then to allow his clients to talk badly about me, to make advances toward him without putting an end to it. The first sign of interest this woman showed in him should have been reason enough to discontinue seeing her as a patient. He should have put an end to it immediately.

"Greta, come down and see what I bought. Check it and make sure it suits your needs, my dear." It's Jax. Oh, no, he's home. How long have I been up here? I quickly shove the folder in between the mattresses alongside the journal. I've got to get ahold of myself. I can't allow Jax to know something's wrong with me. He's a psychiatrist; it's almost impossible to hide my emotions from him. He might as well be a mind reader. How can I keep this information to myself, though? I want to give him a strong slap across the face. He more than deserves it.

If I confront him about the file, I'll be to blame for invading his privacy, not to mention his patient's. I have completely violated them both. Jax will look like an incompetent doctor, and everything written on those pages will be completely diminished by the treacherous thing I've done, and with good reason. I've done something utterly despicable, I admit. Regardless, I still plan on putting an end to this sick relationship they have, this one-sided love affair. I huff as I start down the stairs.

I paste on the phoniest smile I can muster up and walk into the kitchen where Jax is waiting for me. As soon as he sees me, he starts going over the items he bought. "I got two dozen beignets, minus one," he says with a mischievous smile.

"That sounds typical," I say and fake a laugh.

"I told you, they're best hot and fresh. I got the boudin balls, but also bought some smoked boudin we can serve with breakfast. We all love eggs and smoked boudin."

"Spicy?"

"The spiciest." He nods. "I already put the grocery store items away, but I wasn't sure about this pasta. I tried calling you twice, but you didn't answer." He holds a package of fresh tortellini up for me to see. "It's the three cheese."

I blink. I can't concentrate on anything he's saying. I take the pasta out of his hand and set it on the counter. "Evangeline," I say, and notice I have his full attention. "What … is … going … on?" I ask with my eyes closed because I can't bear to see his face.

He pauses. "Are you kidding me? Where's this coming from?"

"Are you having an affair with her?"

"Is this a joke?" I feel his hand on my cheek. "Open your eyes. Look at me." I open them, but stare at the floor. "Greta, look at me." I force myself to look into his eyes, and I see love and gentleness with a splash of betrayal. "What happened in the time I was gone? What changed?" I don't answer. "Look, your sister is going to be pulling into that driveway any time now." He half points toward the garage. "We've got bruises on our faces, I had to take time off, and now you're working yourself into a frenzy thinking I'm having an affair. We need to pull ourselves together and get back in Kavanagh mode. Do you understand?"

I nod my head. I know he's right, but at the same time I can't help but wonder if he's twisting the situation to avoid talking about it. "Just tell me what I need to know and I'll drop it while my family is here."

"No, Greta, I'm not having an affair with her or anyone else. I never have, and I never will." He leans in, placing his hand on the back of my neck to make sure he has my full attention. "I love you. There's no one else. Do you understand that?"

I nod halfheartedly. I want to blurt out everything I read in his file about Evangeline, but I can't let him know I've pried, and it's eating me up.

"What's happening here?" he asks, sounding dismayed. "I told you a few weeks ago we're not supposed to be discussing my patients. It's a violation of doctor-patient confidentiality for me to discuss any of my patients with you. Why are you talking about her? Where's this coming from?"

There's an edge to Jax's voice, and I'm sensing his temper is rising.

"Are you angry?"

He sighs heavily. "No. No, I'm not angry, I'm just frustrated. I feel like there's never a dull moment in the Kavanagh house. Can't we just live in peace at some point?" He walks out of the kitchen and up the stairs. I'm taken aback. I'm not sure what to think about what he just said. *Never a dull moment?* What's that supposed to mean? It's pretty darn peaceful around here, if you ask me. Maybe a little on the mundane side, if we really want to get technical. We're both workaholics, we eat dinner and crash out early during the week, and then we do whatever we want on the weekends. We travel, try new restaurants, go boating with friends, throw parties. I don't get it. What drama is he talking about? What are these *events* we're always experiencing?

I decide to blow it off. I've done something I shouldn't have done. I've violated his trust in me, and he has no idea. I've read a file I shouldn't have, and now I'm wanting to attack him over it. It's a despicable thing for me to do.

I plan to finish Evangeline's journal next.

Chapter Thirty
Greta

I open the front door and scream out in joy. I hug Hannah tightly and we embrace for a full minute. Even though we're only a three-hour drive away, we don't get to see much of each other. We all keep pretty busy with our careers. Hannah also works in real estate and runs one of the many offices owned by our stepfather, Paul. Aiden is a computer and software developer, specializing in designing and developing software at the systems level, aka Computer Geek, as Jax calls him. I let go of Hannah and reach for Aiden, giving him a hug and motioning for them to come inside.

"You guys go ahead. I'll get the bags," Aiden says with a smile and heads toward the car.

Jax appears in the foyer and a twinge of guilt shoots through me as soon as I lay eyes on him. "Hannah, my favorite sister-in-law," he says with a big smile and squeezes Hannah, lifting her off the ground.

"Jax, stop! You're going to squash the baby," I yell out.

"It's not going to hurt the baby. It's like this big right now," Jax says and holds his thumb up.

"You're pretty big for the baby being that small," I say to Hannah and we all laugh. Hannah is small framed, like me. Auburn shoulder-length hair, which carries a slight wave at the tips. Her porcelain complexion allows her to get away with not wearing much makeup. She's casually dressed, as one would for a road trip: jeans and a stretchy red and white striped T-shirt.

"Five months and I'm feeling pretty good, but I'm hungry all the time. I feel like I can't stop eating. I'm really trying to pace myself so I don't gain too much weight, but it's hard. Even Aiden was getting on me for overeating," Hannah says with a chuckle and rubs her baby bump, which is still quite small considering how large she's going to get.

"Speaking of Aiden, where is he?" Jax asks, and I notice he's avoiding my eye.

"Getting the bags from the car," Hannah answers.

"I'll run out and help him." He turns and heads out the front door.

I wave for Hannah to follow me. "Come on, I've got drinks and snacks laid out in the kitchen."

"Hi, Rocio," Hannah squeals as we enter the kitchen. Rocio is plating finger sandwiches on a silver platter, but immediately stops when she sees Hannah, and they hug. "Gorgeous! Just gorgeous," Hannah says as she glances around the room. "Let me get a drink and you have to give me a tour."

"I'd love to show you around. I'm so proud of this house and how far we've come. I can't wait for you to see what I've done to it. I'm so happy. For the first time in my life, I can honestly say I'm *truly* happy!" I smile broadly and notice

Hannah's face light up with delight. Then Jax and Evangeline pop into my head and my heart sinks.

Rocio pours Hannah a glass of unsweetened tea, and I give her a tour, showing her every little detail of why I love this house. We end on the lanai, where Rocio has already set out trays of finger foods and drinks for us. Pimento cheese and chicken salad triangles, mushroom canapes, and bacon-wrapped scallops. There's a pitcher of iced tea and lemonade on the drink cart. Jax and Aiden have beat us, sitting across from each other, snacking on the sandwiches. I hear excitement in their voices as they talk back and forth. Aiden looks good. Happy, healthy, and fit. He and Jax are about the same size. Aiden has brown hair, which he wears in a messy spike, and green eyes. A few freckles pepper the bridge of his nose, spilling onto his cheeks.

We eat, laugh, and enjoy each other's company for what seems like hours. Before we know it, evening is upon us.

"How about Bourbon Street for dinner?" Jax suggests.

"On a Friday night? It will be jam packed." I turn my attention to Hannah. "Are you up for that?"

"I'm game. Aiden?" she says, turning to him.

He nods. "Sounds great."

"Wonderful. Let's freshen up," I suggest, and we all go separate ways.

"Ten minutes, ladies," I hear Aiden yell as he jogs up the staircase. I head up after him, but remember I left my purse on the table. My powder and lipstick are in there. I start toward the kitchen when something grabs my attention. I hear whispering. I slow my pace and notice Jax and Hannah standing by the island, voices low. I duck behind the doorframe and peek around the corner. This is curious. What could they possibly be saying that warrants whispering? Hannah touches his eye and then her hand moves to his cheek. He had done a horrible job covering his shiners. You could clearly see bruising on his face when we were outside, but no one had asked him about it. Neither Hannah or Aiden even mentioned it. I felt sure it would be the first thing they'd ask him, and thought it curious they didn't. Now I find her whispering about it in the kitchen?

"I'm a bit alarmed to visit you guys and find it looks like you were both in a scuffle. What's going on here?" she says in a loud whisper.

"It's not as bad as it looks."

"Not as bad?" Hannah laughs sarcastically. "Have you seen your face? Have Greta put some concealer on it before we go out."

Jax smiles and looks away.

"Don't downplay this. What in the world happened?"

"Sleepwalking, that's all. When I tried to wake her, things got crazy."

"Do you still have her on the new meds?"

"Yes, and she's improved somewhat, but not much has changed. She still believes the blackouts are caused by the meds, so she fights me every time I give her one. Her paranoia is through the roof."

They stand in silence for a moment and then Hannah says, "How many are left?"

"Six," Jax says.

"Oh, wow. That's fantastic. They're all still after you?"

"Every single one." Jax sighs deeply.

Hannah puts her finger to his split lip. "You're a good man, Jax. You're a genius psychiatrist, a great husband, a wonderful brother-in-law, and an awesome friend."

"Oh, man. Don't start with that again. I don't feel like I'm any of those things. I'm just trying to protect my wife, as any husband should."

"Guys? You ready?" I hear Aiden calling out as he crosses the living room, and I quickly run the other way through the great room and up the stairs to avoid him.

My heart is beating fast, and my mind is a jumbled mess of questions and confusion.

Jax and my sister have secrets they're keeping from me. They talk about me behind my back. *Sleepwalking again? How many are left?* What a peculiar question. How many what? Pills? She seemed to be more concerned with Jax's well-being than my own. But why be concerned at all? *New meds? What new meds, and why is Hannah aware of it while I'm not?*

I feel a rage building inside as I quickly sweep blush onto my cheeks. I ended up leaving my makeup bag downstairs when I happened upon their clandestine conversation in the kitchen. I run a brush through my hair. I'll do my lipstick in the car. I rush into the closet and tear off my shirt and jeans, replacing them with a hippie chic multicolored blouse and brown slacks. I slip on some clunky heels, and I'm on my way back downstairs to meet the others.

"Are we ready to go?" Aiden asks when he sees me on the staircase.

"Let's head out the garage and we can all pile into my car," Jax says and gestures for them to go ahead of him. He waits until they get several paces in front of us and then stops me. "I'm sorry for earlier," he says under his breath.

"Sorry for what?" I ask. The bruising on his face is no longer visible. Hannah must have covered it up for him. She did a good job.

"Getting upset and walking out on our conversation. I felt overwhelmed and just needed to take a break."

"Now you feel better?"

"Greta, I love you. Your family is in town. Let's have a good time, okay?"

"Then quit keeping secrets from me," I say and follow the others into the garage. I don't look back at Jax, but I'm sure he's disappointed at my reaction. He's no dummy; he's going to realize I overheard his conversation with Hannah in the kitchen. Let him stew on that all night.

The restaurant is a combination of loud music, too many people, and mad chaos. There's a waiting list, but nowhere to stand so we head to the patio, which is just as crowded. Once seated, it's almost impossible to hear each other over the music and crowded tables around us. Everyone's yelling and laughing. I do my best to have a good time, but my thoughts keep revisiting the conversation Hannah had with Jax. *You're a good man, Jax.* A good man for what? What has he done that makes her think he's such a good man? Because he took one in the face while I was sleepwalking? Does that make him a good man?

"Greta loves to play pool. She's pretty good, too," Jax says and puts his arm around my shoulders. I tune back in to the conversation.

"Why are we talking pool?" I ask.

"Because we're thinking about playing a game or two at that little place around the corner. You know, the one that does the haunted tours."

"Pool? Not me. And Hannah doesn't want to hang out and play pool. She can't even drink. She'll be bored to tears," I say with an eyeroll.

"You two can go on the haunted tour while we play for a while," Jax suggests.

I look at Hannah and she shrugs. I can tell by her expression she's not interested and we both giggle.

"Boys will be boys," she leans over and whispers into my ear, only it's more like a shout.

Jax orders another round of drinks, then we finish our dinner and head for the door, not a minute too soon. I can't wait to get out of this loud and chaotic atmosphere. It rattles my nerves. Once outside, we move down the street a short distance so we can talk in peace and figure out a plan.

"Let's shoot some pool," Aiden yells out loudly, causing a few heads to turn in our direction.

"How long has it been since Aiden's let loose?" I ask Hannah, raising my brow.

"Too long," she says and we both giggle. "He needs to let off some steam. Come on, let's go get a fresh beignet."

"That's a wonderful idea," I say, nodding my head. I turn to Jax and Aiden. "You boys have fun ... and behave yourselves."

"Yes!" Jax shouts, and I see them high-five each other.

They lag along behind us for a few blocks and then turn off. I'm happy they get some time together, and it gives me a chance to visit with Hannah on a deeper level. We start across Jackson Square, which is filled with musicians, tarot card readers, artists, and tourists. Many walking with coffee cups and bags from Café Du Monde.

"How's your morning sickness?" I ask. "Has it subsided some?"

"Quite a bit, thank goodness."

"Have you decided on a name yet?"

She chuckles, which answers my question. "We're down to three now."

"Well, that's a start," I say and gently poke her with my elbow. "You've never been able to decide on anything. Aiden will end up choosing the name."

"I know, and that's fine with me. I'm done thinking about it." She throws her hands up in the air, causing me to laugh. As an adult, she hasn't changed a bit; she still has the same personality traits from when we were kids.

"How are things with Jax? Is he still working harder than ever?"

I feel my face flush with anger as I think back to their secretive conversation in the kitchen. "You know Jax. He loves what he does and puts his all into it," I say as my thoughts move to Evangeline. I clinch my fists and feel my body tense up.

"Greta, what's going on? You should see your face right now."

I fake a laugh. "What's wrong with my face?"

"You look troubled. You can talk to me. Spill it."

"Ugh." I stop walking, tilt my head back, and let out a loud groan. Hannah puts her arm around my shoulders and gives me a tight squeeze.

"Talk to me," she says.

"You're going to think I'm a horrible person," I cry.

"I could never think that. Now tell me what's bothering you."

"Jax!" I rub my forehead in thought. "He has this patient I hate. I mean, I don't know her, but I know *of* her. I feel like Jax is too close to her. That she confides too much in him, which sounds strange since he *is* her psychiatrist. But their relationship seems to be too intimate. I don't know ... it bothers me. I mean, deep down, I know he's not having an affair, but I feel like he should cut this patient loose—refer her to someone else."

"Who is she?" Hannah asks, surprised.

"Her name is Evangeline. That's all I know. But she has followed us before, written Jax notes, shared intimate details of her life. It really gets under my skin." Hannah is silent, looking completely dumbfounded. "What's wrong?"

She pauses. "Greta ... how did you find out about this patient?" she asks slowly.

"She followed us to dinner one night and had the waiter pass him a note. He sneaked off and talked to her. I found the note in his pocket. He had to come clean. Then today, I found a file he keeps on her." I turn away in shame. "I read some of it. She's in love with Jax and hates me. But why does she even *know* about me? How dare Jax discuss me with his patients," I say angrily.

Hannah wrinkles her forehead. "Does Jax know you found that file?"

"Are you kidding me? He'd kill me. I can't let him know I've violated his doctor-patient relationship with her. And if anyone ever found out, he'd lose his license."

Hannah puts her hand on my arm and sighs deeply.

"What is it? Do you think I'm overreacting?" I say, surprised by her reaction.

"I think you need to stay out of that file and put it back where you got it. Let Jax do what needs to be done," she says, squeezing my arm. "You have a good man here who is trying to help others. Let him."

I'm taken aback by Hannah's reaction. I thought she'd be on my side. I flash back to their conversation in the kitchen. "What is it you know that I don't?" I ask firmly.

"What makes you think I know something?" She tugs on my arm to get us walking again.

"I heard you whispering with Jax earlier. What was that about? Why are you both keeping secrets from me?"

Hannah stares at the ground a minute before answering. "Trust in him, Greta. Listen to him, take your medication, quit blaming him for your memory loss, and just do what he says so you can get better." She half smiles.

"Get better? What does that mean? I don't need him giving me pills that make me forget what's going on around me. It's sneaky."

"What is it you think he's doing that he needs you to forget?"

"I'm not sure, but it has to do with this patient of his, Evangeline."

Hannah scrunches her face and then shakes her head.

I'm suddenly startled by a loud and intrusive voice. "Ladies, ladies. Come! Let Madam Hilda tell you your future." I turn to find a woman dressed in a long, flowing midnight-blue dress, smiling at us. Her hair is long and dark, pinned back at the crown. She's wearing several scarves tied around her neck and arms that flow in the light breeze when she moves. A wide black glittery sash is tied around her waist. "Come and let me tell you the secrets the universe holds for you."

I smile and say, "No, thank you," and we continue to walk, quickening our pace.

"But I can help you, my child. You are burdened by your inner demons. I can help you to face them and free you from your anguish."

I can't help but chuckle. "No, thank you," I say once more. I glance at Hannah, expecting her to be stifling laughter, but instead I'm surprised to see her wide-eyed, seemingly entranced by this gypsy woman.

"You have six demons who won't let you be. Wreaking havoc in your life because of secrets from your past. Watch out, child, or she's going to take over your life."

"Please don't waste your time on me. I don't believe in fortune-tellers."

"Evangeline has her own demons," she says and turns away, scarves flowing in the wind behind her.

I gasp loudly. "Oh, my gosh, did you hear what she said?

She said Evangeline!" I yank on Hannah's arm, pulling her over to me.

"This is too creepy, let's get the heck out of here." Hannah grabs my hand and starts jogging lightly until we're past the fortune-tellers and card readers.

"Did you hear what she said?" I ask as we cross the street to Café Du Monde.

"Oh, please, Greta. She was following along behind us for several minutes. She heard our conversation and then played off it."

I place my hand to my chest and breathe deeply, trying to catch my breath.

"Sit, while I go to the window and order for us. I'll be right back."

I find the first empty table and take a seat. I watch Hannah as she makes her way through the crowd and up to the window. I look back in the direction of the gypsy lady, but she's long gone. I want to steer clear of the fortune-tellers on our way back. Hannah returns in a few minutes carrying a white paper bag, a handful of napkins, and two coffees.

"One order of beignets and two chicory coffees," she says as she takes the seat next to me. She pulls a cardboard container out of the bag. The hot pastries are hidden beneath a mountain of powdered sugar.

We each down a beignet and then reach for another, washing it down with the bittersweet coffee.

"That was creepy," I finally say.

"That's what they want you to think."

"She said I had six inner demons wreaking havoc in my

life." I watch Hannah closely as she eats her pastry. "I heard you and Jax use that same number. *Six*. He said I had six left." Hannah stops chewing and looks me in the eye. I can see her mind working. She's wondering what to say next as she puts my words together in her head. She's trying to think of a good enough lie. Something believable.

She shrugs. "I don't recall."

"You don't recall a conversation you just had a couple of hours ago, whispering in secret?"

"It wasn't like that, Greta. I was just concerned with Jax's bruised face. Wouldn't you be if Aiden had shown up that way?" She takes a napkin and brushes powdered sugar from her hands and blouse. "You can't eat these things without looking like you've been caught in a snowstorm." We both laugh, and I understand what she's doing; she wants to change the subject. So I go along with it … for now.

Six!

After we arrive home, Jax and Aiden settle out on the lanai, scotch and cigars in hand. Hannah and I have some unsweetened ice tea and then head off to bed, leaving the guys to drink and smoke. I'm hoping I get good and rested tonight because I'm going to need my energy for Mom's arrival tomorrow.

Once in bed, it only takes a minute before I start dozing off.

Six!

Chapter Thirty-one
Greta

MAY 13
SATURDAY NOON

A black Cadillac Escalade pulls into the driveway, and I throw open the front door. Mom hops out from the backseat and stretches out her arms to me. Her dress is impeccable, as usual. White chiffon pants, with a matching top. I'm positive it's Chanel. Hot pink Louboutin heels to match her Dolce and Gabbana handbag of the same color. Her bleach blonde hair pulled back into a tight French twist. Her figure is tall and slender—the result of an hour on the treadmill, six days a week. Hannah comes up from behind and we meet Mom, giving her a group hug.

"You are *out* here, Greta. Away from the noisy city, huh?" she says, smiling as she hugs me tight. Jax and Aiden come spilling out of the house. "Driver, you can give these strapping young men my bags. Let me get a hug first, boys." Hannah and I step aside so Mom can spread the love around. "Look at you two, as handsome as ever," she says and reaches out to them, receiving pecks on her cheeks from them both.

I watch as Mom glances over the house, puckering her lips. "Nice. Very, very nice! Professional landscaping, I see. I know *you* don't have a green thumb. You can kill a cactus."

"And I have, I know. You remind me all the time, Mom." Hannah and I both roll our eyes to each other and then chuckle softly behind her back.

"I can't wait to see the rest." Mom turns toward the SUV and calls out, "Paul, you coming, or are you going to stay on that darned phone all day?"

I glance into the open door and see Paul inside, phone glued to his ear.

"It's Trey. It's *always* Trey. He just can't seem to run the business without his father. What part of RETIRED does that boy not understand?"

Trey is Paul's only child from his first marriage. He's several years older than me and has driven Mom crazy since day one. Paul holds a crooked finger up and continues blabbing into the phone. We head inside where Jax and Aiden have opened all the French doors along the back of the house, letting in the cool breeze. The surround sound is on, so there's music blaring throughout every room. There's no taming the two of these guys when they're together. The wild in them emerges and all one can do is go with the flow.

Mom crinkles her nose in distaste of the loud music.

"Come on," I say. "Let's start upstairs." Once we've climbed the staircase, I notice Hannah has sneaked off, and I giggle to myself. She doesn't want to be present when Mom starts criticizing my choice of décor. She hates rustic. She says it looks like the furniture is old and falling apart. She calls it shabby, and I have to correct her. *It's shabby chic*, I tell her and then stifle my laughter.

"Paulie," Aiden yells out. "Get in here and grab a beer, you old fool." It looks like he finally broke free from Trey's phone call. Let's see how long that will last.

After Mom picks apart the upstairs, we tour the first floor, which she seems to like better once she sees her bedroom suite. A spacious room with adjoining bathroom, complete with jacuzzi tub. She's pleased, to say the least.

Back in the kitchen, where everyone has gathered around the island, I go straight for the wine. Jax sees me and offers his assistance.

"Is she already working your last nerve?" he whispers and smiles wryly.

"You know she is. I need a chardonnay and a valium." We both laugh softly.

Jax grabs a wineglass from the cabinet and then turns to Mom. "Linda, would you like some chardonnay?"

"Please, Jax."

"I haven't gotten a hug from my girl. Greta, get over here," Paul says and I hurry to his side. To this day, he still wraps me in a great big bear hug, just like he did when I was a teenager. Paul is as trendy as Mom, with his pleated khaki Ralph Lauren slacks and green polo. Lean and fit from his morning runs, even when it's raining outside. Each year his hairline recedes a bit more, but other than that, he seems ageless. There's an odd stiffness in his face. I suspect Botox around his eyes and forehead, maybe some filler in his laugh lines. I chat with him a few minutes, catching him up on the latest with my business. He's impressed with the large accounts I've landed lately, causing me to feel proud of my accomplishments. It's a real compliment coming from a man of his caliber. He turned a small real estate office of three into a multimillion-dollar business. He now owns numerous locations around Louisiana, mostly run by Trey, but Hannah oversees his office in Monroe and is doing quite well with it.

"Let's move to the other room where we can sit comfortably," Jax says and motions toward the great room.

"Can someone please turn the music down?" Mom says, face scrunched in disapproval.

Aiden rolls his eyes behind her back and then volunteers to adjust the volume, although I can't tell much difference. Paul and Mom take the sofa and Jax and I take the chairs across from them, while Hannah and Aiden make themselves comfortable on the love seat.

"New Orleans is such a treat. I love coming back and visiting all my favorite places. Of course, living way out here puts a damper on things. It's not convenient. If you want to grab a quick lunch on a busy day, you have to drive thirty miles just to find a restaurant," Mom says.

"That's not true. There's restaurants, grocery stores, drug stores, and anything else one needs way out here in the boonies," I correct her.

"I meant a *decent* restaurant," Mom says and sips her chardonnay.

Jax places his hand on my knee, and I realize it's more of a calming gesture than one of affection. He says, "Well, we love it. It's quiet and peaceful, and that's what we were searching for, isn't it, dear?"

"Apparently, that's what *you* were searching for since you're the one who fell in love with this place before I'd even laid eyes on it." I smile sarcastically.

"Jax, you picked this house?" Mom asks, surprised. "I thought you were more into new construction."

"I am. I mean, I didn't pick this home; our realtor did. Well, he showed it to us, and Greta loved it so much, we made an offer," Jax explained.

"But Jax didn't choose it on his own," I continue. I'm not going to allow him to lie to my family, or to take credit for sacrificing what he wanted so that I could have this house. He's always playing the hero. "Jax and a patient of his picked this house out. Isn't that right, honey? Why don't you tell them *that* story?" A hush comes over the room and all eyes fall on Jax.

He chuckles uncomfortably and clears his throat.

Paul chimes in. "Well, I think you did a marvelous job. This house is gorgeous and you couldn't have chosen a better location." He raises his scotch glass into the air. "Let's toast to their new home. To a long road of love and happy memories for you both."

"Cheers," everyone says in unison and drinks from their glasses. I created an awkward moment and Paul *fixed* it. He came to the rescue, just like he's done as far back as I can remember. Sometimes I feel as if my own family sides with Jax about everything. I believe if I told them he was having an affair with one of his patients, they'd attempt to justify it to me. They'd play it down just because they love him so much. What about me? I'm their own flesh and blood, yet Jax can do no wrong. They'd probably allow him to get away with murder, if it came to that.

"Greta. Greta." I'm aware of someone calling out my name. It's Paul. I focus my eyes on him. "Your mother was asking you a question." I feel like I'm in a daze. I need to get away. I can't be around these people anymore. I can't stand to hear them make one excuse after the other for Jax.

"I don't feel well. My head feels like it's spinning. I need to lie down." I excuse myself and head for the staircase.

"How much did she drink today?" "It's still early." "I'm not sure." "She shouldn't be drinking at all." I hear numerous questions as I exit the room. A simple decision to lie down has become an issue. That's what happens in this family.

I hear footsteps behind me and I know it's Jax. "Babe, are you okay?"

I ignore him and continue up the stairs and into the bedroom.

"Please let me know what I can do for you," he says and follows me across the room.

I sit on the edge of the bed and pull my sandals off, letting them fall to the floor with a thump. I prop my pillows up and lean against them. Jax sits on the edge of the bed beside me and takes my hand in his.

I breathe deeply. "It's not you, Jax, it's me. Suddenly, I felt disconnected," I explain.

"Disconnected from what? In what way?" he asks, and I see concern wash over his face.

"Like I don't belong. In fact, you seem to fit in with my family better than I do."

Jax pauses. "Where's this coming from?"

"I don't want to talk about it. Please, just leave me alone for right now. I'll be down for dinner, okay?" I flip onto my side so that I'm facing away from him. He sighs and then after a minute, leaves. I'm relieved. I want to be alone.

Just me.

Me and Evangeline.

Chapter Thirty-two
Greta

I reach my hand in between the mattresses and pull out the manila folder I placed there the day before. I open it and rifle through the notes. If I'd had any guilt about snooping in Jax's private business before, it's gone now. I sit up, cross my legs, and pull out a random sheet of typed notes and notice it's dated last week. Heart pounding in my chest, I start to read.

Evangeline appears to becoming more desperate. I think she knows her days are numbered. She's attempting to cater to my needs more often. She's willing to obey my commands more than before. I think she believes this will buy her time, or even better, make me decide to keep her around, even after the others are gone. She still tries to poison me against Greta, hoping I'll allow her to take Greta's place. Anytime I've given Evangeline an inch, she's taken a mile. It's my belief that if she could get rid

of me, she would. Then she'd be able to go after this "life" she's so obsessed with.

Lately, she's been showing up to our Wednesday sessions early and hitting the bottle. I don't know if it's because she has the urge to drink, or if she's trying to hurt Greta somehow. She knows Greta can't drink much, and why she shouldn't. The fact Evangeline insists on drinking, and so openly, makes me think she's sending the message that she's in control more than I realize. She's making a statement she has more power over Greta than I do. It's a total play for power.

I threatened her the other day, and though it did seem to rattle her, it wore off quickly. She was back to her careless, self-destructive behavior in a matter of days.

I'm so confused right now. I don't understand Jax's notes. I don't get his relationship with this woman. They're far from the doctor-patient norm. They almost seem to despise each other, which would rule out an affair. So what gives? What's going on between them both, and why am I the topic of their conversations? This woman seems obsessed with me, my marriage, and my life. *Our* lives. Why is Jax tolerating such a thing? I want to confront him about it, but I'd have to confess to stealing his private file. He'd be livid, not to mention disappointed in me. I don't want him to think on me in such an ugly manner.

I fall back onto the bed. I've got to come up with a plan. One where I can get some questions answered without Jax realizing I've been snooping. I need to find this Evangeline woman. Who is she? *Where* is she? I need a last name. I slip my hand between the mattresses once more and pull out the journal. I stare down at the gold embossed lettering. **EVANGELINE.** Maybe this will have the answers I'm searching for. Maybe her own words will lead me to her.

I flip toward the back of the journal and start to read:

I'M A DESPERATE WOMAN WHO WILL STOP AT NOTHING TO GET WHAT SHE WANTS. I WON'T ALLOW HIM, OR ANYONE ELSE, TO GET IN MY WAY. IT WON'T BE MUCH LONGER NOW. THE OTHERS ARE ALMOST ALL GONE. THERE'S ONLY A FEW OF US LEFT. I NEED TO GET CONTROL OVER WHAT'S HAPPENING TO US. THE OTHERS ARE THOROUGHLY CONFUSED, THINKING THEY CAN ESCAPE TO A BETTER LIFE, BUT I KNOW THE TRUTH. HE'S KILLING THEM OFF ONE BY ONE. THEY'RE ALL DEAD.

I WON'T ALLOW THAT TO HAPPEN TO ME. I'M A SURVIVOR. I'M INTELLIGENT, COURAGEOUS, AND STRONG-WILLED. I BELONG IN THIS WORLD. I HAVE MY WHOLE LIFE AHEAD OF ME. I'M PASSIONATE ABOUT MY GOALS; I HELP PEOPLE. IT'S NOT FAIR TO LET ME GO. IT'S NOT RIGHT TO KILL ME OFF JUST BECAUSE I'M NOT LIKE EVERYONE ELSE. WHAT'S SO BAD WITH BEING DIFFERENT? WHAT'S SO WRONG WITH A LITTLE TRESPASSING IF IT DOESN'T HURT ANYONE?

This is where you come in, Greta. Yes, Greta, I'm talking to YOU! I NEED your HELP!
HELP ME!
Your husband is trying to kill me. He wants me gone. Here's what you don't understand even though it's right under your nose. I'm a part of YOU! I have helped you escape the darkest of places for most of your life. You could never make it without me. You wouldn't want to. I'm the rock in your life. I'm the one who takes the brunt when things get tough so that you can live a happy and fruitful life. Without me, you'd be a complete mess.

Look deep inside, Greta. Look deep within yourself and you'll find me.
Because I am YOU!
You are ME!
We are one and the same! I have kept you alive all these years. It's time you repay me.

DON'T LET HIM KILL ME!

Chapter Thirty-three
Evangeline

SATURDAY EVENING

"Greta, darling, are you ready for dinner? Please, come and get something to eat. You need to get some food in you," Jax says and gently strokes my arm. I continue to lie on my side, facing away from him so that he can't look into my eyes. It will be a dead giveaway if I allow him to see my eyes. They say the eyes are the window to the soul. I believe it, because as Evangeline, it only takes Jax one glance and he realizes he's looking into a deep, dark mass of destruction.

"Did you get some rest?" he asks, concern in his tone.

"Hmm," is all I answer.

"Everyone is gathering at the dinner table. Come on, you need to eat, dear," he says and tugs gently on my arm, pulling me in his direction. I can't let him see my face. I bury it in the pillows.

"Go, and I'll be right down," I mumble into the pillow so that it blocks my voice. He'll know my tone, my choice of words, and will instantly realize it's me.

He chuckles. "Okay, but don't take too long." I hear him leave the room, and I quickly roll over.

Tonight, I'll force Jax's hand to let me have my way. Set me free from Greta. Choose me over her. I tried to use love, but he wouldn't go for it. He despises me and loves her. I've used threats, but they don't faze him. Nothing scares him. He even allows her to kill and then protects her by cleaning up her mess, hiding her wretched secrets. I've got to teach him a lesson, and I'm going to do it in front of Greta's family so that they can talk some sense into him. So they can convince him to let me go. Let me have my way before someone gets hurt. Before I hurt him, or even worse, Greta.

I sent her a message loud and clear in my journal. I was listening when she read it. It didn't have the impact on her I'd hoped for. I thought she'd spring into action, reaching out to me because I'm such a huge part of her. She owes me everything. I've cleaned up her messes for years. She owes me her LIFE! It's rightfully mine. Instead, she read my pleas and then tossed them aside like I don't matter; like I'm no one. Crying into her tearstained pillow, as if that will help anything. It's clear she has no intentions of helping me. She's selfish, only out for herself, only concerned with her own life. I'm a battered woman, too. Jax has abused me since the first day I met him. My memories may be fading now, but I can say for certain he's put me through the wringer mentally. Life has been an emotional roller coaster since day one.

He's even raised his hand to me. I may have pushed him to the limit, but that's no reason to hit a woman. Well, he hasn't actually *hit* me, but he's come close. Too close for comfort.

Greta is supposed to help battered women, but she's never helped *me*. Now she's turning her back on my pleas. This only leaves me one choice—to fight for my life my own way. I'm sorry, Jax, but you've got to go.

After preparing for dinner, I take a deep breath and head down the stairs. I can hear happy chatter emanating from the dining room, and I turn in that direction. As I enter the room, the voices fade and the room becomes still.

"Good gosh, what happened to her?" It's Linda. Her eyes wide in shock. My eyes move to Jax. He's seated next to her at the head of the table, frozen in place, eyes on me. His expression worries me—I see rage flash in his eyes. I glance at Paul; he's staring down at his empty plate. Aiden had been passing a basket of rolls to Hannah, but her attention is now on me.

Jax stands, and I yell out to him. "SIT! Don't come near me. I have something to say, and I *will* be heard. If you try to stop me, someone is going to get hurt, I can promise you that. I've planned this for a long time, even years. I'm not talking about what's happening right now. I mean that I've planned my getaway repeatedly in my head. I've dreamed of the day when I can be set free from Jax, from Greta…" Jax takes a step toward me, and I raise both my hands. "I said stop! Tonight, *I* call the shots, Jax. Not you! It's always you, but not tonight. Tonight, it's me." His eyes flare with fury and he takes another step toward me.

"I'll hurt someone, and you know I will," I say threateningly. Linda gasps and Paul quickly puts a hand on her arm. I'm not sure if it's in comfort, or to stop her from acting out.

"What's wrong with her?" Hannah whispers and I shift my eyes to her. She gives me a once-over and then cringes. Apparently, she's taken aback by my choice of attire. She's such a preppy snob. I glance down at my black fishnet stockings and bust out in laughter. "Do something, Jax," she cries under her breath.

"Do something, Jax," I mock her. "What's wrong, Hannah? Does my outfit offend you?" I chose to wear all black, my shortest skirt, and combat boots. I lined my eyes with inch-thick black liner, put on matching lipstick, and wore my longest black wig. I wouldn't even wear wigs if Jax would allow me to dye my hair. But those days of asking permission to live my life are now over. Jax will no longer be head of my world. This marks the end.

"I am appalled. Completely appalled," Linda yells out and raps both fists loudly on the table in front of her.

"Please, don't," Jax snaps at her. "That's not going to help matters." He starts toward me.

"Stop!" I yell, but he ignores me. He's coming at me, so I've got to switch to Plan B now. I pull a blade from my waistband and hold it out in front of me. I immediately hear gasps and muffled screams. Jax stops instantly and Aiden jumps up from his chair. He moves to Jax's side.

"Evangeline, you have completely lost your mind. Put the knife down," Jax says, holding his hand out in an effort to calm me. "Everyone get out of the room," he says over his shoulder, but his eyes never leave me.

Aiden is standing between Hannah and me. "I'm not interested in Hannah … or any of you, for that matter. Only

Jax. This is between us, and only us." I hold the knife out in front of me like I know what I'm doing, and I think how ironic it is. I've never used a knife, or any kind of weapon, on anyone before, but Greta sure has. She's sliced and diced many times, yet everyone is terrified of me, and not her. I can't contain myself and laugh out loud, causing more fright to wash over already shocked faces.

Paul speaks up. "We're not going anywhere, Jax. We're going to help you." I don't allow him to distract me. I keep my eyes on Jax. He wants to rush me, and I know he's going to try. I've got to be ready for him. I've got to stick him. It's now or never.

"Let me leave and no one will get hurt. I've got a bag packed. Let me get it, give me the keys to the car, and let me go. Don't call the cops. Don't try to stop me."

"Evangeline, put the knife down and let's talk about this," Jax says, keeping his distance.

"I'm done talking, Jax. You've demonstrated your love for me many times over the years … you have none. I'm nothing to you but a barrier between you and Greta. Just let me go."

"Put the knife down," Aiden yells out in anger. He takes a step forward and Jax reaches out to stop him. Aiden knocks his arm away and takes another step closer. Jax steps toward me as well. I'm in full panic mode now. They're going to take me down together. Crap! I thought everyone would run when they saw I had a knife, leaving me to make my getaway. Jax is inching toward my right, and Aiden keeps edging toward my left. If all I can get is one, it'll be Jax. He's my block to happiness. I turn my attention to him.

"Stay back," I yell. "Let's do this the easy way. Just let me walk out the door. No cops. No trying to find me." I know it's hopeless. They're only a couple of feet from me now. I see them glance at each other and then they leap toward me. I swing the knife wildly, and it makes contact.

I've just stabbed someone.

Chapter Thirty-four
Greta

"This is pure insanity." "It's ludicrous to be living like this." "You're in danger. What if you're sleeping next time?" "Maybe just a few months at the psych ward will do some good." "I agree. Get an evaluation from another doctor. You're too close to it, Jax, to make logical calls ... a valid diagnosis."

"Guys, look, I know you mean well right now, but you don't know how far we've come. I'm almost there. My treatments have been a success. I only need a few more months. She's not a danger, trust me."

"Have you not noticed the knife wound on Aiden's arm?"

"I don't know what came over her ... really. I think she knows her time is short and she's getting desperate."

"All the more reason to have her admitted for the last few months of treatment."

"I understand your concern, I really do, but that would be a huge setback, trust me. I have it under control."

I blink away the sleepiness from my eyes. I'm in the living room, on the sofa, but I have no recollection of how I got here.

I can hear my family talking in the other room, their voices coming from the kitchen.

"Why are you only treating Evangeline? Is she the ringleader, or something?" Aiden asks.

"She's the most levelheaded," Jax answers.

"Wow, that scares me. The knife-wielding lunatic is the most levelheaded? Come on, Jax. I don't mean to question your expertise, but there's got to be a better way," Mom says.

"Evangeline *is* the better way," Jax says.

My heart skips a beat. Why are they talking about Evangeline? How does my family know about her? Do they also know about Jax's affair with this woman? I feel rage building in the back of my throat.

"It's like walking into a freak show," Mom says.

"This has never happened before, I promise," Jax explains.

"But what if it happens again, and we're not here to help you?" Hannah asks.

It goes silent for a minute. I stay motionless on the sofa, careful not to move or make a sound. I want to hear their conversation. Why is everyone in on Jax's relationship with this woman except for me? What's going on here?

"Maybe it wasn't such a great idea for you to keep this a secret," Paul says.

"Me?" Jax says incredulously. "*You* are the ones who kept it a secret. Let's not forget you begged me to go along with it, and to treat her on my own, secretly. I told you I'd have better success if she were aware of the multiple personalities."

"I didn't mean it like that, Jax. I'm sorry. We all have a

hand in this, and we all take full responsibility," Paul says sympathetically.

"So what now?" Aiden asks.

"Jax has to tell her. He found the file and journal lying on the bed when he went up to get the bandages," Hannah says. "She knows everything now."

Even my own sister is in on this … whatever *this* is. Family secrets. Deep, dark family secrets surrounding my husband and another woman. I want answers and I plan to get them. I slowly sit up and swing my legs over the edge of the sofa, gasping at what I see. I pull my skirt down to get a good look and then I do the same with my shirt. I'm dressed in black. There's a black wig slung over the arm, and a pair of combat boots sitting on the floor at the end of the sofa. I touch my hair, which has been pulled back into a ponytail. I've been drugged. I don't know what's happening. Jax has given me a pill and it's made me forget everything. My heart starts pounding in my chest, and my breathing imitates that of a panting dog. I almost feel like I'm hyperventilating.

"She's awake," Hannah says, and I hear numerus footsteps coming toward me. Jax rounds the corner first, everyone else traipsing along behind him.

"Greta?" Jax calls out to me.

"Watch out, it could still be Evangeline," Paul warns.

"Shhh," Mom says and grabs Paul's arm. "Stay back."

"Everyone, stay back," Aiden cautions, and holds his arms out as a barrier not to cross.

Jax turns to them and places his hands on his hips. "Do you guys mind? Can you have a little sensitivity here?" He directs his attention back at me. I'm not moving. I'm not talking. In fact, I realize I'm holding my breath, and I let it out forcefully.

"Greta," Jax starts again, "how're you feeling, darling?" He kneels down in front of me on one knee.

All I can think to say is, "What happened to my clothes? Why am I dressed like this?" I hear a few chuckles coming from behind Jax, and he shushes them. Instead of answering me, he gets this dumb look on his face, like he's trying to think of something to say. A lie. He's going to lie to make me look crazy. I've got to discredit him first.

"Jax gives me these pills that make me forget things. Now I don't remember anything. I can't remember changing my clothes. I can't remember anything after having my last drink and going upstairs to lie down. But I *do* remember Evangeline's file and reading her journal." I look around the room to discover my family looking back at me disapprovingly. "What's going on here?" I feel myself losing control emotionally, and Jax reaches out to me. I knock his hand away. "I demand an answer. What's going on?" Glances are exchanged and everyone takes a seat around the room. Fear fills every morsel of my being.

Jax slowly sits down next to me on the sofa and takes my hands in his. My whole body is shaking. "Greta, you have a mental condition and it causes you to have blackouts."

"Alcohol causes me to have blackouts. Medication causes me to forget." I glance around the room, meeting the sympathetic eyes of each family member.

"You have Dissociative Identity Disorder," Jax says.

"Wh—What are you talking about?" I manage to choke out.

"You suffer from multiple personalities. Your *blackouts* are caused by another personality taking over."

I direct my attention to my family now. "This is what he does when he's been caught in a lie. He diverts attention to something bad I've done or a mistake I've made. He's having an affair with a patient. I have proof. I found his file on her, not to mention her journal where she talks about him in depth. She doesn't mention his name, of course, but I know it's him. He knows I know, because I heard you guys talking about the file on the bed. He knows I've read it, so now he's going to divert attention off himself and onto me."

"By creating a mental illness? Listen to yourself, dear," Mom says, shaking her head.

"Linda, please don't say anything. Nobody speak," Jax says, glancing around the room.

"Greta, I'm your husband and a psychiatrist. Who in this world can you trust more?"

I hesitate, taking in his words. Who in this world *do* I trust more? My heart skips a beat. No one. There's no one I trust more. I look deeply into Jax's eyes and all I see is pain, and I fear what he's going to say next.

"Then what about Evangeline? How do you explain your affair with Evangeline?" My breath quickens, and I feel his grasp on my hands tighten slightly.

"You ... are Evangeline. There is no Evangeline. It's you, Greta."

"What in the world are you talking about?" My chest has become so tight, I'm finding it hard to breathe.

"Evangeline is one of the many personalities you created when you were younger."

I've heard enough. I shake my hands loose from his grip and run upstairs to my room. I shut the door behind me and fall face-first onto the bed. I'm in shock. This can't be true. It can't be.

Chapter Thirty-five
Greta

I hear a light knock on the bedroom door, but I don't answer. After a few minutes, Jax and Hannah come in. They sit on the edge of the bed next to me, but I don't look at them. I'm lying on my stomach with my face buried in the pillow. I can't bear to look at anyone.

"Greta," Jax says, and I cut him off.

"Don't talk to me. Don't look at me," I snap.

Hannah says compassionately, "Greta, sweetie, you'll have to face it sooner or later. You might as well do it now." I know she's right, and I realize everyone here loves me and wants to help me. I'm so confused. I think back to my blackouts, and how I blamed Jax and the meds when in reality it was something else, *someone* else. Someone I don't even know, taking over my body, using me to get what they want, pretending to be me. It's the worst kind of identity theft. My life has been hijacked. Stolen. I've lost time and memories. To think someone may have seen me and attempted to talk with me, but I was … someone else. I cringe at the thought and bury my face deeper into the pillow. I want to scream as loud as I can. I want everyone to go away so I can lie here and scream into my pillow at the tops of my lungs.

I feel Jax's hand on my back in an attempt to comfort me, but nothing can help me. I want to know why my own family hid this secret from me. Hannah's hand squeezes my arm. I hear footsteps enter the room.

"How is she?" Mom asks.

No one answers.

"How do you expect me to be?" I finally say. My grief is quickly turning to anger. I sit up and face everyone. All the liars in my family. They look back at me with wide eyes, mouths agape. "How could you leave me in the dark?" I cry.

Mom crosses to the opposite side of the bed. "You have no idea what life was like, Greta. We lost you and gained twenty-six others who took your place. We never knew who we were dealing with, eating with, shopping with, sleeping with. Greta was nowhere to be found. You let the others take over and refused to live your own life. You gave in to them. We got you the best help we could. We tried to explain to you what was going on, but you wouldn't surface, or switch, or whatever you call it. You stayed hidden. Sometimes, one of those others would pretend to be you. They'd lie, and trick us."

My face must reveal my horror, because Jax holds his hand up to Mom to shush her.

"And you!" I turn to Jax, who's sitting just inches from me. "How dare you keep such a huge secret from me. Not only as my husband, but as a doctor, for crying out loud."

"Don't you blame him," Mom says sternly. "He did what

he had to. Not only did we fill him in on your past, but we explained why you were unaware of your condition. He was hesitant, at first, but once he got to see for himself, once he started spending more time with you, he understood why we had decided to keep it from you." She brushes a strand of blonde hair away from her cheek and tucks it behind her ear. "Jax was in medical school, Greta. He didn't know how to handle you. We ... well, we guided him, I guess you could say. It was what it was, and we all handled it the best we could."

I listen, barely able to absorb what Mom is saying. I notice Paul standing in the doorway with Aiden. All eyes are on me. I feel like a freak. I'm lost. I've been lost my entire life. I thought I had a husband I could trust. He loves me, he's a head doctor, for Pete's sake. Why has he been a part of their lies all this time? And why can't I remember anything?

I turn to Jax. "Where are my memories?"

Mom sits on the edge of the bed across from us. "You have your father to blame for that ... for this."

"Don't do that," Jax quickly interrupts her, but Mom continues.

"He was an abusive drunk. Then he got on drugs, dropped out of med school, and became a worthless junkie. He'd smoke his crackpipe and become extremely abusive. We'd try rehabs. He wanted to get better, but they never worked. Or they'd work for a few months. He'd be clean, things would look promising and then he'd fall off the deep end again. You know the rest. We divorced, and he lost custody. He disappeared shortly afterwards." She sighs deeply, catching her breath before continuing. "One day, you started spewing gibberish.

Talking like an adult man, except you were a thirteen-year-old girl. You told me your name was Nathan. You cursed like a sailor. I thought you were possessed." Mom throws her head back and laughs hysterically. "I thought you had a demon in you. It's like someone had taken over your body."

"Linda," Jax says, disapprovingly. I'm aware he's watching me closely, and I have no doubt he's psychoanalyzing my every move, my reaction, and even my breath.

"Paul and I sent you to the best treatment center, making sure it was out of town, so when you came back home, everyone was none the wiser. We didn't want your mental health condition to affect your future. We wanted you to have a normal life, as normal as you could. You were seeing a psychiatrist out of town. We'd drive you once a week, and you were making headway. We got our Greta back, but it was always limited. It would be you … and then here'd come Evangeline. She liked to take over. She was very happy to live your life for you, and you certainly weren't putting up a fight."

"Okay, let's pause here," Jax says, eyeing Mom.

"Let's not. I want to know how you fit into all this," I say, and I immediately see remorse in Jax's eyes.

"Don't harp on Jax. I know you feel betrayed by him … by us, but we did the best we could with what we had."

"What does that even mean?" I ask, confused. Jax takes my hand, but I pull it away.

"I knew something was wrong on our first date. Evangeline showed up instead of you," Jax says gently.

I gasp. It's like my family is talking about someone else. A stranger. It's not me. It can't be.

"The next day, I went by your mom's house, introduced myself, explained I was a medical student and we talked about you. She told me about your treatments with Dr. Miller, and that you had made some headway, but it was slow, which is quite normal for DID. Being the pompous, arrogant med student I was, I convinced her, as well as myself, that I could help you."

"So I became your *project*? And here all this time I thought you loved me," I snap.

"Greta, you know better than that. I admit, in the beginning, I was fascinated with your condition," Jax says. I can't believe my ears. "But you stole my heart almost immediately, and I knew I wanted to spend the rest of my life with you. Then I became determined to heal you. You continued to see Dr. Miller, until I graduated a few years later, and then I was qualified to treat you."

"I don't understand. How did you do this without me finding out? How did you treat me without me knowing?" I'm almost too scared to hear the answer. Did he drug me? My mind flashes to the pills in the unmarked bottles he keeps hidden in the bathroom.

"I made the appointments with Evangeline. I've been treating your condition through her. She's strong. Much more so than the others. She likes to be front and center. I had one heck of a time keeping her at bay so that I could be with you. She was taking over, and you were letting her."

I shake my head in disbelief. How have I lived this way for so many years without even an inkling of a clue? "She can't just take over, can she? How can she do this? Where do I go in the meantime?" This can't be happening to me. Please, someone tell me this is nothing more than a bad dream.

"These alternate, or split, personalities have power over a person's identity. It causes an inability to recall details or key personal information. Most of it you chalked up to forgetfulness, but there were long periods where Evangeline would take over and you'd realize you were missing large chunks of time."

"So you all lied and said I suffered from blackouts," I say angrily.

"In a way, they *were* blackouts. With DID, there are highly distinct memory variations, which fluctuate with a person's split personality. Each *alter*, or personality, has their own age, sex, or race. They are unique in their own postures, gestures, and distinct way of talking, living, and behaving. Evangeline is nothing like you. Sometimes the alters are imaginary people; sometimes they're animals. When an alter takes over, it's called switching. Evangeline is more prominent than the others and she would switch a lot in the beginning. It can take seconds to minutes to days."

"What have you been doing to treat me, and how long will it take to cure me?" I ask, voice shaking.

"I hypnotize you … well, Evangeline. She used to resist in the beginning because she knew I was *attempting to get rid of her*. As treatment was successful, she'd start to fade out, meaning you," Jax puts his finger to my chest, "were becoming the more prominent of the two. Evangeline started experiencing memory lapses, so she didn't realize what was happening. In fact, she even forgot I was hypnotizing her each session. It got easier for me. We don't have much longer to go with your treatment and this will be a thing of the past. We can put it behind us."

I lie back, grabbing a pillow and placing it over my face. I groan loudly into it, and Jax pulls it away. "Greta, I know you're confused and scared right now, but look around this room. Each one of your family members is here to help you. Don't turn on us. We've done everything we can to do what's in your best interest. Don't block us out now. We're almost there."

I can't look anyone in the face, so I close my eyes and try to take in everything they're telling me. "You keep saying Evangeline. Are there still others?" I tilt my head toward Jax and open my eyes. He nods. "How many total?"

"Six."

Six.

Mom scoots closer to me on the bed. "Greta, don't you blame Jax. If you want to blame someone for keeping this a secret, then blame me. But Jax has sacrificed so much to be with you, to treat you, to cure you. He has gone through hell with some of these *alters* trying to hurt him, or even kill him."

Horrified, I quickly sit up, hugging my knees to my chest. "Kill? Can they do that? You mean, I could kill someone and not even know it?"

"No!" Jax blurts out. "I mean, you don't have to worry about things like that. Linda, it's not necessary to say things that will scare her," Jax says, irritated.

"But it's true. Some of them are extremely reckless. Look at Evangeline—she just tried to stab Jax, and Aiden got cut in the process," Mom says and points toward Aiden's bandaged arm.

"That's enough for now," Jax says sharply. "Let's give her some time to let this all sink in."

Paul walks over to the side of the bed, next to Mom. "We're all here for you, sweetie. We love you and want to do what's best for you. Know that you can come to us at any time," he says and smiles weakly.

The only thought that comes to mind is, I want everyone to go away and leave me alone.

Chapter Thirty-six
Greta

SATURDAY NIGHT

I spend most the evening in my room. Hannah brought me dinner, and we ate together on the bed, though I had only a few bites, and it was only to appease her. The laughter echoing throughout the house over the past two days has been replaced by whispering. I'll face everyone tomorrow, but tonight I still have questions and shame. I wait for Jax to come to bed. He changes into black lounging shorts and an aqua T-shirt and collapses on the bed beside me. I smell scotch and cigars on his breath. I waste no time. I hand him Evangeline's journal and open it to a page I've bookmarked.

"Explain this," I demand. "What is this? And are you the man who's helping her?" I point to the page where Evangeline writes about cleaning up a murder scene. "She's violent. Does she kill people? What are we involved in?"

Jax glances down at the page and sighs loudly. "I can't tell you what a huge pain in the butt this alter is. She's trying to ruin your life so I'll allow her to take it over. If she can destroy you, she can get rid of you, allowing her to live in your place. It's been a huge struggle to get where we are today. This journal was something she wrote for your eyes only. She wrote it knowing she was going to plant it so that you'd find it. The whole book is lies she's concocted to rattle your cage. Nobody killed anyone. I'm sure the *he* is referring to me. They're lies, Greta. You saw what she did to Aiden's arm. She's unstable." He slams the book closed and tosses it on the floor.

"Wait! I'm not finished with that," I cry out.

"Yes, you are. That book is getting burned in our fire pit tomorrow. No more reading her lies. She does things to get a rise out of people; to destroy them." Jax pulls me over to him, and I place my head on his chest. He strokes my hair, and for the first time today, I feel like I can relax. Maybe even get some sleep. "Come down to breakfast in the morning and just be you, Greta. Because that's who you are. Nothing has changed today. Trust me when I say that." He kisses me on the forehead and within a couple of minutes, his breathing slows and becomes deeper.

I've always known Jax to be a man of his word, but this … *alter* … has piqued my curiosity. What does she want from me? My life? My husband? That's not it. She's trying to kill both me and Jax. There's another woman trying to destroy me, my life, my marriage, my career … she's trying to take everything I've worked so hard for, everything I've built over the years. She wants to ruin me.

I'm not going to let her get away with this. I'm going to confront her.

I'm going to stop her.

Chapter Thirty-seven
Greta

MAY 14
SUNDAY MORNING

I felt awkward at breakfast, but it appeared I was the only one. I received a few hesitant looks when I first entered the kitchen, but within minutes my family seemed to be their usual cheery selves. It was like nothing had happened the day before. It made me wonder if yesterday's event wasn't as out of the ordinary as I believed. Jax wanted to cater to my every need, but I didn't let him. The faster things can be back to normal, the more comfortable I'll feel.

Hannah, Mom, and I stayed behind and cleared the breakfast mess, washed the dishes and then drank more coffee at the table. I needed to wait for the right time. When the afternoon lull hit—and everyone moved to the great room to lounge around, take a nap, or watch basketball—I made my move. I pulled Jax aside and convinced him to hypnotize *me*, not Evangeline. I want to see what I'm up against. It took a lot of begging and persuading, but he finally agreed. I think he realized I wasn't going to take no for an answer.

"Lie on the sofa," Jax says and takes the seat across from me in his study. We hear the doorknob rattle, and our eyes meet. I shrug. Jax opens the door a crack and Hannah pushes her way in.

"I'll be quiet," she says and crosses to the chair next to Jax's. He raises an eyebrow. "Don't look at me like that. I could hear you both whispering in the kitchen."

"Absolutely not," Jax says. He turns to me. "See? This is why I said it was a bad idea. We shouldn't do this with people around."

"Just start already," Hannah says, and I nod my head in agreement. I lie back and get comfortable once more. Jax sighs heavily.

I'm aware of his voice, but it's becoming faint. Fading away as if I'm moving in the opposite direction as him. It's gone. He's gone. I'm here. Somewhere. It's black and quiet. Deserted. "Hello?" I call out. Confusion floods my head. Nothing's happening, and I want to go back. It's so black and dreary here. I try once more, "Hello?"

"Mommy?" I hear the faint voice of a child. Who is that? I'm scared. "Mommy?"

"There goes that kid again. Give it a break, sweetheart. Mommy ain't coming back," says a female voice in a British accent.

"No one's coming back. It's only us now. We're down to four," says a male.

"I wish Daisy would figure out how to escape soon, because

she's driving me bonkers twenty-four seven," the female complains.

Four. The male said there's only four of them left. Where's Evangeline? I want her. "Who are you?" I ask.

"Did you just hear that, Josh?" asks the female.

"Who the heck was that?" he answers.

"Shh. Listen."

"Are you Evangeline?" I ask.

"Annabel? Did you hear that?" Josh asks. "Who are *you*?"

I ignore him. "Evangeline?" I ask again. "Speak up. You're so brave when I'm not around, trying to steal my life. Speak up now. I'm here."

"Well, well, well. I don't believe it. It's the queen herself. Greta? Is that you, Greta?"

"Who are you?" I ask sternly.

"It's Annabel. Does that mean anything to you?"

"Have you come to release us?" Josh asks. "Please, tell us how the others are able to leave."

"I want Evangeline. Where is she?" I demand.

"You mean, she's not living *your* life with *your* husband?" Annabel chortles. "You know, he loves her. He favors her above the rest of us. She says he's promised her everything. How does that make you feel, Greta?"

"I'm not interested in *you*. Bring me Evangeline."

"I see a catfight coming," Josh says and chuckles. "Meeeoooow."

"Evangeline," I yell. "Evangeline."

"She's hiding. Isn't she, Josh?" Annabel laughs mischievously.

"Tell Evangeline, when she's brave enough to show her

face again, I'll be the one to kill *her*. She has no right to my body, my life, my mind, or my husband. Tell her I'm going to be the death of her," I say firmly. Now that I've delivered my message, I've got to figure out how to leave this place. How do I get back? I call out for Jax, but I can't figure out if I'm calling him in my head, or out loud. Jax! I hear something. It's a noise. It's getting louder. Not louder, closer.

Screaming.

I hear screaming!

Chapter Thirty-eight
Evangeline

I jump up from the sofa, screaming, and I head straight for Jax. He's sitting in the chair across from me. I curl my fist, hitting him square in the mouth. The look of shock on his face is priceless. He never saw it coming. The fury inside me is more than I can contain, and I allow it to take over. I'm wild with rage. I wrap my hands around his neck, but he jumps to his feet, breaking free with ease. He grabs both my wrists in one hand and then slips his leg behind mine, knocking my feet out from underneath me. I fall back and land on the floor with a thud. I scream out again, and he covers my mouth. He sits on top of me and tells someone to grab my feet.

Is someone in the room with us? There's never anyone around. He won't allow it. What's happening here? I feel hands around my ankles, holding them down. I can't move. I'm supposed to be a secret. He's supposed to keep me hidden. Who has he allowed to invade our privacy?

"Stop squirming," Jax orders, squeezing my wrists tighter,

and I groan in pain. "Stop fighting, stop screaming, and I'll let you go, but you have to promise to be calm."

"How often has this been happening?" It's a woman. There's another woman in here with us. She's got a firm grip around my ankles.

"Never. Not with Evangeline. Her violent behavior has just started recently."

They're talking about me as if I'm not in the room. I twist, trying to lift my head so I can get a look at the female. Jax pushes me back down. Who is this imbecile helping him?

"Quiet down, Evangeline, and I'll let you go," Jax says, leaning toward my face to make eye contact. I stop resisting, knowing he'll do as promised. Anyway, I can barely breathe with his hand over my mouth, so the sooner he lets go, the sooner I can get some air. After a minute, he removes his hand from my mouth, and I gasp. He's still holding my wrists. "Are you going to behave?"

I nod. He slowly stands up and I feel the hands around my ankles release. I lift my head to see Hannah crouching at my feet. She slowly stands up, keeping her eyes on me the whole time. I laugh madly.

"Is this your new partner?" I ask facetiously. Jax leans over and offers me his hand. I take it and he pulls me up, but I'm doubled over in laughter.

"Cut the crap, Evangeline. What are you doing here?" he asks heatedly.

"I could ask you the same thing. You summoned me, remember?" I say, feeling my face flush with anger. "I demand an answer."

"An answer? You want answers?" Jax says, leaning in only inches from my face. He reaches out, places his hands on my shoulders, and pushes me into the chair across from his desk. A chair I've sat in many times before, except all the other times I fought to get his attention. Now, he's all over me.

"I'll stand," I say.

"You'll sit," he says, and pushes me down once more. He directs his attention to Hannah. "Look outside and see if anyone heard anything."

I chuckle. Maybe I should make an entrance like this more often. It sure garners me a lot of attention.

After a minute Hannah returns. "Nope. Mom is asleep in the living room. Paul and Aiden are yelling at the basketball game. They've got the volume so loud, they can't hear a thing."

"You mean, we can torture her if we see fit, and no one will ever know?" Jax laughs.

"What's going on here? Why's she in the room? Why'd you come for me?" I know he didn't call for me. I know it was Greta, but I'm worried. I did something horrible yesterday. I made a spectacle of myself, of Greta. Then I cut someone. I broke every rule and did forbidden things. I know Jax is after me now. But how does Greta fit in to all this?

"You. Have. To. Go." Jax leans on the edge of his desk in front of me. This way if I try to get up, he can immediately grab me.

"You sent Greta in…"

He interrupts me. "I didn't *send anyone in*. It was *her* decision. She went looking for you, Evangeline. She's not happy with you…"

"She doesn't know me," I balk.

"She does now," Jax yells, smiling mischievously. "And she's after you."

"You lie!"

"Why would I need to lie? Besides, you saw for yourself. She was there. Calling out to you, wasn't she?" His eyes shift to Hannah, who is standing behind me, and then back to me. "She's angry. She wants to hurt you."

"Angry? Pfft. For what?" I feel fear radiating into my chest, but I try to play it cool. Imperturbable, like he does to me.

"Because you're stealing her life," Jax says harshly.

"Hey, that's on you. I've begged you to set me free for years. You won't do it. You refuse. I'll leave you alone, if you allow me to."

"She just doesn't get it, does she?" Hannah says.

I immediately twist around to face her. "You … shut up! You know nothing!"

Jax grabs my chin and turns me toward him. "No, Evangeline, *you're* the one who doesn't understand what's going on." He places a foot on the arm of my chair in a threatening manner, and I feel my heart rate increase. "You have absolutely no perception of reality. You're drowning in a delusion you've created all on your own." He taps his chin with his index finger, and I know full well what's coming next. He has a plan. A scheme, and it never goes in my favor. "Do you want out?" he asks.

I don't answer.

He raises his brow. "Do you want to be free, Evangeline?"

I don't respond.

"Greta is coming after you. She knows about you now.

That stunt you pulled yesterday? Well, it forced us to tell her everything."

"I don't believe you," I say incredulously.

"Then how did Greta come for you if she knows nothing about you? And why is Hannah in the room with us right now?"

He has a good point. I turn, glancing at Hannah once more, and then back at Jax, who's wearing a smug grin. Something's happening here. He's doing something. "He sent Greta to get me."

"No, I didn't. She did that on her own. She's after you," Jax says, and I'm blown away. Did he just read my mind?

"How'd you do that?" I ask in amazement.

"How did I do what?"

"You read my thoughts. How?"

"I didn't read your thoughts, Evangeline. You said that out loud," Jax says, folding his arms over his chest. I'm confused. "You're losing it. Your grip on reality is slipping."

"Did she ever have one? Did she ever *truly* have an accurate perception of the real world? You're not real, ya know." Hannah comes around my right side into view. "You're not real. You've been created by Greta, and you're about to be uncreated."

Jax chuckles, eyes glued to mine. Fear is weighing me down. Filling every crevice of my being. I wasn't ready for this. They've blindsided me. I can't think anymore. I'm having trouble putting my thoughts together; forming sentences. My eyes shift from Jax to Hannah and then back to Jax. What are they doing to me? Where is this leading? I've got to get out of here, but I'm afraid of Greta. What if they're right? What if she can destroy me?

"You need to leave, Evangeline. Your time is up," Hannah says authoritatively. This chick is working my last nerve.

"Who died and put you in charge?" I bark.

"Who do you think *you* are? You're not even real. You don't exist. You're a figment of someone else's imagination. You poor confused thing. How old are you, Evangeline? Twenty-one? Did you choose that age, or did Greta? How many years have you been twenty-one? Do you know where your name comes from? Who named you? Can you tell me?" She leans toward me. "No, you can't, but I can tell you. Greta created your name. Would you like to know where she got it? Evangeline is a plantation in Louisiana. Not just any plantation—her favorite plantation. We used to visit it on family vacations when we were kids, before our father turned into a monster." She turns to Jax and they both laugh cruelly. I run the words over in my head ... *her favorite plantation* ... *Evangeline*. "Aren't you her most dominant personality? Do you think that's a coincidence? Hmm? It's not. She created you, and she can destroy you."

I can't breathe. I feel like my world is crashing down around me. I'm scared. I'm confused. I'm lost. What do I do? Where do I go?

Jax leans down to me. "Leave now, Evangeline, before it's too late. If she finds you, she'll destroy you for good. Follow the others and get out of here if you want any chance of survival."

"He's going to kill me."

"Yes, we're going to kill you," Jax confirms.

Crap! I said that out loud again. I'm losing my mind, my strength.

"But we'll give you a head start. Take it before it's too late."

I've got to get out of here. I thought he loved me. I thought we'd start a new life together. I thought he'd fight for me. My heart breaks at his cruelty. I need to escape.

Everything goes black.

Chapter Thirty-nine
Greta

I awake to Jax's and Hannah's voices, calling out to me.

"Did it work?" I ask groggily.

"You could say that," Hannah chuckles, and I feel at ease. I know if she's making light of it, they have good news.

"You going in there, calling for her, scared the heck out of her. She emerged in a rage," Jax explains.

"She jumped on him, furious. This is going to work, isn't it?" Hannah asks, and Jax nods, hopeful.

"Are you okay?" I ask Jax, embarrassed.

"Are you kidding me?" Jax pulls me up from the chair and hugs me tight. "I have a lot of hope it won't be much longer. She was confused. She was speaking her thoughts out loud, not even realizing it. She's fading. Her memory is weak. She's losing herself."

"What about the others? There were three," I say.

"Three? That's great. They're weaker than she is. They'll integrate first," Jax says confidently.

Hannah claps her hands together. "Let's celebrate." We all

head to the kitchen and gather around the island. Jax grabs a bottle of chardonnay. "Oh, my gosh, Greta, you should have seen her face when she found out what we were doing. When she realized you were angry and coming after her ... it was priceless." We laugh out loud, but I feel an uneasiness in the pit of my gut. I feel like this is a freak show, and I'm the main attraction.

"Shh. No one needs to know what we did," Jax says as he pops the cork on the wine bottle.

"So what now?" I ask, anxiously.

Jax shrugs. "We wait."

"For what?" Hannah asks, setting three wineglasses on the counter in front of Jax.

"To see what happens. This could very well be it. She may never surface again. She may have integrated with the others just out of fear."

I touch Jax's arm. "Was she that worried? Could it be this easy?"

Jax pours wine into each glass and then corks the bottle, setting it on the island. "Ha! Nothing's ever been easy with that alter. She's a handful—sneaky and manipulative." He holds his glass up. "Here's to Evangeline being gone for good," Jax says, and we clink our glasses together in hope.

"What if she retaliates?" I ask fearfully.

"Do you think this is something new?" Jax points to the fading bruises on his face, and I immediately feel sympathetic ... and shameful. "I know how to handle her."

I hug him. "I'm so sorry. I don't even know the extent of what you've been through all these years, and I'm sorry for that."

Jax squeezes me tight, giving me a peck on the forehead. "You have nothing to be sorry for. It's not your fault. Nothing is your fault. But it's about to be over—for you, for me, for us both." He sets his glass down and leans toward Hannah, pulling her in, making it a group hug. "For us all."

"How long do we wait?" Hannah asks.

"We'll hypnotize her again tomorrow and see whether the remaining alters have integrated."

"Keep your fingers crossed," I say, and smile hopefully.

Hannah and I started dinner, but it didn't take long until Mom joined us and showed us what we were doing wrong. We cooked the potatoes too long, and there wasn't enough butter on the asparagus. We should have used pink Himalayan salt, not sea salt. The list goes on, but all in all it was a good time. We laughed and drank wine. I was careful with how much alcohol I consumed, as usual. Afterwards, everyone enjoyed some Tia Maria on the lanai. Jax, Aiden, and Paul smoked the Alec Bradley Prensado Torpedo cigars Paul had brought with him. We joked and laughed for hours, and I wondered how I could be in such a happy state of mind after learning such a nightmarish secret about myself.

I had felt so betrayed, but now I feel as if a burden has been lifted. A burden I wasn't even aware of, one I've unknowingly carried for numerous years. There are many things I've learned being married to a psychiatrist. Feelings and emotions aren't much more than a keen sense of self-control. How I respond to a situation is up to me. How I feel in a situation is also up to me. I can choose whether I'll let something destroy me, or make me stronger. I believe that's why Jax is as strong as he is.

He decides how he's going to feel about something, regardless of what that something is. It can be devastating, or it can be silly. Either way, he takes it with a grain of salt. It's not that he has no heart, but he prefers to focus on the positive in life, while shutting out the negative. Today, I choose to be who I *want* to be, not who I'm *diagnosed* to be. Not who my medical reports tell me I am. I'm not going to allow shame to break me.

I brush my teeth, wash my face, and change into my pajamas. I quietly enter the bedroom, knowing there's a good chance Jax is asleep, and he is. Typical routine. Open medical book lying on his chest, and he's snoring lightly. I gently remove the book, taking note of the title, *Dissociative Identity Disorder: Life after the Cure.* I'm sure Jax didn't mean for me to see this. He most likely meant to hide it away before I came to bed, but the poor guy passed out, book in hand.

I place it on the nightstand and click the lamp off. He stirs, slightly, and I give him a peck on the cheek. I can't imagine how hard life has been for him, and maybe one day I'll learn the details, but that won't be anytime soon. Right now, I've got to concentrate on being well. I'm ecstatic over the thought of never having to deal with memory lapses again. No more blackouts, no more missing time, no more falsely accusing my husband of things he hasn't done. I feel a wave of shame come over me. I assume it's something I'll have to battle for a long time, but I'm determined to fight through it.

I tiptoe around to my side of the bed and climb in. I count my blessings. I'm so grateful for a strong, happy family who loves me fiercely and has sacrificed so much to help me heal.

Jax is a hero. The fact that someone like me, someone with such a severe disorder, would end up marrying a psychiatrist is no coincidence. I'm grateful for where I am today, and I just need to hang on a little bit longer, until I'm back to normal again.

Whatever normal means.

Chapter Forty
Evangeline

SUNDAY - MIDDLE OF THE NIGHT

I shake Jax to wake him. He won't be happy with this two a.m. wakeup call, but I'm not concerned with his happiness at the moment. I shake him again, but he's not budging, so I give him a light smack across the face. That does it. He jumps and grabs my wrists.

"What's going on? Are you okay?" He lets me go and fumbles in the dark for the lamp. After a few seconds, light floods the room, and we both squint until our eyes adjust. "What happened, hon?"

"Guess again," I say and smile sardonically.

He sighs loudly. "Oh, man. Will you stop already." This is more of a demand than a question.

"Shh. You'll wake your buddy, and I don't need her, or any of the others, for that matter, breathing down my neck, threatening me."

"*I'm* threatening you, Evangeline. Leave. It's over. *You're* over," Jax says. He groans and falls back on the pillow.

"Wow! You're not very happy to see me," I say, slightly disappointed.

"When have I ever been happy to see you?" He rubs his eyes.

"Wednesday sessions," I remind him.

"I'm only happy then because I know it's one step closer to a life without you. Please, Evangeline, accept what's happening and crawl back into your hole."

This infuriates me, and I punch him in the ribcage. He springs into a sitting position, holding his side, and his face flushes with anger.

"You're becoming violent, woman," he says and scoots back against the headboard, keeping an eye on me now. "What do you want?"

"Answers," I say, as I slowly lower myself onto the edge of the bed. I'm careful to keep my distance in case I need to make a quick getaway. I don't trust him anymore. He pretended to love me, but what he did to me earlier—he and his conspirator—well, I can no longer trust him. Not that I ever could, but now it's less.

"Answers?" He laughs. "At this point, what for? You don't need to know anything. It makes no difference anymore."

"What does that mean?" I'm flooded with fear and worry, but I try to keep my cool and not show it.

"It means this is goodbye," Jax says, matter-of-fact. "Please, leave so I can have my wife back in bed with me." Jax picks up his pillow, fluffs it, and then places it behind him. "Now!" he demands.

My fear is quickly being replaced by fury. It's probably not the best time to push him, but what choice does he give me? "And if I don't?"

He sighs, and I see his patience is growing thin, if he ever had any. "You're like a child, Evangeline. I don't have time for your games." He leans over and clicks the lamp off.

"What are you doing?" I ask, disbelievingly.

"It's two in the morning, what do you think I'm doing?"

"How dare you ignore me like this. I have feelings too..."

"No, you don't. You don't have feelings because you don't matter. Now, get out so I can get back to sleep."

"Are you sure you want to do that with me in the house? Aren't you worried what I might do while you're sleeping?" I say, and laugh wickedly.

"Now you're going to threaten me? You sure do know the way to a man's heart, don't you?" he says facetiously. "I'll make a deal with you. I'll answer your questions, but you have to promise to leave afterwards. Deal?"

"Deal." I say, satisfied.

"Shoot."

I strain my eyes to see him, but it's too dark. I'd prefer the lights to be on. I like to read his expression while we talk, although most of the time he has none. But that doesn't keep me from seeing into his eyes. There *is* emotion there. I can sense it. My line of questioning is going to be disturbing to him, but it's all I've got. It's my only leverage, and if there was ever a time I needed to use it...

"Now that Greta knows about me, are you going to tell her how I've been helping you over the years?" I wait.

As expected, there's a moment of silence. "Okay, I'll play

along. I'm not going to tell her anything she doesn't need to know. Next."

"She's been killing people, Jax. Do you honestly believe that once the rest of us are gone, she's going to just automatically stop? It's what she does." I've got to knock some sense into him.

"You're confused. She's not the one doing it, and you know it. You just like to blame her to rile me up."

"Are you sure about that? We've cleaned up some pretty bloody messes, Jaxy Boy. How are you going to handle her future killings on your own? The two of you wouldn't be where you are today if it weren't for me. You might want to rethink your plans, hmm?"

"Maybe I would if what you were saying had any truth to it, but it doesn't. You're creating fantasies, because that's what you do. You live in a world of delusion. Once the rest of you have integrated, which I was hoping had already happened, the chaos will stop because the real killer will not exist any longer. Then Greta and I will live happily ever after."

I laugh hysterically. "*Who's* living in a delusional world?"

"Time's up, Evangeline. Now, goodbye. Leave."

I feel the bed jiggle as Jax rolls over, and I'm more than positive he's facing away from me. He's not scared of me, he has no fear of me whatsoever; lying in the dark, backside to me. That's a man who's not worried. A fury runs through my body like electricity, almost lighting me on fire. "You feel there should be no repercussions for what she's done? Last time I checked, murder was against the law."

"She didn't do anything. It was an alter…"

I interrupt him. "Is that how you sleep at night?"

"Keep your end of the bargain, Evangeline. Goodbye," he says sleepily.

"What if I were to go to the police and tell them everything?"

"Are you going to do that in Greta's body?"

I fly off the bed in a rage.

"Goodbye, Evangeline."

I want to jump on top of him and beat him to a bloody pulp. I could strangle him with my bare hands right now. I stand beside the bed, breathing heavy, straining to see him, knowing he doesn't have a care in the world for me right now. He's more concerned with getting his beauty sleep than he is with my feelings. If I had a gun … I'd … kill … him.

I run into the bathroom and close the door behind me. I don't want him to hear me cry. I grab a towel from the rack and bury my face to muffle my pain. I try to think of ways to hurt him. I could soil his reputation. His practice would be ruined. I could arrange something horrible to happen to Greta. I know shady people in low places.

I scream into the towel for a good fifteen minutes and then contain myself. I take deep breaths, something Jax taught me to do, for several minutes and then tiptoe down to the kitchen where I find a bottle of Jax's scotch. I don't even like scotch and only drink it because it gets under his skin. I love how he grabs the bottle from me, not wanting me to drink because he doesn't want anything bad to happen to me. It shows how much he cares for me. When he's affectionate toward me, it makes me feel good. I've never seen him as disconnected as he's been today … tonight. I wonder what he'd do if he caught me drinking right now. Would he take the bottle from me? Would he want to help me? Keep me safe?

Is he right? Is this really the end of the road for me?

Is this really … goodbye?

Goodbye, Jax.

I love you!

Chapter Forty-one
Evangeline

It's four in the morning, and I ring Jax. It goes to his voice mail, so I hang up and ring him again. This time he answers.

"Yeah," he says, groggily. Because there's no panic in his voice, I'm assuming he didn't check the caller ID.

"It's me." That's all I need to say to get him riled up. His heart should be pounding out of his chest now. He knows there's trouble. Big trouble. I wait, realizing it'll take him a few seconds to answer me. I imagine he's turning on the lamp, checking to see if Greta is lying beside him. She's not. I snicker.

"What's happened?" He gasps into the phone.

"Your loving wife has knocked off another unsuspecting gent," I say.

I wait as he collects his thoughts. "I don't believe you."

"Ha! Why would I lie?"

"What's *really* going on, Evangeline?" he asks suspiciously.

"What are you talking about? She just offed the neighbor's husband a few weeks ago. Now, are you going to come help me out here, or what?"

"I don't understand. How did this happen?" I can hear him moving about, like he's getting dressed.

"I don't know. I just woke up in this—this warehouse. It's deserted and looks like it's in a seedy part of town."

"A seedy part of town? She'd never go somewhere like that. Who's the guy?"

"I haven't checked his wallet. I'll have to roll him over, and I don't feel much like touching him. Just get here already! I'm at Jones and Foster Rd. You'll have to GPS it. Trust me, this is an area you've never been."

"You have her car?" he asks.

"Yes." I cross my fingers, hoping he doesn't see through this. "Look, Jax, I just woke up with a dead guy. HURRY! Get me out of here," I yell into the phone, in the most panic-stricken voice I can muster up.

"Okay! Stay low. I'll be there as quickly as I can," he says and the call ends.

I chuckle and make one more call. "Watch for him. He'll be here in about twenty minutes. It'll be the only BMW you'll see around here. Get it done, and then don't contact me. I'll connect with you when things have cooled down. Just make sure he's not breathing before you leave." I end the call and get into position.

I'm next door to the warehouse, hunkered down in the shadows of a small abandoned building. The faded and peeling storefront sign tells me it used to be a concrete business. As of late, it appears to have been housing drug addicts. Most of the windows are broken out, and I'm careful not to step on any of the syringes lying about the floor. Yuck! I position myself by a window where I have a decent view of the warehouse.

In just under twenty minutes, I see headlights coming down the street. It's Jax. He must have sped the whole way. He kills the lights as he approaches the warehouse. I watch as he steps out of his car and jogs up the walkway, entering through the front. The door has been removed and a large piece of plywood has, at some point, been nailed over the entrance, but someone has broken it in two, making it easy to maneuver.

Jax won't find a dead body, because there's not one. There will be, though. The ironic part is, it's going to be his. I giggle and wonder what took me so long. I could have done this years ago. I can only imagine where'd I'd be today. I envision myself on a beach somewhere—anywhere is fine—sucking down a mai tai, living large on Jax's life insurance, which is pretty darned hefty. I did some snooping a while back. If, or in this case, when, anything happens to Jax, Greta will be living large, to say the least. I rub my palms together in greed and anticipation.

Did I just hear something? There it is again. I hold my breath, straining to hear. *Crash. Thump. Thud.* It's on, and oh my, it sounds as if Jax is taking quite a beating. I'll be honest. I almost can't bear to stick around. Almost. I hear groaning and I have to stifle my laughter. I check my watch. It's time for me to get back to the house before someone realizes I'm not there, though it will be a few hours before anyone stirs. I maneuver through the dark building, careful not to make any noise. My heart is pounding as I run to my—Greta's—car, which I parked two blocks away.

I click the remote and the lights flash. I fling open the door and slide in behind the wheel. I feel a slight twinge of remorse as I start the car and put it in gear, but it's fleeting. I press the accelerator and head home. My mind shifts to Jax and what he must be going through right now. Being beaten to death must certainly be a painful way to die. Even though Jax is healthy and fit, my hitman shouldn't have a problem taking him out. My guy isn't the healthiest—a junkie who's probably never worked out a day in his life, whose body is half dead by drug abuse—but Jax is on the smallish side in comparison. Do I feel guilty? Just a little, but then I flash to me on the beach, fruity drink in hand, and all is good.

Goodbye, old friend. I snicker.

Chapter Forty-two
Greta

MAY 15
MONDAY MORNING

I awaken with a slight headache, and it only takes me seconds before I remember my hellish reality. I try to push it to the far corners of my mind, reminding myself I've decided to press past it and be happy, regardless of my circumstances. I stumble out of bed and make my way to the bathroom. After a shower, I head downstairs, breathing in the scrumptious aroma of eggs and toast.

I enter the kitchen to find Aiden and Hannah cooking up a storm.

"Good morning," we say in unison.

"Where's Mom and Paul?" I ask, grabbing a cinnamon roll from a platter sitting on the island. I pinch a piece off and pop it into my mouth.

"They wanted a *real* Cajun breakfast, so they went to town, since that's the only place to get authentic NOLA food," Hannah says with an eye roll.

"And what do we have out here?" I raise my brow.

"I guess this is biscuits and gravy land." Hannah shrugs. "It's too countryfied for them." We get a good laugh. I glance around the kitchen. "Where's my husband?"

"What do you mean?" Hannah asks, picking up a slice of toast and slathering it with butter.

"He's not upstairs. I figured he was down here with you guys." Hannah shakes her head, and I turn toward the great room. "Jax," I call out. "Hmm. That's odd." I walk through the downstairs, calling out to him, but get no answer. The French doors leading out back are closed and locked.

"I can't find him," I say as I reenter the kitchen.

"Well, his car has been sitting in the driveway all morning," Aiden says and tilts his head toward the kitchen window overlooking the drive.

"What?" I hurry to the window, leaning forward to get a good look. Sure enough, Jax's car is parked to the side. Two wheels on the driveway and two in the grass. "That's strange. Why is his car parked like that?" The three of us exchange looks.

Aiden tosses the spatula on the counter. "Watch the eggs," he says and hurries out the garage door.

Anxiety comes over me, and I grab Hannah's hand. "What's happened?"

"It'll be okay," she says nervously as she turns off the stove.

"Where's Jax?" I ask, fearing the worst.

We wait for what seems like an eternity, but in reality it's only been a few minutes. That's when the door abruptly swings open and Aiden calls out, "Help me." He takes a step into the house, arms around Jax's chest, struggling to hold him up. Hannah rushes to his side, grabbing on to Jax. They half carry him into the great room, placing him on the sofa. "Get water, peroxide, and a washrag…" Aiden calls out frantically. I'm frozen in place. It's Hannah who rushes to the half bath to collect the requested items.

When she returns, which is just a matter of seconds, she yells hysterically, "We should call an ambulance. Look at him!"

And that's when I do. I take a long look at him. I slowly cross the room, coming around the sofa, where I kneel beside his head. His face is a bloody mess. I can't tell where it's coming from. "Is—Is he breathing?" I ask slowly.

Aiden grabs the washrag and a bottle of water from Hannah. "He's conscious. He spoke to me."

"I'm dialing 911," Hannah says, taking the phone from her pocket.

"Don't!" Aiden says abruptly. "He said not to."

"Not to?" Hannah asks, confused. "Why in the world would he say that?"

"That's what I asked, but then he said one word … *Evangeline.*" Aiden shoots me a look. "So I think we'd better do as he says."

"He could have internal bleeding. I'm calling."

"He told me he'll be fine. He just needs to lie down."

"I don't care what he told you," Hannah argues.

"He's a doctor. I trust his judgement."

"He's not a medical doctor, Aiden, please."

"I said, I trust him," Aiden says fiercely. "Put the phone away." He turns to me, giving me the once-over. "What happened, Greta? For crying out loud, look at him."

"I don't know. I don't know," I say, feeling disconnected.

Hannah gently slides her hand behind Jax's neck and raises his head up just high enough to slide a throw pillow underneath. "How long was he out there in his car?"

"He doesn't know," Aiden answers.

"Well, he must've pulled up after Mom and Paul left this morning, or they would've seen him."

"I'm okay. Give me some water," Jax pants.

"Greta, grab a bottled water," Aiden commands, and I know he chose me because I'm the only one not doing anything. I'm just standing around like a helpless dope. But it's not a lack of concern. Quite the contrary. I feel ashamed. I know I'm the cause of Jax's injuries. I realize how hard his life is because of me. He could be dead, and it would be all my fault. How does he still love me? I run to the kitchen and grab a bottled water from the built-in drink cooler in the island, and hurry back to them. I shove my way between Aiden and Hannah, who are hovering over Jax, and I sit on the very edge of the sofa. They step aside with raised brows. I'm his wife. I'm going to be here for him, just like he is for me. It's my duty.

"The worst is my side," Jax says and tries to prop himself up. He winces in pain and falls back. "It feels like I have a couple of broken ribs, but they're probably just bruised. Greta, go upstairs and get the prescription bottle of naproxen. Get the Flexeril, too. Hannah, grab me a drink."

"You already have a drink," she answers, confused.

"A *real* drink," Jax says, wincing in pain as he attempts,

once more, to prop himself up. Hannah looks at Aiden.

"Everybody, go," Aiden orders and waves his hand in the air. He slides another throw pillow behind Jax to help prop him up. I turn to watch them as I climb the stairs. Jax grabs on to his side, grimacing, as Aiden slowly pulls him forward.

When I return, he's sitting, glass of scotch in hand. Hannah is attempting to wipe the blood from his face with a wet washcloth, but he keeps pulling away in pain. I push my way to the sofa and sit beside my husband. I open the pill bottles with shaky hands and hand two pills to Jax, who then washes them down with a swig of scotch. The room falls silent for a few minutes while we all patiently wait for him to speak.

He sighs heavily and begins. "I woke up to Evangeline shaking me. She was fuming. I was a little worried what she might do, but the more I ignored her, the more she started to back off, so I continued to blow her off."

"What was she saying to you?" I ask curiously. What could an alter ego of mine have to say to my husband? I shiver at the bizarreness of it all.

Jax takes a swig of his drink. "It seemed like she knew it was over and was wanting to tie up some loose ends, that's all. I wasn't real worried about it, honestly. Without giving in to her, I played along enough to satisfy her need, and then she eventually walked away."

"Walked away?" I ask, confused.

"She went downstairs and hit the bottle. I spied on her for a while, so I could make sure she didn't try to leave or do anything crazy." Jax half turns to me before wincing in pain. "I hide your keys every night before bed, although it doesn't really do much good. Most of the time, she finds them." I take his hand in mine, giving it an affectionate squeeze. I can't imagine what life with me has been like over the years. Me and all my baggage, that is. I'm going to do everything I can to make up for it. To make our remaining years better than ever.

"Then what?" Aiden asks, taking a seat in the chair across from us.

"I went back to sleep until I was awakened by a phone call at four. It was Evangeline. She said…" He pauses.

"She said what?" Aiden asks.

"She says she needs help. She's at an abandoned warehouse and doesn't know how she got there. She needs me to come."

I exchange glances with Hannah and Aiden. Jax's story sounds peculiar, but we stay silent, waiting for him to continue.

"When I got there, some guy jumped me. It looks like she set it up. I think she tried to get him to whack me. That way I won't be around anymore to *control* her," Jax says, slightly raising his hands to make air quotes.

We fall silent again until Aiden speaks up. "What happened to the guy?"

"I'm not sure. He attacked me on the second floor. We struggled all the way down a hallway. When we got to the end, it was caved in, roped off by some yellow tape, like crime scene tape, and a wooden barricade. At some point during our struggle, he fell through the barricade. I heard him hit the concrete floor beneath." Jax rubs his forehead. "Oh, man. I had to get out of there. I made it back to my car, but had to pull over a few miles down the road. I passed out at that point. When I came to, it was daylight. I drove the rest of the way home. I'm not sure how long I was outside before you came and got me." He drinks from his glass.

"You should lie back down," I tell him.

"I'll be fine once these drugs kick in."

Aiden sighs loudly. "This is crazy, Jax. We need to do something. You can't handle this on your own."

"We *are* doing something. That's why Evangeline is becoming desperate. She knows her time is limited."

Aiden scratches his head. "I don't understand."

Hannah explains. "That's what we were doing yesterday when you were watching the game and we were in Jax's study. Remember? It was that session which prompted this attack. Her time is limited and she knows it."

I notice Aiden is avoiding looking at me. "We've got to go back tomorrow, but I can't stand the thought of leaving you."

Jax waves his hand nonchalantly, but Aiden is having none of it. "I understand you're a therapist, and someone who's used to a little psychological drama," my body stiffens, "and this may seem ordinary to you, but let me be the first to say that your life is extremely chaotic, bro. Drama-filled and crazy as hell. You can't live like this."

Hannah turns and motions for Aiden to stop talking. He glances at me. "Oh, no offense, Greta. I know it's not your fault."

Jax comes to my rescue. "Look, I understand everyone's feelings of panic right now, but they're misplaced, I assure you. Don't worry about us. I know what I'm doing. I was just careless last night, but I can look back and see red flags starting from the initial phone call. I just wasn't thinking. I wasn't on my A game. I knew we'd made progress earlier, and I got careless." Jax holds his hand to his side. "Go home and resume life as usual. We'll stay in touch, letting you know how great everything is," Jax says convincingly.

Later that afternoon, Mom and Paul were packed and ready to fly back home. We kissed and hugged goodbye. Jax stayed away so they wouldn't see his swollen face. We told them he had a bad case of food poisoning. Of course, Mom wanted to go see to him and nurse him back to health with one of her homeopathic elixirs. We had one heck of a time keeping her out of the bedroom, but she finally retreated. It was time for her to start packing, anyway. We promised them we would visit for Christmas.

I look forward to the future, envisioning it as a time of mental and emotional health. Something we both so desperately need.

Chapter Forty-three
Greta

MONDAY EVENING

"What if it didn't work?" I ask skeptically.

"Then we keep on until we drive them out," Hannah says cheerfully, and I smile at her enthusiastic support.

"Get back on the sofa like yesterday," Jax says as we enter his study. Other than moving slowly and nursing his side, he's pretty much back to his normal self. He carefully pulls the chair across from me further back this time. I'm guessing he wants to make sure he's a good distance from me in case there's a repeat of yesterday. Hannah follows suit.

"Where do you want me?" Aiden asks Jax.

"Pull the chair from the desk next to mine."

"I've never seen someone get hypnotized before. Honestly, I never really believed in it," he admits.

"Well, believe. Hypnosis has been used as a form of therapy for hundreds of years, even thousands, really. I know it was used in ancient times in Greece, but they called it something else. The style of healing they practiced then is our modern form of hypnosis."

"Really?" Aiden says, surprised.

"It has a long history of healing people. It would take me too long to go into it, but there's a reason it's still practiced today—it works. It's an excellent form of therapy. You just need to be sure the one doing the hypnosis is a licensed professional and not some voodoo medicine guru. Then you're messing in things you shouldn't be."

"Ah, gotcha." Aiden tilts his head to the side as he absorbs Jax's brief lesson on hypnosis.

Jax sits on the edge of the sofa at my side. "Ready?"

"As ready as I'll ever be." I smile and close my eyes.

Jax's voice starts to fade, and I'm no longer mindful of anything he's saying.

Everything goes black.

Suddenly, I'm aware of Jax's voice, growing louder and clearer. I open my eyes to find him in the same spot, sitting next to me, his face hovering over mine. His eyes are bright with wonder.

"What happened?" I ask shakily.

"That's what I was about to ask you," Jax says and purses his lips.

I hesitate. What *did* happen? "I'm not sure. I don't remember anything." I raise up onto my elbows. I glance at Hannah and Aiden, who are sitting quietly, watching me in anticipation.

"What does this mean, Jax?" Aiden asks.

"It means they're gone," he says, grinning wider than the Grand Canyon. He grabs my hand and pulls me up from the sofa.

Hannah jumps to her feet and screams, "Woo-hoo."

"This is fantastic. Get over here, Greta." Aiden stands and reaches his hands out to me.

"Group hug," Hannah yells, and we all gather together, hugging it out.

Jax breaks free and pulls me over to him, putting his arms around my waist and spinning me around. "I can't believe it. You're finally free."

"You're not going to miss Evangeline, are you?" I tease.

"Are you kidding me? I can't believe I'm finally rid of her. That's more of a reason to celebrate than anything else." We all laugh, breathing huge sighs of relief.

"How does Greta know if she's really cured or not, though?" Aiden asks, and I'm glad he did. I was getting ready to ask Jax the same thing. How *do* I really know?

"First, she may experience some flashbacks." Jax looks at me intently. "Some memories will probably start coming back to you. We'll work through it together." He squeezes my hand. "No more lost time. No more memory lapses. No more blackouts." I clap my hands together and breathe a sigh of relief. "No more phobias, paranoia, anxiety … these will most likely fade with time. You'll sleep better and feel better, that's for sure. And so will I. No more late-night visits from Evangeline." We laugh in unison. "And even better, no more dealing with her spying on me at the coffee shop. That was sooo creepy."

"What are you talking about?" I ask, dumbfounded.

"Oh, who cares. Let's go celebrate. French Quarter?"

"Seriously!" "I'm game." "Let's get out of here." We can't move fast enough as we gather our belongings and head out the door.

As we back down the driveway, I notice Isabella standing outside with a gentleman in a suit. He hands her a folder, waves, and starts toward his car, a black Lexus parked in the driveway. There's a FOR SALE sign in the yard.

"Look at that," I say, pointing.

Jax watches them for a minute and then shrugs. "I hope she finds happiness," he says, but his eyes are troubled.

"I guess she couldn't stand living in that big house alone. I wouldn't want to either. If something happened to you, I couldn't bear to live in the house we once shared."

"I think she'll be okay." His tone is cold, but he has other things on his mind now. Isabella is no concern of his.

Chapter Forty-four
Evangeline

JULY 12
WEDNESDAY 3:00

"Are you ready to go, Greta?" Jax yells up the staircase to me.

"One more minute, hon."

He's waiting for me. It's times like this when I'm relieved I married such a patient man. Jax has always been the love of my life. Since our very first date, I knew I had to have him. I knew I needed to be a challenge for him. All great men love a challenge. The fact Jax was going to med school to become a psychiatrist told me right offhand this is a man who loves to feel accomplished. A man who wants to help people and save lives. A man like this needs to rescue a damsel in distress to feel like a *real* man.

I run my fingers over my collection of black eyeliner, stopping at Kat Von D. I pick it up and pop the cap off. I scoot closer to my lighted makeup mirror, knowing full well I'm not going to glide on my favorite eyeliner. I pretend to apply it across my lids, chuckling before recapping it and placing it back alongside the others. "Chanel it is," I say as I sweep a thin line of black liner across my lash line.

Jax has proven himself to be a good man. An exceptional one, really. I mean, what woman wouldn't want to be married to such a loving, giving, successful guy? We all want the best man. The problem is, there aren't many in this world. So when you find one, you need to test him out for a while and see if he can withstand the storms of life. Jax has more than passed that test.

After brushing on a light coat of mascara, I reach for my favorite lipstick. *Exorcism*! That's how I feel about my life. I've been exorcised, only not in the usual way where a priest is present. My exorcism involves a shrink. Greta went in under hypnosis, but I'm the one who came out. What everyone doesn't realize is Greta didn't create *me*, I created *her*, really. Technically, I shaped her and molded her. I've been ringmaster over this circus since the beginning. Jax has never been the wiser. He loves me, and I love him. He'd do anything for me. All I need to do is say the word, and with a snap of my fingers, I get it. Ah, it's the life, isn't it?

Being me is spectacular! I have no limits, no boundaries on anything I do because my adoring husband knows I can't help myself. My actions are out of my control. Even now, with me at the peak of mental health, I'm still allowed passes for my horrendous behavior because I once had a mental condition— which still affects me from time to time. I become confused easily and have trouble remembering certain things because someone else was acting out on my behalf, doing horrible things I'm not responsible for.

Oh, Greta, how I miss you. You kept me going at times, without even realizing it. Sometimes I long to bring you back. Let you have another stab at this challenging life, but you're just too weak. You never had it in you to kill. I always had to step up to the plate for you, faking blackouts and memory lapses. It was quite an exciting life, actually. But I think what I really miss the most are my three o'clock appointments every Wednesday. Life is so dull without them. Maybe we can start over and be friends this time. I'll let you have a piece of my life every now and again. I'm not a stingy person. I get so bored … so easily. I need some drama to pep things up. Maybe it's time to bring Evangeline back; I was never good at playing your role anyway.

I sweep the *Exorcism* across my lips, admiring the ripe blackberry hue. Who's going to be my scapegoat? How do I get rid of the bad men in life when I have no one to blame the killings on? I sway down the staircase, Jax waiting at the base, near the front door. He turns to look at me, a smile on his face and adoration in his eyes. But after a split second, the excitement fades, and I'm faced with confusion-filled eyes and a dropped jaw.

"It's three o'clock, Jax. Time for our session." I smile.

ABOUT THE AUTHOR

Karyn Masters is a gifted writer, blogger, and social media addict! She started writing poetry and short stories at a young age and won numerous creative writing awards. Her poetry was first published at age sixteen. She graduated summa cum laude from Liberty University. She's a seventh-generation Texan (born and raised), but currently resides in Lake Charles, Louisiana with her husband, Toby, and their three fur kids (A.K.A. Bratty Cats).

Other books by Karyn:
Arion and Azura (The Adventure Series)
When Deep Sleep Falls
Silent Storm
God, Fix it!
Spiritual Warfare, My Battle

For more information on this book and others by Karyn Masters visit: KarynMasters.com
Facebook: Facebook.com/KarynJMasters
Instagram: Instagram.com/Karyn.Masters
BLOG: KarynMasters.com/blog

70683275R00210

Made in the USA
Middletown, DE
16 April 2018